Where Tigers Roam

Augustus John Roe

ISBN: 978-1-9995966-2-0

DEDICATION

Dedicated to the many incredible characters and martial artists
I have met on my travels that inspired me to write this book.

ACKNOWLEDGMENTS

Thanks to all of the people who have contributed to the writing, editing, and inspiration for this book.
In particular, I would like to thank Ann Roe, David Bell and Le Thanh Ha for the ongoing support and encouragement during writing. Also everyone who helped with early drafts and marketing, including, Grant J Riley, Jasper Roe, and Jonathan Chappell. Finally, thanks to Dejan Lekic, Nguyen Que Anh, and Pawel Kardis for their illustrations and cover artwork respectively.

CHINA

Hong Kong

The Port

Xi River

The Citadel

The Mountain Clearing

Minh's Village

Red River

Tonkin

South China Sea

N E W S

PROLOGUE

'MURDERER!'

Peter's voice echoed through the cavernous hall. Anger stung his throat, but pain was a feeling he'd come to know well.

In less than a second his enemy had covered the few yards that lay between them, the first blow smashed him across the jaw, the second thundered into the side of his head. A ringing in his ears plunged Peter's thoughts into chaos, and a heel in the chest slammed his body against one of the thick wooden columns that lined the chamber.

It took a moment for Peter to realise where he was. The dust tickled his lungs, narrow shafts of sunshine pierced the shutters above, illuminating the red and gold panels that ran from floor to ceiling. A trickle of warmth crept across his face and dripped down onto the cold, white tiles below, staining them with droplets of crimson. *Get up*.

Peter forced his body to its feet, every inch of him was crying out in pain, but he chose not to listen. The impossible twists of fate that had led him here couldn't all have been for nothing. *Could they? Remember your training*, he thought. *Calm your mind*.

Slowly, Peter exhaled, he felt the fear and anger leaving his body, rising upwards like a balloon through the shadowy rafters of the castle and out into the depths of the blue sky beyond. Every tiny detail of his surroundings lit up; the shimmer of the statues that lined the room, the earthy aroma of incense that burned on a stone altar in the corner, the whisper of a flute playing in the distance, and the iron sting of blood on his lips.

By the time his eyes focused, the enemy was hurtling towards him. Peter felt his weight sink through the soles of his feet deep into the earth below. His teeth gritted and muscles tensed. *Live or die, it all ends now. I'm ready.*

CHAPTER ONE

I hate boats, Peter thought watching the bow rising and falling in the gentle swell. A grating laugh cut through the creaking and straining of the vessel, it annoyed him how happy she was. Sophie, his sister, and two off-duty members of the crew were kicking around a shuttlecock trying not to let it touch the ground. *She's never going to win, why doesn't she just give up?*

He wondered how many rematches the crew could put up with before getting bored themselves. Peter had no desire to socialise with them, though he couldn't help but feel a pang of jealousy as he sat alone in the morning sun. He didn't find it easy meeting new people or making friends, so sticking to routines kept him comfortable. In the weeks since they had set out, his days had been busy enough spent reading, cleaning, and studying.

The Princess Helena, a private cargo ship, had left Portsmouth in January 1934. Just a few weeks before, Peter had been standing in the shadows as his parents sat around the oak dining table in the kitchen. Their voices echoed off the wooden floorboards and down the hallway of their modest, but attractive home. 'According to Collins it's like herding cats,' his father laughed, 'most of them are determined to stick to their old ways, and the others are too scared to even speak out about religion. He's got only a handful of converts in the last few years.'

'Well, all the more reason we should go and offer our support then,' his mother had replied, 'they'll soon get used to the idea.' Peter grimaced, to him the idea of going into a foreign country and trying to convince people to change their way of thinking seemed unfair. It was something his family had done for as long as he could remember, and now seeing the glimmer of excitement in his mother's eyes he knew he wasn't going to have any say in the matter.

'Do you think it's safe enough?' his mother said, her face returning to a familiar look of concern.

'Yes, of course dear. The reverend is a good man, if he's having no trouble I can't imagine we'll bring it to him.' Just then something caught the corner of his mother's eye. Her gaze followed the length of the table towards the hallway and locked with Peter's in the shadows behind. He knew he'd been caught, but compared to the misery of the trip they were discussing, being in trouble seemed like the least of his worries.

'What is it?' his father asked.

'Nothing dear, thought I heard a noise.' She smiled at Peter, as if to tell him he had heard enough. Silently, he crept down the hall and up the stairs, climbed into bed and shut his eyes, but his thoughts were far from sleep. *Again?* he wondered. *Just as I start getting used to something.*

CHAPTER TWO

Sophie was buzzing with excitement as she belted up the staircase to the cabins. They had just been given the hour warning for port, and even though she loved travelling, being stuck on this dank old boat for weeks was insufferable. Peter barged past her in the narrow corridor, as though he couldn't wait even a second longer. *He's so self-absorbed*, she thought.

'Finally, I get to stand on dry land again,' he said with a sigh arriving at their shared cabin.

'Good, because you can't stand here very well,' Sophie smirked and shoved him from behind. Peter tumbled into the doorframe, just managing to stop the fall with his hands. His face reddened with anger and embarrassment, even though he knew there was no one around to see it.

'Hey-' he started, but the scrape of the boat's rudders on the land below cut him off. When the creaking and groaning of the metal finally halted, Sophie made her way out onto the deck. Every member of the crew was rushing around manically, shouting, securing ropes, and dropping sandbags.

The first thing she noticed as she crossed towards the port side was the heat of the air rising up from the dock; it hit her like a brick wall. For weeks she'd had the sea breeze blowing in from all angles, but finally being stationary meant the humidity was choking.

Just then, a gust blew across the deck, it carried a sweet and fruity aroma that triggered memories of her time at the mission in Algeria. Every day for more than a year, Sophie had walked with her friends down the dusty trail towards the sand-coloured dome of their school, laughing and joking while Peter followed a few steps behind. As they crossed through the market square in the outskirts of Constantine, she would enjoy the rich scents of dried dates and plums that were piled high on the vendors' stalls. Although she was just over a year older than him, Sophie had resented having Peter trailing along behind her and her friends. He was awkward and stubborn, but for some reason she was always the one that got blamed for causing trouble.

A stench of rotting meat wafted in shattering Sophie's pleasant thoughts and she retched in disgust. Her hands wrapped around the rusted metal guardrail and as she peered over at the hub of activity below, her grimace gave way to a grin. A cacophony of sound rattled the ship, voices blared across the crowd competing to be heard, whilst dockyard workers scurried around heaving and crashing cargo up and down the quayside. Sophie stared in disbelief at one tiny vehicle trying to barge its way through honking then skid to a halt, barely missing pushing a man into the water. *Ha-ha Seriously?* Just the notion of trying to drive here seemed ridiculous. *How are we going to find one man in this?*

Her father was already helping the crew to unload crates of supplies onto the main deck of the boat, whilst her mother was frantically grabbing bags and stuffing items into any space she could find. It reminded Sophie of the panic that would precede a guest arriving at their cluttered home back in London. She couldn't care less about tidiness, but always offered to help. She knew it was a matter of pride for her mother whose home, wealth, and ideals were all inherited from her Grandfather.

The family followed a few steps behind as Sophie's father led the way down the gangplank with bags in hand. 'Keep an eye out for the reverend,' he called back, and almost as he spoke, she noticed a face smiling back at them from the crowd. Through the heaving throng of short, dark-haired workers, the tall, mousey-brown haired man waving his arms towards the boat stuck out like a sore thumb.

'Do you recognise him?' Sophie yelled at Peter over the ruckus. He shrugged. She had only vague memories of the reverend, he was telling them a story about pirates and his adventures in the Far East, but she couldn't recall any details, only the excitement she felt whilst listening. Maybe it was because he was surrounded on all sides by dockworkers, but Reverend Collins looked much taller and thinner than she recalled. Sophie glanced back at her lanky brother stumbling down the gangplank and couldn't help but smile at how similar they seemed.

CHAPTER THREE

'Keep up, easy to get lost here,' Reverend Collins called back as he pushed his way through the throngs of people. They burst out of the crowd and onto a cobbled street that was illuminated by the mid-morning sun's yellow glow. The reverend stopped in front, allowing them a moment to enjoy the less-stifling air. 'You two will have to watch out,' he said looking first at Peter, then to Sophie, who had stopped just beside him. 'There are plenty of thieves about. Hold onto your bags and stick close behind me.'

We're not stupid, Peter thought, his gaze met Sophie's and the smile creeping across her face showed she was thinking the same. A sudden commotion in front shifted his attention back to the street; a horse had bucked, kicking over a stack of cages. Peter watched as the chickens scattered and the owner pursued them in an equally erratic manner. *This is going to be a really long trip.*

Reverend Collins led the family across the street to a waiting horse and carriage, both of which appeared to have seen better days. The horses looked mangy and old, while the carriage was streaked with cracked varnish and mud, almost obscuring the faded paintwork on its doors. The driver, a shabby man in a straw hat, leapt down from his platform at the front, performed a quick bow and snatched the luggage from Peter and his father. The cases were unceremoniously swung onto the roof and another worker tied them down.

As quickly as they had arrived at the madness of the docks, they were leaving it behind. The hard, wooden bench of the carriage didn't offer much relief and bouncing up and down through the pothole-filled streets soon had Peter wincing with every bump.

'Going by train or car is definitely the more comfortable option,' the reverend said seeing the pained expression on his face, 'but where we're going they wouldn't get far.' As the carriage squeezed through the narrow alleys that skirted the harbour, it made several stops. The first time they pulled up to a group that were clearly waiting for the party. They had what Peter guessed were camping supplies held together in a dark-green canvas wrap, and pots and pans strung on a line, which they wasted no time fastening onto the roof of the carriage. By the second stop, the sun was directly overhead and the scents of fruit and meat cooking in the midday heat wafted in, adding to the nausea of the bumpy ride.

'We can't take vehicles in here,' Reverend Collins said, clambering down from the carriage. Behind him an upward-curved roof straddled two faded yellow pillars, marking the entrance of what looked like an open-air market. 'Who wants to come and collect the food with me?' The look of the street ahead, buzzing with flies and the dank aroma emanating from it was less than appealing, but a rumble in Peter's stomach spurred him on.

'I'll come,' he answered. *Maybe I can choose some of the food.* He shuddered thinking about the sheep's eyes they had been invited to try in Algeria.

'This is a delicacy, be polite and don't upset our hosts,' his father had instructed through a forced smile. Sophie had been in hysterics at Peter's cringing, when he saw an eyeball burst between her teeth and shoot out juices.

'Come on then, we've a long way to go today,' Reverend Collins said, and turned to Peter's father, 'you had better stay with the ladies. Foreign women are unusual around these parts so we don't want any trouble.'

What does he mean 'trouble'? Peter felt a hint of concern as he tailed the reverend through the bustling street, but brushed it off. Every pavement in the market was lined with dark-haired old women hunched over stalls that were covered in colourful fruits, vegetables and meats. Some Peter recognised, whilst others didn't even look edible, one fruit in particular was the size of a football, covered in razor-sharp barbs and stank like mouldy cheese, forcing him to hold his breath and walk quickly as they passed.

'This way, we need some dried meat, pickled vegetables, rice and fruit,' the reverend said walking up to one of the stalls. Peter stayed a step behind, fearing he'd be asked to talk with the ancient-looking woman. Despite weeks of studying on the boat, it dawned on Peter just how few words he recognised as Reverend Collins talked with the vendor. From their body language it was obvious that the stony-faced grocer was driving a hard bargain. After a couple of minutes Collins dropped a handful of rusty coins into a green ceramic beaker on the table, picked up the jar of what looked like pickled cabbage and left. Peter grimaced, *Urgh, I'd rather eat sheep's eyes.*

Reverend Collins glanced around at the other market vendors who were waving their hands in an attempt to call him over. They visited the meat and fruit stalls on the opposite side of the street where the same routine happened.

'Is shopping always such hard work?' Peter asked.

'Ha-ha, I'm afraid so,' said the reverend, 'but it's the culture to bargain, it's all about pride, by looking like they offer a discount and I pay more than I wanted too we all save face. That's one reason why it's so hard for Britain to establish good trade here, the way we do business is so different.' Peter nodded, wondering if their pride over selling fruit and vegetables in the dockside market was really worth the effort.

As the reverend proceeded to another stall, the crashing of cymbals and drums somewhere close by caught Peter's attention. It was similar to the sound of marching bands that would sometimes parade through the streets of London, but somehow more frantic. A memory of sitting on his father's shoulders watching the parade go by flashed through Peter's mind and almost instinctively, he followed the entrancing rhythm. At the end of the narrow market lane, a square opened up and a cool sea breeze gusted through.

In the centre of the square lay a circular stone platform, around twenty feet across. Around the outside of the circle sat a handful of musicians, while on top a Lion Dance performance was beginning, Peter recognised it from descriptions he had read. Vibrantly dressed performers were playing different parts of the animal, the men acting as the legs were throwing each other up, jumping and kicking while the man on the front danced around wearing an enormous, almost-comical lion head. Another dancer, armed with a wooden sword rolled and dived in front of the beast, miming a battle as he avoided its jaws, swinging and slicing. After several minutes, the crashes of the cymbals slowed and softened as both the lion and the fighter wore each other down.

The group bowed to the few onlookers and made their way down from platform. Two bearded men then sprang up on either side of the circle and strode to the centre, stopping just a foot or two apart. They both bowed, almost horizontally, with their hands clasped together. After a second of silence, the beating of drums began and the men started throwing fists and feet at one another, dodging and weaving around strikes in time to the rhythm. Peter had seen boxing matches before but never anything like this. They moved gracefully but with power, launching kicks higher than his head and throwing punches that cracked with speed. A tight grip clasped Peter's shoulder and he jumped in surprise, he had been so caught up in the action.

'You shouldn't wander off on your own boy. You've only been here five minutes. Honestly, I thought Sophie was the naughty one.' Reverend Collins' expression was grave.

'Sorry...' Peter paused, knowing he shouldn't be making excuses, 'I saw the lion dance then this fight started and I wanted to see how it ended.'

'Not to worry, no harm done this time,' the reverend said relaxing his tone. 'Anyway, we had better get back to your parents now. We've got a lot of ground to cover before we get somewhere safe to stop this evening, these parts can be dangerous.'

What is he so worried about? Peter wondered. He glanced around at the bizarre scene of the market, yet strangely normal-looking faces of its vendors, performers, and customers. He forced the nagging thoughts from his mind and trailed the reverend back through the gates

CHAPTER FOUR

As the carriage trundled through the outskirts of the town, Peter gazed out at the landscape before him slowly transforming into countryside. His mother and Sophie were sat to his right whilst his father and Reverend Collins were squeezed in opposite, leaving him barely enough room to straighten his legs.

'We're in for a long ride I'm afraid,' Collins said, 'three days west at least, and then up into the highlands north of the great river.' Peter had been waiting for answers for weeks, he despised feeling ignorant, so even this scrap of knowledge was comforting.

'The people there are a different tribe,' the reverend continued, 'in my village they'd never even seen a foreigner until the mission last year, they weren't very welcoming at first either, but once they saw the goods we'd brought they quickly came around.' Peter's father nodded as though he expected as much, his calm demeanour helped ease the tension in the carriage. 'It's up in the highlands,' the reverend continued, 'kind of a no-man's land between the central government in the north and the French Indochina to the south. Most of the travelling is done on foot there so we should expect a lot of questions and staring from the locals, but remember they don't mean any harm by it.'

Oh great, Peter thought, he felt isolated enough already without being the odd one out in some desolate village.

'Your father told me you learnt some of the language already?' the reverend said looking to Sophie, 'you can practice with the drivers if you like, at least until they hop out at the province border, they'll be really impressed… ' she feigned a polite smile but clearly wasn't keen. Meanwhile, Peter's interest was piqued; he focused on the voices outside of the carriage. The endless lists of words they had practiced every day on the boat had seemed impossible, but hearing the men chatting happily just beyond the partition felt a lot less daunting. While studying with the ships porter, Sophie had picked up a few phrases almost effortlessly, but Peter had struggled the entire time. It's easier for her, she's older, he had reassured himself, embarrassed at how long it had taken to make any progress. Without realising, he imitated a sound from the driver 'oohay.' Everyone turned to him and Sophie cackled hysterically, 'Ha-ha, you sound like a monkey.'

'Shut up,' Peter muttered, his face glowing red.

'Come on you two, I thought you agreed to get along after last week,' his mother said. They had argued for days on the boat, eventually culminating in a fight in which Peter had thrown a pair of Sophie's shoes overboard and she had slapped him around the face in front of the captain. He muttered a half-hearted apology, turned away and rested his head on the wall of the carriage grumbling then closed his eyes.

Peter jolted, knocking the side of his head against the wooden window frame. His eyes felt heavy, but the bright glow outside shook his mind awake. We've stopped moving.

Sophie and his mother were asleep pressed up against the far wall. His father, Reverend Collins, and the drivers were nowhere to be seen. The only sound was Sophie's snoring over the faint whistle of the wind. Peter creaked opened the carriage door and stuck his head out; his vision was struck with the soft orange hue of sunset. The daylight was dropping behind majestic limestone mountains in the distance, each seemed so high it almost blended with the clouds above. They looked like how Peter imagined the stone columns of Olympus in the Greek legends he had read at school. Before them lay fields, countless pointed, emerald stems swayed in the gentle breeze which was laden with a bitter scent, almost like freshly cut grass. A dyke, barely the width of a person, cut through the sea of green like a bridge, leading to the track on which they had stopped.

A voice to the rear of the carriage caught Peter's attention and a burst of adrenaline distracted him from the beauty of the landscape. For a moment he panicked, unsure whether he was meant to be in charge of his mother and Sophie's safety or vice-versa. His father's laugh was carried in on the breeze and a sense of relief washed over Peter as he and the reverend came into view carrying a bundle of sticks.

'We're stopping here for the night lad,' his father called out. 'I'll get a fire started, you grab the tents from the roof... the local lads hopped off a way back.'

Peter nodded, still feeling unsure of himself, and climbed up the side of the carriage. He wrestled to release the canvas sack from its ropes, but just as it was beginning to loosen, his foot slid from the window frame and with a complete lack of grace, he tumbled down onto the ground below. 'Sorry,' he murmured, but the old friends were too busy reminiscing and didn't take much notice.

Just as the last strands of daylight were slipping away over the distant peaks, Reverend Collins sparked a fire with a flint run across his knife. Peter's father brewed tea, while Sophie and his mother prepared some potatoes and fish that had been produced from the market bag. The heat of the day finally started to fade, but as night fell mosquitoes swarmed the camp, keeping comfort at bay.

Exhausted and ready for sleep, Peter lay in the tent trying to ignore the bloodthirsty creatures buzzing around his head. 'I hope the village isn't like this,' he muttered, and looked over to Sophie who was snoring away again. I've had enough, he thought after an hour of counting the holes in the canvas above him waiting for sleep. He lifted the leathery flaps of the tent and scanned the camp. The fire was smouldering, barely, and the tree line to the west was buzzing with the croak of cicadas.

Peter walked, not far but just enough that his legs began to feel heavy. The road that ran alongside the fields was straight, the moon was bright, and his eyes had adjusted. I'll have no problem finding my way back. He pondered the day's events, wondering where they might be tomorrow and what it might be like. *I've been to worse places*, Peter eventually decided, thinking back to the time he saw a thief beaten to death in the streets of an Algerian market. The image of the man's eyes before he was dragged into the mob had burned itself into his brain. Thankfully, tonight, he managed to force the thought from his mind as he walked into the darkness.

CHAPTER FIVE

Chatter outside slowly tugged Peter awake. By the time he had dragged his groggy body from the tent, the rest of the campsite had already been bundled into the canvas wrap, which lay open on the floor awaiting his own contribution. Sophie and his parents were loading everything else back onto the carriage while Reverend Collins fed the mangy-looking horses that had spent the night tied to a tree a few yards from the camp.

'Come on sleepy, we haven't got all day,' his mother said. Peter smiled back weakly and nodded. I can't believe it's only spring, he thought feeling the warmth radiating up off the floor and the sun beating down overhead. It barely ever got this hot during summer in Britain.

The group plodded on through fields and rice terraces for two more days. By the evening of the third day, they were traversing slopes and mountain paths that verged on sheer drops. A cool breeze blew through the hills offering Peter some relief from the muggy weather. But cooler temperatures meant more energy and Sophie, who was always bored after more than five minutes, was taking it out on her brother, trying her best to wind him up at every given opportunity.

'I know she can be difficult sometimes,' his father said, as the two of them constructed the tents that evening. 'She's so much like her mother,' he smiled and shook his head, 'but you'll have to hold on to your frustrations for a few more days until we reach the village.'

'But why is it always me who has to hold on or fit in around what everyone else?' Peter knew they were all just as tired and frustrated as he was, but still felt the way she got away with everything was unfair.

'That's one of your strengths, you're flexible, you adapt quickly, like me,'

'-not out of choice.' His father smiled, but his face looked weather-beaten and tired, it was obvious arguing about it wasn't going to help. Maybe he's right. Peter wasn't sociable like Sophie, but he was happy with his own company and was certainly used to change.

That evening, he rolled out the ground sheets and his sleeping bag, lining them up perfectly with the tent door, before helping Reverend Collins stockpile enough wood to last the night. There was pleasure in the process of repetition, the sense of stability it offered made life simple. The same as every night, he ate dinner then lay on his back, counting the ever-growing holes in the canvas over his head. Peter thought about his life back in England, and how, despite never really fitting in, he still missed it. Six months until I'm lying in my nice soft bed. His back was aching from sleeping on the solid ground, separated by only a thin mat. He climbed over his sister and poked his head outside. The fire was still going strong. Getting better every night, he thought staring at his handiwork. All around was quiet, there were fewer flies and mosquitoes too, *maybe it's the height.*

Peter ventured further than he had done the past few nights, the track was winding, and more ups and downs kept him focused on remembering the route. After an hour or so, a high-pitched yell was carried in on the breeze. *What was that?*

Peter stopped in his tracks, remembering that Reverend Collins had briefly muttered a warning about wild animals. A few more seconds passed. Another noise, this one was clearer. *A shout.*

It's people? What are they doing out here? They hadn't seen a soul for two days. Peter froze, he held his breath and strained to listen. There were hooves too, the regular beat was unquestionable. Even worse, they were getting louder, fast. *Are they coming this way? Do they know I'm here?* A barrage of questions rushed into Peter's head but one thought cut through. *RUN!*

He took off back towards the camp as fast as his legs would carry him, the blood rushed to his face making him even less graceful than usual, and the sounds of hooves echoed behind him, growing louder with each passing second. Voices to his rear became shouts, and the orange glimmer of burning torchlight caught the corner of his eye. Worry and confusion transformed into blinding fear, Peter's eyesight became a tunnel, focused only on the dark track in front of him whilst the shouts and gallops converged into a deafening symphony at his rear.

Get off the path. Peter peeled to the right, he stumbled into a ditch and lost his footing. A desperate scramble to his feet ensued, and after what felt like minutes he clambered out of the other side and broke into the tree line running blindly. He glanced over his shoulder to see only darkness. *No one's following me.* His eyes flicked forwards just as an enormous shadow tore through the trees beside him. BANG. His vision shook and started to blur, a warm sensation ran down the back of his shirt.

I've been shot... I'm dying. Peter's thoughts spiralled, they made no sense. The ground sped towards him. He felt the warm dirt on his face, its bitter taste in his mouth. All the questions running through his head melted away as the world faded into darkness.

CHAPTER SIX

The sound of hooves beat the ground. Their pulsing rhythm reminded Sophie of the weekly rides from the parish into the impoverished suburbs of Constantine. She would chat with her mother, trotting along side by side, while Peter was always on the front of her father's horse leading the way. When the oval-arched bridge that marked the city border eventually appeared on the plateau ahead, they would pick up speed into a gallop, smiling and laughing as the road behind them was obscured under a blanket of yellow dust.

Sophie's memories seemed fractured and chaotic. She recalled the familiar thuds of her ride into town, but something felt different. Now they were in a frantic gallop, faster than she had ever been before. A stab of pain shot into her ribs as they went over a bump. *I'm lying on the horse,* she realised, *this is all wrong.* Another stab in her chest forced a gasp for air, and the horrors of the night came back to her. *I can't breathe.*

A horde of soldiers had torn through the trees, scattering embers across the camp. In the pandemonium of fire, screams, and gunshots, she had been dragged by her hair into the darkness. Blows rained down on her until she had lost consciousness. The next thing she knew she was being heaved onto a horse. As they sped off into the darkness, she heard her father's shouts growing more and more distant. A gunshot echoed through the trees. Then silence.

The rope was cutting into Sophie's wrists, a coarse woollen bag covered her eyes and mouth, making breathing hard, and seeing impossible. Maybe it was the deprivation of her other senses, or the adrenaline still coursing through her veins, but she could hear everything. Shouts were being exchanged from one rider to another, at least five horses stomped along beside her, and the wooden wheels of the trailer that she had got to know so well rattled along behind them. Tears ran down Sophie's cheeks, pooling in the top of the hood before dripping through the weave towards the floor. She bit her lip as she fought back the urge to scream. Only now, Sophie realised how uncontrollably she was shaking, she had never felt anger like this. *I* need *to get free.*

CHAPTER SEVEN

Minh nodded keeping his lips pursed, and the old woman's stern expression changed to a smile of blackened teeth that was barely visible in the shadows of the hut. *Ha-ha, no way*, he thought.

Minh loaded up his hunting basket. A handheld crossbow, a water bottle made from the figure-eight shaped fruit of a gourd plant, a ball of sticky rice wrapped in banana leaf, and his machete. He threw the vine-strapped basket onto his back and set off towards the dusty path out that led out of the village. As soon as he was out of view Minh immediately turned east, straight into the thick forest that lined the hillside. He knew why Thi didn't want him going there, the forest had often been a hideout for bandits and criminals that fled to the mountains, as well as far more fearsome creatures, but it was also where the best hunting was found.

He crunched barefoot over the sticks and leaves that blanketed the forest floor until his soles were black and his legs ached.

A squirrel zigzagged through the undergrowth like a bullet. The crossbow bolt in its side had slowed it down, but there was plenty of life left in the creature and it was determined not to be an easy meal. As his prey paused in the shadows of a bush collecting its energy for an escape, Minh crept forwards. He swallowed a deep lungful of air, trying to catch his breath without giving his position away. Just as he pounced, a glimmer of light caught the corner of his eye, the squirrel sped off and Minh crashed through the bushes landing hard on the leaf-carpeted ground. *Damn.*

It was going to be difficult explaining how he had been gone so long without a catch, but something else had caught his attention. *What* was *that?* He rolled over and turned his gaze to what appeared to be a pool of water under the leaves a few feet away. *Its spring, there shouldn't be any water here.* Minh limped over, his side hurting from the fall, and swiped the leaves aside. He gasped as the corpse of a bizarre-looking man lying beneath came into view. His white shirt was torn and covered in smears of mud and blood. *That's what it was, glasses,* Minh realised. He had seen them before on the foreign missionaries that came to his village when he was young, but never up this close. He studied the face below him for a few moments and decided he must be a boy, similar in age to himself.

'*Ban la ai?*-Who are you?' Minh said aloud. *Either way, you're dead as a bag of rocks...and much worse looking.* He stifled a laugh and glanced around making sure there was no one to hear him. *You don't need them anymore. Thanks,* Minh reached out to take the glasses from his face. As his finger brushed the boy's nose, his face twitched. *He's not dead!*
Minh's excitement quickly turned to apprehension as he pondered how much the skinny boy could weigh, *I could always drag him, it's not like he's going to get much dirtier anyway.*

The sun was beginning to set as Minh approached the outskirts of the village. He soon had a couple of farmers helping him carry the foreigner and within minutes, they were winding down the pathway that led into the village square. The commotion caused by their arrival drew the entire community out of the stilt houses that stood elevated over their workspaces and animal pens. Questions of 'Is he dead?', 'Where did he come from?' echoed through the crowd.

Yai bustled to the front of the congregation.

Bring him here quickly,' he called out to his nephew, and directed the carriers towards the ladder of the hut he and his small family shared. 'Did anyone see you with him?' Yai asked, the fear in his uncle's voice caught Minh off guard.

'I don't know...'

CHAPTER EIGHT

Lord Tan leaned forwards on one of the dark hardwood seats that lined the receiving room. His forehead rested in one hand, while the other tapped on a tiny porcelain teacup. Any other day he would have been strategising with his generals, doting on his son, or drinking with guests. But today he needed to keep his head clear. What felt like hours dragged by and his thoughts ran wild, first through confusion and then rage. *Who are they? What are they doing in* my *land?*

Finally, the familiar sounds of soldiers' shouts and hooves were carried in on the breeze offering him a moment of respite. Lord Tan swallowed the last sip of his bitter green tea and rose to his feet. He paced through the sunshine of the courtyard, ignoring the servants that had stopped to bow on their way to clean the room he had departed.

The official report will be prepared in moments. Lord Tan knew the process, he counted the minutes, picturing the soldiers dismounting, then meeting with their general to be debriefed, before making their way through the citadel and finally into the main hall of the castle. Lord Tan had done the same many times over the last thirty years, first as a soldier, then as a ruler. But things were different now, time was not on his side. More of the foreigners were coming to his lands each year, attempting to establish trade routes—by force if need be—or feed lies of religion and salvation to his people. In the past Lord Tan had been unconcerned, simply cutting the tongues from their mouths and releasing them to die of thirst in the forests, but today, something felt different.

The soldiers burst through the iron doors of the main hall, shattering the forced aura of calm their ruler was hopelessly fighting to instil inside. General Khang strode the length of the room, stopping a few feet before the dais, a red and gold platform that elevated Lord Tan's throne three steps above the floor. He bowed deeply with his arms crossed as a sign of respect. Lord Tan could barely restrain his tongue, as he waited for news of the captured foreign spies or soldiers. His men dragged forwards a bulging sack and clattered its contents onto the floor. Lord Tan eyed the heap for several moments, the initial sense of relief he felt realising they were not as he suspected, soon turned to anger. He hated the foreigners' religion, but even more so the cheap, useless equipment they brought.

'Books we can't read, cooking pots, and a few cheap metal crosses,' he murmured forcing the room into silence. 'WHAT DO YOU CALL THIS?' the veins on Lord Tan's face bulged as fury overwhelmed him. 'I want guns, and gold, not this worthless pile of junk.'
Lord Tan ripped his sword from the sheath slung over one side of his throne, and swung blindly at the forward-most soldier. Before he knew what had happened, a flash of steel caught his blade. It was held steady, just inches from the man's throat when General Khang's eyes met his own. Both glanced around the room, and a deadly silence was cast within.

'My Lord, this man is not to blame,' the general said, his voice calm and low, 'they were travellers not soldiers, they had very little. Please take my squad's wages to make up for this error.'

'Fine,' Lord Tan replied through gritted teeth and lowered his weapon, 'but next time you come across rats like these in my lands I expect you to return with their heads.'

The soldier who had been inches from death spoke, his voice trembling, 'please accept my humble apologies, Sir. But, we also took some-'

'-we have a prisoner,' General Khang interrupted. He signalled to a group of men who had been waiting silently just outside the almost-closed door of the hall. They fought to keep their grip carrying a thrashing and kicking figure towards the foot of the throne. As the soldiers approached, a flailing foot connected with one man's jaw causing him to stumble backwards. The captive thudded down on the floor in front of the dais and all went quiet. The first soldier pulled the bag from the prisoner's head and several swords were trained on the throat and abdomen of the girl.

Blood and dirt covered her face, whilst her blonde hair was knotted and blackened from smoke. Lord Tan had seen foreigners before, but very few foreign women, and even as a mess this one looked pretty. *This does make things better,* he thought running his eyes over her as though examining a pig in the market.

'Hmm, very well,' he nodded, 'take her away and clean her up.'

'Thank you sir,' General Khang replied, 'I'm sure your father would have acted just as mercifully if he were still with us.' Lord Tan rose to his feet and glared down at the ageing soldier before him.

'You have done well general, but remember, I am in charge here not my father, and if you *ever* question me again it will be your head my sword is swinging for.'

CHAPTER NINE

Yai sat watching the boy's chest rise and fall as he lay on a wicker mat in the corner. For three days and nights, they had done all they could, cleaning his wounds, feeding him rice soup and coconut water. Yai prayed the boy would come around, but knew if he wasn't awake by now he may never be. 'Still like a corpse,' he sighed looking over to Thi on the far side of the long stilt-hut, his grim tone reinforcing the expression on his face.

Another day passed before a wandering peddler arrived bringing news, he was directed to Yai after talking with the villagers about an attack just a few miles to the east. Sitting in the old man's hut the he explained, 'Bandits attacked the group, hunters found their bodies nearby.'

'What of the camp?' Yai asked.

'Ashes,' the peddler sighed, 'the whole area was burned to the ground.'

The old man's fists clenched. He took a deep breath and hung his head until the anger he felt began to subside. He thought long and hard about what he would tell the boy if he ever woke up.

They weren't bandits, they were soldiers. Not that anyone would dare say it. Thinking about Tan's men sent a shiver down the old man's spine. Not for himself, but for Minh, Thi, and the villagers who would face torture or death if they were found to be sheltering the boy. Tan was known for being a great warrior, but over the years it seemed his paranoia had grown, as had the strength with which his iron fist clasped onto power. Those that opposed him were killed, those that supported him became rich, and those of no use, like Yai and his village were simply expendable. The safest thing they could do was to keep quiet and hope that there was no reason for his men to take notice of them.

He must have known about the foreigners, we can only pray that they counted the boy dead, Yai decided. He tried to meditate, as he always did when facing tough situations, but his mind was fogged with anger, and when night came he lay awake with scenarios running through his head. We could leave him in the forest; the animals will make short work of him... but what about his family? Without veneration the spirits of his parents would be forced to wander eternally as hungry ghosts, starving but unable to eat, dying of thirst but unable to drink, a fate worse than the lowest level of hell. Yai cursed his conscience.

As the morning sun rose, revealing the sea of green trees and rice paddies the lined the hillside, he found a new perspective. It is Karma that brought him here, and we too must accept our own. If Buddha is smiling on him, he will never wake.

CHAPTER TEN

Pillars of sunlight stretched through the cracks in the thatched roof and crept across the floor, illuminating the wooden panels inch by inch. As one ray worked its way up onto Peter's eyelids, he blinked.

There was a searing stab of pain, but darkness. *Am I blind?* His memories rushed back to him. *I was dying, am I dead?* He couldn't see, he couldn't move, his entire world was agony. It certainly felt like how he imagined death would feel. After what seemed like an eternity, the pain began to fade. Peter could sense his hands and feet twitching, as though his body was slowly returning control of them to his brain. *Smoke?* was his next thought. There was a fire burning, it wasn't close enough for him to feel its heat, but for some reason the familiar smell and crackling was comforting.

After hours of darkness, shapes began to emerge from the gloom. He was lying on a woven mat in some kind of a hut, half in the shadows. The walls were brown tubes of bamboo and a kettle sat over a fire in the corner which, almost as he focused on it started to simmer. Peter recognised the sound from his dreams, there had been strange voices talking over it too.

I can't remember anything else, he realised, and a fresh wave of fear gripped him. *Don't panic. What's your name? Peter.* He remembered the faces of his family sitting close around him as they moved in some sort of vehicle. But where they had been going or what he was doing there were mysteries.

We were on a boat! He thought back to the rocking sensation of the waves, but his mind felt clouded and numb.

Come on, focus, then what? A voice just outside the door shook him from his thoughts. Peter tried to move but his arms and legs were locked stiff. He seemed to be looking down at his body from above, staring into his own eyes as an old man rushed towards him, then darkness again.

A gasp of air hit Peter's lungs as cold water splashed his face. A smile cracked through the beard of the old man, spreading wrinkles across his dark skin. A woman sitting on the mat beside him smiled through a mouth of blackened teeth that he couldn't tell if he had imagined or not. *I can move!* Peter shot back into the corner, pinning his arms and legs in close.

'Who are you? Where am I?' he blurted but was met with blank faces. The old man leaned forwards pointing towards his face and muttered something.

'What?' Peter gritted his teeth in frustration. *Why am I here? Who are these people?* A ringing in his ears and searing pain forced his head back down onto the mat.

It felt like just a few minutes had passed when he woke again, but now it was dark. The only light came from lamps burning in the corners of the hut, filling the room with an eerie orange glow. The old man called his wife over and started speaking slowly. *I can understand some of the words...* Peter realised, it wasn't many but one or two stood out. *Why? It doesn't make any sense.* The old woman offered him a wooden bowl containing some kind of soup and a cup of brown water, filled with herbs and seeds. He drained the liquid in one, 'more please,' he gestured rubbing his throat, suddenly aware of his overwhelming thirst. When he had finished eating and drinking, the old man sat down on the mat beside him. 'Yai,' he said patting himself on the chest.

'Peter,' he replied and tapped his head shrugging, trying to explain he didn't remember anything. After several minutes, a boy clambered through the entrance of the hut. 'Hello. My name is Minh,' he stated proudly in a thick, awkward-sounding accent.

'You can speak English?' Peter croaked with as much excitement as his weary body could provide.

'Say slowly... little English.'

'How?'

Minh made a gesture of prayer to the sky. 'The... err-'

'-missionaries? They're here?'

'No. Three years,' he held three with his fingers and wafted his other hand backwards.

'Three years ago? Are they still here?' Minh shook his head.

With a combination of broken English, the odd word Peter knew and gestures, Minh explained how he had found his body in the leaves of the forest, and brought him back to their hut. The woman, Thi, remained stony-faced and barely spoke, while Yai and Minh tried their best, but getting any information across was difficult. Peter asked about his parents several times but Minh didn't know anything and for some reason the old man refused to answer, just telling him, 'rest first.' Peter's thoughts circled. *He knows something, why isn't he telling me?* But the frustration was exhausting and it wasn't long before his eyes closed again.

It was afternoon when Peter next awoke. The sound of the ladder outside creaking shook him from sleep and shortly after a man wearing a long European-style jacket and carrying a leather bag entered, adding to his confusion.

'I am Sang,' the man muttered in an almost British accent, 'I 'm a doctor.' He reached forwards to shake hands, Peter responded but was unsure what to make of the visitor.

'Do you know what happened to me? How did I get here? Where are my family?'

'First, I need to check you,' said Sang, pulling a small glass vial and syringe from his bag. He pierced the lid, drew the liquid up and reached for the patient's wrist. A sudden wave of panic caught Peter off guard, he jumped back pushing Sang's hand away. *Maybe he's here to finish me off?*

'It's only painkillers,' Sang said in a calm voice with his hands out flat. He seemed like a doctor, but Peter didn't know who he could trust. He was shaking so much he barely felt the needle enter his skin, but as Sang went on to probe his head, it burned with every touch. After a few minutes, the doctor seemed satisfied and went over to speak with Yai. They stood in the far corner of the hut where the kettle continuously simmered. The solemn expressions on the two men's faces as they talked were making him anxious and Peter dug his fingernails into his palms, *Will somebody please just tell me what's going on?*

Eventually, Sang walked back over, he let out a long breath, lay his leather bag on the ground and kneeled down beside Peter.

'Your group was attacked. I'm sorry to tell you this… but they are dead,' the doctor said with sadness in his eyes. 'A provincial lord named Tan, likely ordered you all to be killed, his ruthlessness is widely known.' Peter couldn't believe what he was hearing.

'No. You're lying!' But the look on Sang's face was too full of genuine sympathy to deny. He gasped for breath and tears welled up in his eyes. The faces of his family felt fresh in his mind, he could picture them clear as day. *I'll really never see them again*? It was unbelievable. For a long time, there was silence. A storm of anger and sorrow swelled inside Peter until he could control it no longer. He cried and screamed until his weakened body had nothing left to give and finally succumbed to the fleeting relief of sleep.

CHAPTER ELEVEN

Peter ran his hand over the back of his head, wincing as his fingers felt the depth of the wound. Glimpses of the ground speeding towards him flashed through his mind, but it was all too brief for him to make sense of. He struggled, trying to force his brain to recall any details of the night they were attacked. *Nothing. What am I missing?* A noise outside caught his attention just in time to see Minh manoeuvring through the narrow doorway of the hut. The last day and night he had felt cut off from everything he had ever known, but seeing Minh's friendly smile as he approached was reassuring. Although difficult, their combined knowledge and use of sign language went a long way towards having a conversation and for the first time Peter could remember he was glad to make small talk.

Other than the throbbing wound on his head, his injuries were minor cuts and bruises and as the days went by he gradually began to feel stronger. With each conversation his language ability also grew, it started with simple items, water-*sui* and rice-*gao*, but over time he learned more and more from the family. As Peter recovered he stayed alongside Thi, who was always cooking or repairing clothes, while Yai and Minh were helping plant rice or hunting. After sometime she finally agreed that he was well enough to work outside, and one morning sent him off with her nephew.

On his first venture out beyond the steps of the hut, Peter was led towards a rocky outcrop. The purpose became clear as they climbed; the peak offered a panoramic view of their surroundings. The village was high in the mountains, to the west lay steep rice terraces which ran down into a valley, and to the east was the forest in which Minh had found him, an endless sea of greens and browns stretching into the distance. Peter gulped as the sheer scale of where he was sunk in. *How will I ever get home?*

As the days ran into weeks, the heat of early summer grew intense. Most days were spent working out in the fields to ensure the rice harvest was a success, and while they went about their jobs Peter got to know the lifestyles and customs of the villagers well. People were hardworking and resourceful, but superstitious; from the fragments of conversation he understood they seemed to be nearly always discussing omens and signs from the spirits.

At first the ways of the village had seemed so unfamiliar from his old life, Peter had wanted to give up even trying to understand, but he was used to change. Eventually, he found that just going along with the routine day by day was the best method to keep himself distracted from the sadness that threatened to swallow him up.

Each morning they would be up at dawn, working for a few hours until the sun was almost at its peak, then they would eat a simple meal, sleep through the hottest part of the day, and continue with farming or hunting till sunset. Some evenings the whole village would eat and drink together around a fire, other times Peter just sat and practiced speaking with Minh, reasoning that if he was ever going to escape he'd need to know to communicate properly. He didn't know if it was down to his lack of memory, the fact he had never really fitted in at home, or if his brain had somehow been rewired by the injury, but with each passing day, Peter felt less and less like an outsider.

One afternoon, as the heat of the summer day was condensing into storm clouds overhead, the pair were on the trail of a fox. Minh had tracked the animal for hours as it led them farther east than Peter had ever ventured before. After such a long chase he knew there was no way they could quit empty-handed. As the trees began to thin, a scene in front sparked Peter's memory; it was like a shot of electricity cutting through the fog.

'I know this place,' he said and without another word broke into a jog. *We came this way, in the carriage.* Fragmented shards of places and conversations returned. *Sophie, my parents, the reverend we were all here.* He took off sprinting down the path in front, hoping in some desperate way that it might lead back to his family.

After more than a mile, a noxious odour filled Peter's lungs, it burned his nostrils and the back of his throat as he panted, struggling for breath. The path twisted in front of him and turning a corner, he burst into a clearing. The ground was black and the air reeked, specks of charred earth and ash swirled in circles around the camp, carried by the winds of the approaching storm. Blackened items littered the hellish landscape, without hesitation Peter was on his hands and knees hunting for anything that survived. As Minh caught up and entered the clearing, the colour drained from his face.

'*DI, NAY!*- GO NOW!' he shouted, Peter could see the look in Minh's eyes begging him to leave.

'I… I can't,' he said, 'I need to know what happened.'

Minh grabbed him by the shoulders and started dragging him up and back the way they had come. *What's that?* A glimmer in his eye pulled Peter back around. He shook off Minh's grip and shot down towards it. His hand stretched out for the glimmering silver pendant that lay almost obscured amongst the charred debris. *My mother's necklace.*

Peter paused, suddenly aware of the silence. A breeze rustled treetops in the distance, but there were no sounds of life, not even the chirping of a bird or the buzz of a fly. In a single moment, the true nature of the situation dawned on him. *They're dead. Nothing survived.* He snatched the necklace from the floor and fastened it around his neck. *Only this. And me.*

Accompanied by an explosion of thunder, Peter's cries of guilt and anger ripped through the forest. Finally, the black clouds burst as though offering to wash the ashes away in sympathy. By the time he had composed himself, the pair were both drenched. Minh put a hand on his shoulder and slumped down on the blackened grass at his side. Peter's body was shaking with anger and through gritted teeth he vowed, 'I'll kill the man who did this to my family. If this is the last thing I ever do, I swear, I'll do it.'

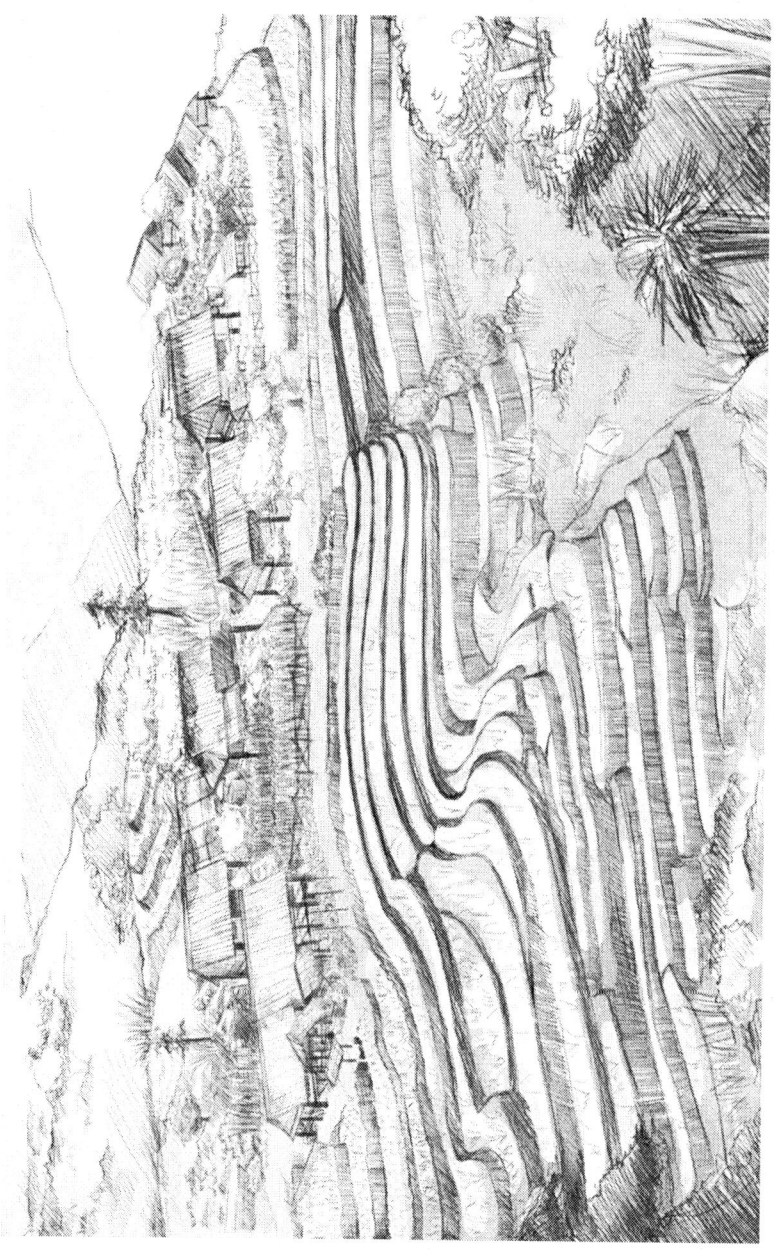

CHAPTER TWELVE

'Never!' Sophie spat, 'I'd rather die,' as yet another whip from the rattan cane snapped against her shins causing a crimson stripe to rise from her skin. No more than an hour passed before it started to dawn on her, *I might actually die here.*

Almost a month had gone by since Sophie's new life inside the castle walls had begun. Up until now, she had remained defiant, but as her body began to break so did her will. Hunger, grief, injury, and depression had left her beyond exhausted. Slowly she came to accept that her choices were to do either as she was ordered or face death.

The castle was an octagonal structure centred upon a courtyard. On all sides were rooms that housed the hundreds of Lord Tan's servants, advisors, personal guard, and wives. The main structure was surrounded on all sides by a low wall, then a flower garden, and a high outer wall dotted with watchtowers. Beyond this was a town of some sort, Sophie could hear the noise of a market and people going about their lives from the gardens, and from time to time labourers entered the castle.

It must be fifty feet high, she finally concluded after days of staring up the grey stone blocks of the wall and trying to picture the drop on the far side. Most of her time was spent alongside Tan's wives, although they seemed more like slaves, working from sunrise to sunset cooking, cleaning, and serving guests. There were five of them in total, the oldest wife Chi, was the mother of Tan's sole heir, the nine-year-old Lord Cau.

Sophie didn't know if it was because she had managed to give him a son or if her relationship with Tan went deeper than that, but Chi wasted no time making it clear that she was untouchable. She acted like an elder sister to the others, keeping the younger women in line, and teaching them how to act in the presence of dignitaries and guests. Sophie was certain she overheard her muttering to herself a few times in French, a language she had picked up at school in Algeria, but Chi only ever ordered her around in her mother tongue.

Sophie was squatting down in a shaded corner of the courtyard, reluctantly following her orders to wash vegetables one afternoon, when the sound of approaching footsteps caught her attention. She glanced up to see Chi pacing over with her head held high. She muttered something too quietly and quickly for Sophie to make out and the blank expression on her face made Chi repeat herself three times to no avail.

'Me comprenez-vous maintenant, petite fille stupide? Savez-vous comment servir le thé?-Do you understand me now you silly little girl?' Chi sighed. 'Do you know how to serve tea?'

I hate you, Sophie thought gazing up at her repulsive face. *'Je pense que je sais*-I think I know,' she mumbled. Sophie had seen some of the women pouring tea for the officials that had arrived earlier in the week. There was ritual to it; they poured the tiny porcelain cups in order of both the age and level of importance of the drinkers, which seemed obvious by how ornate their robes were.

'Good, tonight you will serve our lord and his guests.' Sophie wondered what the punishment would be if she refused. Just a week before she had seen the whip marks on one of the younger wives' back as she changed her clothes, apparently she had embarrassed Lord Tan in front of a guest.

Chi spent the next several hours bossing Sophie and two other of Tan's younger wives around as they were being dressed and made up. Except for Chi, and Yen—the only woman who hadn't taken an immediate disliking to her—Sophie could barely tell them apart. She watched the reflections of the two wives on either side of her, and those rushing around behind. To her right sat Nung, the youngest of the harem. She was stunning, even despite the permanent scowl on her face. *Beautiful-Nung,* Sophie dubbed her. The other, Hao, was tall and spindly, with arms that appeared too long for her body, *Lanky-Hao.* Sophie bit her lip to hold in a smirk.

The three women were forced into tight silk dresses, 'I can't breathe,' Sophie explained pointing to her chest and panting. Chi hushed her, making it clear comfort was not a priority, and the cords that held the dress were strained further, almost to breaking point. Powder was padded onto her face, filling the room with a cloud of metallic, noxious-smelling dust. *I look like a ghost,* she thought catching a glimpse of herself through the fog. She had never used makeup before and this made her appear sickly pale, but Beautiful-Nung glared at her, whilst applying thicker and thicker layers to her own face. Sophie kept her eyes forward, being surrounded on all sides by the spiteful group was intimidating, it made her feel small. Someone to the rear muttered something obviously insulting, several of the wives sniggered and Sophie's cheeks burned red through the chalk-white makeup.

Chi was tying her hair as they made eye contact in the mirror, 'Nung is jealous,' she said in French, 'she thinks Lord Tan just wants you around to show off.'

'I DON'T CARE!' Sophie snapped. Her eyes immediately shot to the floor realising that she had gone too far.

'They're right,' Chi growled through gritted teeth, and caused Sophie to wince as she tugged tightly on her hair and pinned it up on top of her head. 'You are a novelty with which our lord will soon tire.' Sophie smiled back with obvious spite. Just then, the ringing of a bell from the courtyard pulled her thoughts back to the torturous evening that awaited her. Chi tugged Sophie up by her shoulders and nudged her in line behind the other women that were starting for the door.

CHAPTER THIRTEEN

When the guests began to arrive, Sophie was sat seething on the benches that lined the courtyard. She was struggling for breath through the combination of humidity and the ridiculous silk dress she had been forced into. Yen approached and with a sympathetic smile, signalled for Sophie to follow. 'Don't worry,' she whispered, leading Sophie towards the wooden-arched corridor that ran from the courtyard to the main hall, 'I was nervous too.' Yen mimed anxiety, putting her hands to her face clenching her teeth to ensure she understood.

Why would I be? I'm furious you idiot! Sophie managed to swallow her anger and force a weak smile; Yen was as close to a friend she could hope for, and she certainly didn't need yet another enemy. Chi and Beautiful-Nung were waiting at the entrance alongside two guards in decorative red robes and woven hats. A feeling of panic came over Sophie as they approached the carved dark-wood doors of the hall that lay ominously ahead. It was where she had been thrown onto the floor at Tan's feet on that first day. *Was it really was only a few weeks ago? It feels like years.*

The doors heaved open, inside was lit up by the glow of lanterns that hung from every wall. It looked beautiful, like a different world. Chairs and tables carved from the polished roots of enormous trees were laid out in the centre of the room, while the rich scent of lacquer and fragrant burning wood filled the air. Lining the walls were several plinths dotted with decorative vases, statues of deities, and a seemingly random selection of European items interspersed between them. A grandfather clock ticked away softly on one side, a musket that must have been a hundred years old was in the centre, and beside it a three-foot long, ornate gold crucifix, *obviously stolen from a church*. As Sophie examined the strange array of valuables around the room her stomach knotted, she realised she *was* part of this freakish collection.

Sophie followed the others as they moved between the tables pouring tea in the hour that followed. *They look like pigs,* she thought as a seemingly endless parade of fat, red-faced old men in silk gowns entered the hall and found their places around the tables. Their eyes upon her made Sophie's skin crawl, she wanted to cry but was determined not to give them the satisfaction. As the hours ticked by, the guests grew fatter and more drunk. Endless plates of boar, porcupine, and other unrecognisable animals, along with copious jars of liquor were delivered to the hall. Sophie had been praying that when the eating had finally finished she would be able to slip out unnoticed, but Chi obviously had other ideas and ushered the serving women to the back of the hall. She dragged Sophie by the wrist to the front beside Tan's throne, smiling and bowing to the guests as they went.

'Kneel there,' she ordered pointing to a mat by his side.

'No.' Sophie glared, she was exhausted, her feet were screaming in pain, and there was no way she was going to kneel at the feet of the man that killed her family whilst his court of swine leered at her. Chi's eyes burned, through her forced smile she snarled, 'kneel now or you will be carved in half on the spot.'

Is she serious? A wave of fear washed over Sophie as she noticed the engraved golden sword bouncing up and down on Tan's lap as he laughed. Sophie kneeled. A palm waved in front of his guests silenced them immediately and Tan turned to her. The stab of worry and anger she felt as their eyes met her own was almost too much. He picked up a green and gold lacquered cup from the table that rested in front of his throne. He raised it above his head with both hands and then to his lips draining it in one. *What on earth is going on? Are they going to kill me?*

Tan rose to his feet, swaying as he did, and then passed his sword to Chi, who thrust it into Sophie's hands. *Maybe they're testing me?* Unsure how to respond, she laid it beside her on the ground and glanced at the faces upon her hoping for any clue of what was going on. A servant rushed over and refilled Tan's cup. He raised it to the room once more, before turning to Sophie. 'Drink it,' he growled, the stench of alcohol on his breath was noxious. She bit her lip to hold back a retch, but didn't move. 'Do *not* embarrass me,' Tan whispered, his tone was grave. Sophie's trembling hands reached out and received the ornate porcelain. As she lifted the cup to her lips Chi pushed it higher pouring the revolting liquid down her throat. Sophie gagged, fighting the urge to throw up, it burned her throat and tasted like death. Tan raised both arms above his head, and the room erupted with shouts and cheers.

'What happened? Did he poison me?' Sophie whispered.

'Don't be stupid,' Chi spat back, whipping the sword away from her.

'You were sharing wine. You're married.'

'WHAT?!'

'Shhh.'

A stab in her gut forced Sophie to double over in pain. She buried her head in her hands and spluttered to get air into her lungs. *This was my marriage? THIS?* Sophie's face burned red and her eyes clouded. The embarrassment was crushing, her swell of tears burst and before Sophie knew what was happening she was running towards the door. Tan roared with laughter as the room erupted once again.

'Lord Tan wants to see you in his quarters,' Chi called out to her as Sophie lay curled up in the darkest corner of the courtyard. Even in broken French, the jealousy in her voice cut through. Silence.

'Did you hear what I said?' It is your Lord's request. Do not leave him waiting.'

'Please don't make me go, I'll do anything,' Sophie begged. She had never hated anyone more in her life and the thought of being trapped alone with this drunk, murderous, dog made her want to die. From the twisted grimace on her face, it seemed Chi didn't like the idea much either, she stood in thought for a moment, then turned and paced away back through the courtyard towards Tan's personal quarters without a word.

It was only a few minutes before she returned. 'He's drunk and has fallen asleep, now get out of here quickly,' she said, her face twitching unsure whether to be relieved or angry.

Sophie lay on the edge of the wicker mats that the 'new' wives shared in their communal quarters. For the first time since her arrival, she prayed. *Thank you God for not putting me through that.* She prayed for the souls of her mother, father, Reverend Collins, and finally for the strength to escape. Whether it was desperation or sorrow she did not know, but she wasn't ready to pray for Peter. *Where were you that night?*

CHAPTER FOURTEEN

It had been weeks since Peter visited the charred camp. The summer was in full swing and the stepped terraces were thick with the blades of maturing rice plants. Farming was hard work, but as the autumn harvest drew closer they spent more time out hunting and trapping than in the fields. Through necessity alone, Peter's language skills were developing faster than he could have ever imagined.

One evening the whole community—nearly a hundred people—had gathered to eat and drink around a fire on the rocky outcrop Peter had climbed during his first few weeks in the village. Yai had explained how the days of the full-moons were auspicious as they were closest to the heavens, and tonight its outline was vast overhead, bathing the village in a soft white glow. They chatted and laughed over the meal for several hours and as things began to quiet down, the relaxed atmosphere spurred Peter to bring up a question that had been on his mind for some time.

'What happened to your family Minh?' he asked. Peter knew they were dead, but up until now no one had mentioned them.

'We buried them when I was young,' Minh answered in English. The pair often flicked between languages when they didn't want anyone to overhear. Although there was sadness in his voice, the look on Minh's face was one of pride. Yai saw it too, even in the dark of the evening there was no getting secrets past the old man. He looked into the flickering flames ahead and took a deep breath almost as though preparing himself.

'Minh's village was on the far side of the valley. There used to be many here like ours.' Yai sighed turning to look at his nephew, then to Peter. 'One season the rains came late and the harvest was low. Tan and his men tried to take the larger-village's reserves to feed their own people, but many fought back, so that their children might live. We offered our help to take in the young, to hide them from the soldiers-'

'-Minh is our son now,' Thi smiled, 'and we are lucky to have him.' The tale conjured up memories of Peter's family, and as he thought back to happier times the sorrow he had been carrying with him felt momentarily lifted.

The next morning Minh's snoring woke Peter. He lay on a mat in the corner whilst Yai and Thi slept on the far side nearest the entrance. As rays of sunlight began to spill over the horizon and filter through the bamboo-pole walls, a realisation came over him. He didn't know where he was, what day it was, or even how long he'd been here, but he was alive and free. *How many others can say the same?*

As everyone eventually awoke, the usual tasks of feeding the animals and fetching water began. Mid-morning Thi ordered Peter and Minh to visit the market, the heat and humidity meant nothing kept for long and food needed to be restocked daily. Minh greeted the market vendors with a wave as the pair strolled along the track towards the village square. Peter had felt like an outsider the first time he had visited the market, people had gawped and pointed at him, chattering in hushed tones, but by now, the novelty of having a foreigner around had worn off. He was talked to just like anyone else, albeit slower, but with each conversation he learnt a little more of the language and about their way of life.

The sun emerged from behind the clouds as they entered the village square and Peter squinted through the glare to see what was going on. A crowd had gathered in the centre, thirty or forty feet from them. *What if they've come back for me?* was his first thought.

'Let's see what's going on,' Minh said and jogged off without even pausing for an answer.

'Wait,' Peter called, but he was already out of earshot. *Calm down, nobody knows you are here.* He felt angry at himself for being so worried, there were often travellers and peddlers passing through the village and it was almost definitely just one of them drawing the crowd. As they closed the distance, there was too much noise emanating from the small group of spectators, something felt strange. Peter peered over Minh's shoulder in front of him, eager to be reassured of his safety. An old man was in the centre of the circle, his long white beard and dark-blue robes looked out of place even by the village standards. He was twisting and lunging almost like a dance. Peter recoiled as the sunlight glinting off the sword in the old man's waistband caught his eye. He began to edge away backwards away hoping to have gone unseen, but Minh caught him by the arm and pulled him back in.

'Ha-ha, I can't believe he's here so soon,' his friend said with a grin.

'You know him?'

'Yes, he's a wandering monk and doctor. He passes through every year, trades medicines and reads fortunes.'

Almost on cue, the old man began to sing in a monotone too deep and too quiet to make out any clear words. Within a fraction of a second, his sword was whipped from his belt. He circled it around his head, striking the floor again and again. Peter glanced around the crowd; everyone seemed in awe of the old man's show.

'He's praying, asking the spirits to reveal the future... he's never wrong.'

'Never wrong? Seriously?' Peter's face twisted in disbelief.

'Yes,' Minh shot back seeming almost upset. Peter had gone along with plenty of strange rituals since his arrival, but foresight was one step too far, especially for a doctor, which Peter assumed he must have misheard.

'Hmm,' he nodded, deciding to save his argument until the noise of the crowd dropped down. After a few minutes, the fortune teller's dance came to a stop, he bowed to the onlookers, lowered himself onto the ground sitting cross-legged and took out a tube of rolled paper from his bag. A paintbrush and pot of dark-blue ink slid out of the roll. It dawned on Peter just how rare it was to see anyone writing around the village, *I haven't actually read anything since I arrived!*

The old man licked the paintbrush, dipped it into the pot, and unceremoniously scribbled for several minutes. He then stretched out his arm, handing the paper to an old woman without even turning his head and he uttered a few words, her face burst with joy at the result. *What could he possibly have told her?* The fortune teller stood up, walked over to a patch of shade in the corner, and lay down with his head resting on his bag. The crowd began to disperse.

'Let's go and talk to him,' Minh whispered.

'I don't believe in fortune telling, and I definitely don't believe that this old man could tell me much by dancing around,' he said, but Minh was already on his way.

'Oi,' he called out. Peter winced, he knew the greeting was polite, but to him it just sounded aggressive. The fortune teller turned his head to the side and peered out of the corner of an eye fixing his gaze on Peter, he knew just what the old man was thinking. *You're a long way from home.* The fortune teller flicked his eyes back to Minh, 'You shouldn't interrupt an old man resting. He frowned revealing the wrinkles on his weather-beaten face, 'what do you want?'

Peter was wondering if he expected an apology when Minh burst out with a barrage of questions. The old man immediately swiped his hand through the air, signalling for silence. He responded as though he was giving a lecture, but his dialect was bizarre and Peter recognised virtually nothing he said. Minh was nodding along at first, but slowly looked more and more baffled as the old man continued. *What is he talking about?*

'Leave the master alone, he has enough to worry about without your questions.' A familiar voice rang out from across the square, Yai approached the pair and bowed to the old man. 'Will you join us for a meal Master?'

'I was waiting for someone to ask,' said the fortune teller, smiling and rocked to his feet with surprising vigour. Yai led the group back to their hut.

'His name's Master Hong,' Minh whispered to Peter, translating the old man's words as he spoke. 'He's requesting accommodation, in exchange for medicine or guidance, he never accepts money though. He comes through on a pilgrimage at a similar time each year.'

'Pilgrimage? Where to?' Peter said, wondering how this grouchy old man could ever be considered pious.

'We don't know, it's the secret of the monks,' Minh said, 'you have to become one if you want to find out, ha-ha.' Peter tried to listen as Yai and Hong talked. He seemed different, abrupt, almost rude, yet a strange air of calm surrounded him.

'He was asking Uncle Yai about you,' Minh hissed, 'where you came from and if you can understand the language.' After only a few minutes of listening in, Thi ordered the boys out to ask around the village if anyone could spare a bed for the old man. As they walked away from the hut, Peter could hear the conversation continue, he was certain they were still talking about him, but brushed off the frustration he felt.

It didn't take long to find Hong accommodation, just a few dozen yards down the road Yai's neighbours were excited to put up the honoured guest.

'Why do you think they wanted us out of there?' Minh asked as they headed back towards the hut. Peter smiled, surprised at his perceptivity, but a tremor of suspicion echoed through him. 'I don't know.'

CHAPTER FIFTEEN

As he followed Minh up the creaking bamboo ladder and entered the hut, all eyes were on Peter. Aside from the croaking of cicadas that filled the warm evening air, all was silent.

'Come and join us,' Yai said beckoning them over to where he, Thi and the fortune teller sat in the centre of the hut, 'Master Hong has some news.'

'Thank you brother,' Hong nodded and turned to Peter who sat down opposite.

'You must understand, this is only a whisper among the villagers, but brother Yai and I decided you should know. There is word that Lord Tan has a new wife. A foreigner. Were there women travelling with your party?' Peter was on his feet before he even realised, his face alight with excitement. 'Yes! My mother and sister, are they okay?'

'I know nothing for certain,' Hong said, 'but as I heard there was only one prisoner a young girl.'

Learning that Sophie may still be alive changed everything. Peter was overwhelmed with joy, but at the same time struck with sorrow. There had always been a tiny shred of hope that his parents had survived. Now it was gone.

For hours Peter sat and listened to the conversations around him, but he felt thousands of miles away. After some time, the fortune teller sat down at his side, he pressed a cup of warm tea into Peter's hand and as if reading his mind, Hong spoke, 'No matter what we do, the past has already happened. You can run and hide from it, or embrace it and learn from it, the choice is yours.' The old man's words rang true, there was nothing that Peter could do to change what happened and now he knew it was only a matter of time until he needed to make a decision. *If I ever hope to see Sophie again it'll be down to me alone. But what can I do? I'm no one...*

For the next few days, a typhoon laid siege to the mountainside, blasting it with winds and rain the likes of which Peter had never seen. He spent the time buried deep under the weight of his thoughts. *Do I stay or go? Do I search for her or run?*

Minh idled away the hours listening to stories of the fortune teller's travels. As he questioned Hong about every detail, it became clear just how badly Minh wanted to experience the world outside of the village. *I think it's better here, simpler at least,* Peter thought. He wished he could stay, maybe out of fear alone, but somewhere deep down he knew, *I can't hide here forever.*

On the afternoon of the fifth day, he and Minh were helping to lock up the chicken coops beneath the wooden slats of the hut when the sun, that had made a brief appearance, was once again obscured by black clouds. The rain fell lightly at first, before a torrent lasting more than an hour beat down on the thatched roof above them. Finally, as the downpour began to subside, the beat of hooves echoed in the distance. Peter bolted to his feet and Yai's eyes met his own, even in the darkness of the hut, the fear on the old man's face was clear.

Peter's mind screamed at him to run, but Yai had other ideas. Under the far corner of the hut, he was boosted into a wooden crate. It was dry and well hidden, while a crack in the slats provided a view of the track that led towards the village square.

'Don't move and no one'll know you're here,' Yai whispered. Peter prayed he was right.

As the gallop of the riders approached, it was clear they were moving at speed. He stifled a sharp breath seeing the sunlight glinting off their blades in the distance. *Soldiers.*

Two men rode up the swamp-like track from the village square and towards the row of stilt houses, whilst Yai and another elder walked down to greet them. They both did their best to appear as friendly as possible while trying not to lose their footing in the mud. Yai bowed almost horizontal as the soldiers slowed their horses and came to a halt side by side in the path. The older of the men spoke first, 'I am Captain Phu. On behalf of Lord Tan we are conducting a search of the villages in this area and expect your complete cooperation.'

'Please sir, no need to wait on ceremony,' Yai replied, 'come and get dry, then we will be glad show you around.' Peter was concerned, he sounded *too* confident. The soldiers dismounted, and the four men talked in hushed tones for several minutes before Yai called Minh over. A few seconds later he jogged off again, banging on the wooden struts that held each hut up until the whole community had emptied out onto the path.

The soldiers combed through their homes one by one, every dwelling in the village was only one or two rooms, so nothing was left untouched or uninspected.
By the time the pair had reached the fifth building, they carried an armful of family heirlooms and hunting equipment

that had been deemed illegal. All the villagers could do was watch politely as their most precious items were whisked away. Peter stewed in anger watching them abuse civilians this way, but his fear far overwhelmed the rage. His heartbeat was pounding in his ears. *Any minute they're going to see me.*

They entered the sixth hut—just a few dozen feet from where he was hidden—there were muffled voices coming from within. Every set of eyes in the village were searching to see which loved one or friend was absent. *Calm down, breathe, and don't get stupid now,* Peter thought as he battled the adrenaline in his veins that was urging him to run. He tried to focus on a happy memory from his childhood to calm his spiralling thoughts. It was a warm summer afternoon, he and Sophie were racing to climb a tree in the garden, whilst their parents laughed and cheered from the lawn beside them. He focused on the sounds of their voices, the scent of the oak tree, and the singing of the birds in the distance until he felt as if he was almost there.

A sharp bang broke Peter's concentration, he saw a flash of blue as a figure tumbled into the door frame just inside the hut. *Who is it?* A fraction of a second later the perpetrators identity was revealed by the white of his beard. *Master Hong.* Peter squinted to see through the gaps as the soldiers followed him out, Hong wasn't resisting but he certainly wasn't making it easy and the younger soldier had to practically drag him from the entrance and onto the muddy ground outside. *What's this crazy old man doing? He's going to get us killed.*
Peter wanted to scream at Hong for being such a fool, but he knew it would be a death sentence.

'Hand over the sword. Now,' the captain said, pointing at the weapon tucked into Hong's waistband. *It's not even sharp*, Peter thought praying the situation would end without incident. In a strange way he liked the fortune teller, at the very least he didn't want to see him die. Hong began to reach for the weapon in his belt, just as his fingers found the buckle, something caught the captain's eye. He started for Yai's hut with his gaze fixed on the crates. *He's seen me, I'm going to die.* Peter gritted his teeth and squeezed his eyes shut.

'NO.' Hong's voice echoed across the silent path, stopping the soldier in his tracks. The captain spun on the spot, and his eyes nearly popped from his head as he saw the fortune teller fastening the weapon back around his waist. Hong stood opposite with his hands on his hips, looking defiant yet serene, almost smiling at the captain's brewing anger.

'Don't make us hurt you old man,' growled the captain and began to approach from the side, 'give us the weapon.'

Hong didn't say a word. The embarrassment was too much for the younger soldier, he lunged to grab the sword from the old man's waistband, but Hong twisted sideways leaving his attacker grasping only air. The soldier lunged again, this time aiming to grab him by the throat. Hong stepped back, just a fraction out of range with flawless timing.

'YOU FOOL!' The captain whipped his sword from the sheath by his side and in one fluid movement swung it at the old man's neck. Maybe it was the burst of adrenaline from his impending fate, or the speed of the attack but Peter's brain barely even had time to register what happened.
Hong's body arched backwards almost horizontal to the ground and the look on the captain's face turned to panic as

he realised he was cutting nothing. BANG. Hong's right foot streamed up from the floor his heel smashing the captain under the chin so hard his feet left the ground. Stunned, the younger soldier froze, it was barely a second before he regained his composure, and charged forwards, screaming, with his sword raised high.

Hong sidestepped his attacker and in one fluid motion, fired off four blows to his ribs and head followed by an elbow, which landed with a sickening thud and dropped the soldier to the ground. As both men lay face down in the mud there was absolute silence in the village. After what seemed an eternity, Hong adjusted his robe and turned directly to Yai who was standing wide-eyed at the front of the group. 'I apologise for bringing this violence to your people, but I could not let them continue. I will bury the bodies then head to the mountains… no more lives will be put at risk.'

Oh no, how does he know they are dead? Peter glanced towards the crumpled bodies and retched. The whole fight had lasted only seconds and just like that two men had become nothing more than piles of flesh and bone lying in the mud. He felt bile rise into his throat, the acidic taste burned as Peter fought the urge to throw up.

Hong bowed to the villagers, then to the bodies. *'Namo Amitabha*-Praise to Buddha,' he said, and turned back to Yai.
'I will take the boy, he'll die if he stays.' Hong's gaze pierced through the cracks of the crate locking on to Peter's own. As their eyes met, he started to shake.

CHAPTER SIXTEEN

'*Chao bui sang*-Good morning,' Tai waved to his neighbour as he wheeled the cart past his house and onwards down the bumpy track towards the village. Since dawn he had been shelling rice and netting the crabs that lived in his field in preparation for the weekly market trip. In previous years, the few buckets and baskets on his cart would have been an almost-daily harvest, now he struggled to make enough once a week.

Tai had grown up in the lowlands that surrounded the citadel, life there was simple and he enjoyed it, for the most part. But occasionally he would look towards the grey walls on the horizon and imagine what it would be like living within them. When he was young, he and his father had visited the town to trade a handful of times, but for now it seemed his fate was living day to day and just making sure he had enough to get by.

As Tai rounded a bend in the path, a familiar figure came into view a walking in the opposite direction.

'What have you got today?' Soc said, closing the gap between them and leaning in for a better view of the buckets. 'Hmm, what do you want for the crabs?'

'Four hundred,' Tai replied.

'You've got to be kidding! I'll give you two.' Soc scattered a handful of rusty coins into a cup at the front of the cart and helped himself to the bucket.

Good start, Tai thought trundling on.

As he approached the bamboo fences of the village, something seemed odd. *Why's it so quiet?* Normally the bartering on market day could be heard half a mile from the square.

He rounded the corner and the problem became clear, a pair of soldiers were trotting on horseback along the stall-lined path, probing at the products with sheathed swords, and questioning the vendors. Tai continued on as discreetly as he could, the buckets on his cart clunked over the uneven ground, but as he passed the soldiers on the far side of the path they didn't seem to pay him the slightest bit of attention.

Just as Tai was commending himself on a job well done, a voice stopped him in his tracks. 'What have you got there boy?' the officer called. He glanced back over his shoulder and it took a second for him to realise the question was directed elsewhere. Tai set his cart handles down and turned to see a boy, who couldn't have been more than ten years old, stood frozen behind a stall about twenty feet behind where he had stopped.

'Pass it here,' the soldier ordered, leading his horse across the path and over to the boy.

'Pass wha-'

'-you know what. Don't test my patience.'

'I can't, it's my mother's,' the boy pleaded, still grasping the melon-sized clay pot that he had been attempting to hide beneath the counter. Tai rolled his eyes. *Don't be an idiot.*

The soldier dismounted, and paced the remaining few feet, his sword and leather armour clacking together as he went. He tore the pot from the boy's hands, scattering the few coins inside across the floor. The child's lip began to shake, tears welled in his eyes and he quivered with anger. *He's going to get himself killed.* Almost on instinct Tai sprinted over, grabbing the child by the wrist an instant before he threw his fist.

'Nephew, relax. We all need to pay our taxes,' he said in as soft a voice as he could muster. He turned to the soldier, smiled and bowed his head. 'I'm sorry sir, my nephew didn't understand you were just doing your job, please accept my apologies.' Tai glared into the boy's confused, tear-filled eyes as if to order him, 'let it go.' The officer's hand pushed his partially drawn sword back into its sheath.

'You should raise your children to respect their superiors' peasant.'

'I will sir, thank you,' Tai nodded.

'This should cover the taxes,' the officer waved at the coins scattered across the floor.

'Clean them up then lad,' said Tai tutting like his own father would have done. The boy set about picking them up one by one and placing them back into the pot.

'Now what about the insult?'

'Please take my products,' Tai said pointing out the cart that was sitting on a few yards further down the path. The soldier stared him out.

'I suppose that'll do,' he growled, 'but don't expect us to be so lenient next time.'

Tai bowed low, gritting his teeth into a fake smile. The boy handed the pot to the officer, not daring to look up from the floor, whilst the other soldier tied his cart behind his horses.

'I didn't need your help,' the boy hissed as soon as the soldiers were out of earshot.

'You were about five seconds from dying. You certainly did need my help,' he scolded, 'they have no sympathy for you, they'll skewer you like a pig and won't lose a wink of sleep over it.' The boy grumbled and returned to sitting behind the stall. *Typical. That's the thanks I get for sticking my neck out.* Tai glanced over to where his cart had sat. *Bastards.*

CHAPTER SEVENTEEN

Sophie resisted with everything she had, scratching, biting, and kicking as the guards dragged her through the courtyard and towards Tan's quarters. It had been less than a day since the wedding.

'Ah my beautiful wife,' he laughed, as the guards struggled to restrain her thrashing body. Sophie ripped an arm free and threw her whole weight behind it, her fingernails caught Tan's face scoring three deep red lines just below his eye. He yelped with a mixture of pain and surprise, pinning a hand to his face. A second later Tan's palm smacked into Sophie's temple sending her vision spinning for the few seconds before everything went black.

Sophie awoke on the flower-patterned tiles of a darkened room. She had no idea how long she had been there. Her head was throbbing, but the feeling of defilement as she lay unclothed on the floor was what truly hurt. Unable to move or speak, she waited there suffocated by shame and guilt, for almost an hour. Finally, two guards dragged her back to the wives' quarters, where she was dropped onto a mat and her bundled clothes thrown on top of her. A similar story played out many times in the following weeks. Sometimes her defiance paid off, on other occasions she didn't have the strength to resist and simply let her mind go to a less-abhorrent place. But, as the weeks rolled by she was called upon less often, thankfully, it seemed as if her novelty was starting to fade.

What's going on so early? Sophie thought, a commotion coming from the courtyard had awoken her. There were calls of roosters already coming from the citadel, but outside it was dark as night. She stepped into the pre-dawn courtyard to see Chi hurrying back towards the section of the castle Lord Tan and her son shared.

'Excuse me. What's going on?' Sophie asked, hoping she was not in her usual foul mood.

'Some soldiers went missing searching for more of your friends,' Chi answered, glaring as though she was personally responsible. Sophie's heart skipped a beat.

'Who are they? where-'

'-I don't know, and I don't care,' she snapped, 'and neither should you. You are the property of our lord and shouldn't be concerned with such matters.'

Blood streamed to Sophie's cheeks as she fought the instinct to explode. But from that moment on, escape occupied every waking second of her thoughts. *Whoever they are I have to find them, it can't be worse than this.*

She had thought about running away before, but knew on her own she would never get far in the wilderness, now a glimmer of hope gave her new resolve. Sophie decided if she was to make it to freedom she would need to be trusted by Chi, who watched her like a hawk. *You'll have to be like them, become one of them.* She shuddered at the thought. *It won't be long, then you'll be free.*

Within a week Sophie had seamlessly moulded into her new role. She understood how people thought and once she had managed to swallow her pride, it was easy. Sophie bit her tongue instead of cursing under her breath, and even forced a smile onto her face in front of Tan and his guests. As the days ticked by she got almost to the point of considering Yen and Lanky-Hao her friends. *This isn't who you are,* she had to remind herself often, fearing she might become too accustomed to life within the castle.

One afternoon, Sophie was sitting on a bench in the courtyard working through a pile of broken garments. *The joke's on them,* she thought looking down at the terrible job she had done of fixing a ripped robe. Although she had learnt to sew with her mother as a child, Sophie considered it one of the most tedious activities conceivable. Muffled shouts coming from the main hall on the far side of the courtyard interrupted her thoughts. She always sat here, because it was cooler she told the other wives, but in reality it gave her the perfect position to eavesdrop, and any snippet of information could be her key to escape.

He's such a child. His temper is going to be his downfall, she thought listening to one of Tan's tantrums. The almost-daily outbursts put the entire castle staff walking on eggshells, praying they wouldn't end up as one of the bodies that were carried from the hall with increasing regularity.

As Sophie reached further down into the warm wicker clothes box, her fingers felt something cold. *What the..? It's metal,* she thought, feeling the weight of the item. Sophie withdrew her hand grasping the handle of a tailor's knife, it was a six-inch-long, single piece of steel, ending with a razor-sharp tip. *Lucky I didn't cut my wrist,* Sophie thought. She realised someone must have left the blade there by mistake, who and when didn't matter. Now she had a weapon.

Sophie waited until the sun was setting, and when she was sure no one was watching, tucked the blade into the silk wrap that acted as a belt, and made her way to shared wives' quarters. Her space was a corner near the door, home to extra mats and covers, which were rarely needed in the heat of the summer, and she was certain that if she hid the knife deep enough under the mat no one would see it.

Sophie's face dropped as all five of the wives, who were sitting in a circle on the floor talking about something, turned to see her enter the room. *What can I do now?* She couldn't sit down without removing the blade or getting cut. Sophie feigned a pain in her stomach as an excuse to stay standing and after a while the conversation seemed to lapse. Yen wandered over to where she stood by the door.

'Maybe you're pregnant?' She said sounding excited, 'I knew one of us was bound to be eventually, where does it hurt?' she reached out to touch her stomach.

'NO.' Sophie panicked, realising Chi was eyeballing her.

'Sorry… it's just painful,' she answered, guiding Yen's hand to just above where the blade was hidden.

'Don't be a fool,' Chi spat, 'we all know he's dry as the desert. I wouldn't let him hear you talking about it either if you know what's good for you.' She huffed and turned back to her conversation. Sophie sighed with relief.

'Thank the Lord,' she mouthed when the lamps were finally extinguished for the night. She lifted up the corner of the mat, and slid the blade as far under as she could. *Don't get found. I'm going to need you.*

CHAPTER EIGHTEEN

A root sticking out of the ground sent Peter tumbling to the floor, he clambered back to his feet, and wiped the mud from his stinging palms. Noticing he'd nearly lost sight of the old man in the darkness of the forest he jogged a few steps. *How is he so fast?* Peter thought, struggling to keep up with Hong's pace over the rugged terrain. It seemed impossible for a man of his age.

Hong and two other men had dug graves in the forest a few miles east of the village. It was dense enough that any more soldiers were unlikely to venture through, and far enough away that it wouldn't be clear who had buried the soldiers there.

Did they really have to die? Peter had wondered as he stared at the lifeless heaps slung over their horses' backs. *They were people too... what if they had families?* He had to remind himself that they only died because of their actions, but it did little to ease the sense of guilt he felt. Minh had helped to unsaddle the horses and set them free, while Hong performed a blessing for the spirits of the dead men, a kind of last rites. He had lit incense over the graves and knelt down chanting a prayer, it reminded Peter of the fighters he saw paying respect to each other in the square on the first day he arrived. Hong's chants were slow and melodic, but tuneful, almost too pleasant sounding to be for the people he had just killed.

'Even the souls of evil men can be purified with mantras, a type of Buddhist prayer.' Hong explained as they began to walk south from the graves.

But you killed them! Peter thought in disbelief. He knew if Hong hadn't acted then it was likely they would both have been caught, and that the soldiers may even have deserved to die. But for a religious man to be so well practiced at killing, particularly the one he was now following into the depths of the forest, scared the life out of Peter. He replayed the fight continuously in his head, until he was no longer sure what was real and what he had invented. After what seemed like hours of it pressing on his brain he finally snapped.

'Why did you have to kill them? How do we know their lives are any less valuable than ours?' Hong stopped. His shoulders sunk as he turned and his eyes searched for Peter's face that was barely visible, just a few feet away.

'I did not *want* to kill them. Men of religion must avoid violence wholeheartedly, especially out of hate or rage.' Hong's calm tone made it hard for Peter to be angry at him.

'I had no choice, they found me without even meaning to. They would certainly have found you... they were looking for you, and then Lord Tan would have ordered the village destroyed. The lives I took today were with Karma in mind, by sacrificing the spirits of the two soldiers, we will have saved many more. Like all powerful people we tread a fine line, balancing between life and death'.

We? You more like. Peter was glad to be alive but he knew the image of the lifeless men staring up at him as the soil showered down and covering their faces would haunt his dreams forever.

As they left the highlands that surrounded the village, the paths narrowed until there were only animal tracks and the temperate forest turned grew thicker and more humid with each step. 'Where are we going?' Peter asked, trying to steer his thoughts from death.

'Talk later boy, now we need to cover distance. More soldiers will be coming soon. We have one or two days at best or our fate will be worse than theirs.'

Peter winced. *I don't want to die, I've got so much left to do, I could have been a scientist, or a doctor. Now I'm stuck here, probably forever...*

'Stop worrying about dying and start caring about living.' Hong called back, almost as if he knew, 'first thing you can do is pray.'

CHAPTER NINETEEN

Peter and Hong spent the night under a huge Indian-almond tree that reached high into the starlit sky of a clearing. The ground was wet and outside of the thick forest it was cool, feeling less like summer and more like autumn. Swarms of ravenous ants and mosquitoes ensured it was a long night as they feasted on Peter's wrists and ankles. Between the cold and the insects, it was impossible to get more than a few minutes of sleep before waking up and starting the long process again.

By the time sunrise came, both men were sat cold and exhausted, eagerly awaiting its warmth. They gathered up their possessions; Hong had his sword and bundle of medical supplies, mainly just bottles of herbs and balms. Peter wore his mother's necklace, and in a wicker backpack, carried a long shirt and trousers given to him by Minh, a few pieces of fruit, and a ball of rice. Hong passed Peter the final gulp of water left in his gourd bottle and they began to walk.

'We're going south, there's a mountain I spent a few years training on as a younger man, Hong said, 'they will be coming for us, and it is only a matter of time, but should we be caught there, we will be able to fight from the high ground.' *Fight?* thought Peter, the idea of more soldiers was terrifying. *Did he say a few years?*

'How long will we be there?'

'Hard to say. If they do not find us first, a season at least.'

Peter swallowed his fear and nodded, the glum expression spread clearly across his face. *I should be back in England already. I miss my comfortable bed. I miss my family...* a lump swelled in his throat as he fought the urge to cry. In that moment, the absurdity of the situation hit him, stopping him in his tracks. *Is this really how I'm going to live my life?* He wondered, *like a child crying for my home and my mother? I have to find Sophie and we can escape, together.*

The last few days had been so overwhelming he had barely thought about her. Peter promised himself that when they made it home, there would be a proper funeral, and his parents would get the mourning they deserved, but now was not the time. He needed to be strong.

'Get down boy,' Hong hissed pulling him by the back of his neck into the bushes that lined the path, 'someone is following us.'

'Soldiers?' Peter whispered.

'No. It's too quiet. Maybe a tiger.'

The colour drained from Peter's face along with his short-lived burst of confidence. *Seriously?* Hong peered up through the gaps in the leaves scanning for movement. A faint rustle gave away the position of their stalker. They were definitely human footsteps, the breaking twigs and rustling seemed ungraceful, even to Peter, who lay flat on the ground struggling to control his breathing. In perfect silence Hong rolled over onto his back. He drew the sword from his waistband keeping it flat to his chest. Step. Step. Step. Almost upon them. Hong spun on his shoulders, with both legs sweeping in a semicircle just above ground level and narrowly missing smashing Peter in the face. The assailant yelled as their feet were whipped out and they hit the forest floor hard. Hong leapt up, his sword streaming towards the throat of the enemy as a killing blow. In the very last moment, the blade stabbed into the ground a fraction of an inch from the attackers' face.

'YOU FOOL. I almost killed you!' Peter pulled himself to his knees. In front of them, frozen stiff, with the exception of his bottom lip trembling, Minh's face stared back.

'I...I...I'm sorry,' he barely managed to get the words out, 'I wanted to help.'

'Help? How could you help you bumbling oaf?'

As he regained his composure, the look of distaste melted from Hong's face and he took on a more peaceful tone. 'You are in danger travelling with us, you will be in even more danger returning home on your own...' he sighed, sounding exasperated more than anything, 'we have no choice, you must come with us. Although now there are more tracks for them to follow.'

Peter was still shaking from the experience, but seeing Minh's face break into a nervous smile, helped ease the heavy atmosphere that had been hovering over him ever since they left the village. Just at that moment, the sound of a distant gunshot echoed through the trees, Minh's smile fell and both boys looked to Hong.

'We need to move. Now.'

CHAPTER TWENTY

When he was younger, Minh had always been by his father's side as he and the other villagers hunted, sometimes for days at a time. Walking long distances and sleeping rough was the hunters' way of life, but now after three straight days of marching, the humidity of the forest coupled with a lack of food and water was taking its toll.

'Get up there and take them,' Hong barked as Minh pointed out a cluster of fruit growing in a tree above. *Keep your beard on old man.* If there was anything Minh hated more than being told what to do it was hunger. He ran up the tree, his hands around the trunk and his feet flat on the bark, determined to prove that he wasn't useless; seconds later he dropped back down to the ground in front of them with the fruit in his arms.

'They're wild bananas,' he said to Peter, 'not exactly delicious, but better than nothing.' He handed a couple over and watched the disappointment on his face as he peeled the skin to find the thick potato-like flesh and bundles of black seeds inside.

Within hours, the gentle slope of the forest had grown steeper until they practically had to climb from tree to tree. In front of them, the trees opened up revealing the peak of a mountain that dominated the skyline. The sloped hillsides were dotted with shacks and rows of neatly trimmed lime-green bushes.

'Tea farmers,' Hong said, 'they grow here because it's cooler, better for training too.'

Training? What training?

They rushed through the open tea fields keeping quiet and low, then passed bundles of bamboo and bushes that grew thicker and thicker until they were surrounded by yet more forest. Minh's legs were burning as they wrestled their way up the steep path through the undergrowth, it was more than hour before it levelled out into a plateau. Trees lined every side and dangled overhead, as if a cave had been carved out of the forest. A stream trickled down the rocks from the peak above and formed a pool, twenty of thirty feet across, in the centre of the clearing. Minh knew the danger; *anything could have died in it upstream.* He was too thirsty to care and plunged his face into the cool water. Hong tutted, shaking his head. 'Luckily, the water is safe to drink. We're near the top.'

The group rested for a while in silence before Hong led them around the pool to the far side of the plateau, he pushed aside the overgrown bushes to reveal a narrow, perfectly-hidden stone staircase.

'One way up, one way down.'

The worried expression that had been almost permanently stuck on Peter's face since they left seemed to relax slightly, as he realised how obscured they would be. The stairs were steep, uneven, and seemed to run forever.

'This was once the site of temple,' Hong continued, 'on this peak, a sect of warrior-monks lived, trained, and died.' His voice trailed off. 'Anyway, no point in wasting more energy. You'll get to know these stairs very well.'

What's that supposed to mean? Minh wondered. He had never been this far from the village, and although he was unsure what lay ahead, the freedom was exciting. He had decided long ago that a life of farming wasn't for him and with each step towards the peak he became more and more certain. *There's a reason why all this has happened. My parents' death, finding a new home with uncle Yai and Thi, rescuing Peter, and meeting Hong. Everything has been leading me here, to this... It's my Karma. My destiny.*

CHAPTER TWENTY-ONE

I hope we don't have to that again anytime soon, Peter thought, dragging his heavy legs up the final few steps. At the top of the moss-covered staircase, lay a clearing. It was nearly a perfect circle, approximately a hundred yards across. It seemed miraculous that such a large space could be so obscured from the outside world, but there it was. The sounds of chirping birds and chattering monkeys rang out from the trees that grew high around the clearing; the green and brown of their early-autumn leaves shaded its edges from the afternoon sun.

The pair followed Hong across the clearing, stopping in front of a stone altar that lay in the centre. Peter gazed at the massive chunk of weathered marble. He ran his hands over the edges that had been worn smooth by centuries of wind and rain. Barely visible, but intricate patterns and inscriptions suggested it was sacred.

'How did this get up here?' he asked.

'The monks dragged it up, one step at a time,' Hong answered, 'in ancient times this mountain was a pilgrimage site for shamans and warriors alike. The highest peaks were considered holy, and the temple that once stood here was dedicated to the spirits of martial arts.'

'Martial arts? Like fighting-' Peter said.

'-more than just fighting. Martial arts are the cornerstone on which we work towards spiritual prowess, when our bodies are strong, our minds can be too. When we have mastery of both, our power can become limitless.'

Peter stared at Minh with his eyes wide as if to say 'this guy is mad,' but he was captivated by Hong's speech.

'So you're saying that by doing martial arts you can become magic?'

'Not magic, but when you are in complete control of your body and mind you will be able to do things that seem impossible.'

'Can *you* do this?' Peter questioned in a condescending tone.

'Did you not just see a frail old man take down two heavily armed soldiers with ease?'

'Yes,' Minh said and grinned Peter's reddening face.

'And not if, but when they come for you,' Hong said, 'wouldn't you prefer to do the same rather than roll over and die?'

'YES!' Minh shouted, unable to control his excitement.

'I don't know.' Peter knew he was right, but the thought of more soldiers was too terrifying to even think about.

The old man shook his head, muttering to himself, and walked over to a battered stone hut that lay on the north side of the clearing. He dropped down his bag and rummaged about for a few seconds before revealing two apples that apparently he had been hiding.

'Gifts,' he called back. 'You two, put these on the altar and pray to the spirits of the mountain, maybe they can help our fortunes.' Even though it seemed ridiculous, Peter decided it was better to do as Hong ordered than risk his wrath.

'Just copy me,' Minh whispered and stood in front of the altar with his eyes closed.

'Please allow us to live on your mountain,' he said out loud, 'please help us with our training and help to watch over those we left behind.'

Peter was stood beside him with one eye open looking uncomfortable. *This is stupid.*

'What am I supposed to do?' he said.

'Pray.'

He thought back to the prayers that had been etched into his mind as a child.

'Our Father who art in heaven, hallowed be thy name...' Peter sighed at how hollow his words felt. He took a deep breath, and decided, stupid or not, he needed all the help he could get. *Please allow us to live on your mountain and protect us from our enemies, help Sophie stay alive, and more than anything let my parents rest in peace.*

After a few minutes of quiet, the pair's eyes met, and with a silent nod they agreed enough has been said. They walked over to the stone hut, fifteen yards or so to the rear of the altar, where Hong was using his feet to clear the spider webs and leaves lining the floor.

'Minh, go and fetch some firewood,' he called out, 'Peter, go down to the pond, use this bamboo to carry as much water as you can.' He stamped on a length of dried bamboo and it split at the top dividing into even, cup-like segments.

The stairs? Peter rubbed his aching legs. *Not again.*

Laden down with the heavy bamboo tubes, it took him the best part of an hour before he was even halfway back, and as he walked his thoughts continued to spiral.

I'm stuck in the wilderness with a killer. My sister is either a slave or dead, and any day now an army are coming to kill me... how could things get any worse? After a hundred or so steps, he remembered his decision not to live this way and tried to focus on a happy memory. It was Christmas, back in England. His family were playing a game of charades in their warm, sitting room. The scent of sage and onion floated through the house and mixed with the pine fire that burnt in the hearth, bathing the room in a soft orange glow. *I don't even have a picture of them...* Peter realised, he concentrated on remembering every tiny detail of his parents' faces to make sure he wouldn't forget them.

His arms were cramping as he entered the clearing. The sun was just about to disappear over the treetops, but a campfire was already on the steps just in front of the shack, its flames swirling in the cool breeze that wafted through the open space.

Minh had found some sweet potatoes growing just past the tree line and skewered them on sticks to roast over the fire. He and Peter ate as if it was their first meal in months, whilst Hong silently chewed, savouring their warmth and sweetness.

'Yai told me about your family,' said Hong swallowing his final bite, 'and yours before them Minh. It is clear our journey is one that will not end peacefully.' Peter looked at his friend, in a strange way it was comforting to know they had so much in common.

'Men who are driven by hatred and killing can rarely be stopped with peace, eventually our situation will come to a climax and death will be inevitable.'

'Who's death? Ours?' Peter blurted.

'I can't say. It's up to you to choose the path you walk.'

Why doesn't he just tell us what he means? He thought growing frustrated with Hong's cryptic answers.

'Now, they will come to find us, of that I am certain. Here we are on the border of the southlands, hopefully that will buy us some time. In the meantime we will start your training'.

'Martial arts right?' Minh said, his face lit up with excitement in the firelight.

'You must learn to defend yourselves, both of you. If you hope to see your homes again you will need to be prepared.' Peter gulped.

CHAPTER TWENTY-TWO

A nerve in Peter's neck twinged as he peered towards the door. It had been an uncomfortable night on the cold stone tiles of the shack, while the physical exertion and stress of the previous few days had pushed him beyond exhaustion. He pulled himself to his feet, yawned and stretched his arms, hoping it might clear the fog from his head.

In the light of day, it was visible that the hut had also once been a sacred space, the beams overhead and now-decrepit stone walls displayed the remnants of detailed carved patterns and text. Peter winced as he stepped outside, there was a lingering stab of pain in his head as his eyes adjusted to the morning light. He crossed the clearing towards where Minh was kneeling forwards working on something. *Is he gutting an animal? How long was I asleep?*

Peter's throat scratched as he swallowed. 'Do we have any water?'

'Glad you could join us,' Minh said, 'no, but the old man is getting some, while I make breakfast,' he said skewering some kind of squirrel-like creature. Peter squatted down beside him, and for the first time really took in his surroundings. Under the warm glow of the sun, the clearing was beautiful. It was spacious and green, alive with the sound of the animals in the trees and insects running at their feet.

'I would have been worried about all these insects before,' Peter mumbled with a smile, as he remembered the panic of finding what Minh called a 'baby-sized' spider crawling up his leg in the village.

Their hut sat on the north side opposite the staircase. A cracked and overgrown pathway ran across the centre of the clearing, meeting the altar and linking all three together while the rest of the ground was grassy and flat. As Peter gazed off into the distance, trying to estimate the area of the clearing in his head, Hong skipped up from the steps looking nonchalant. He was carrying two poles over his shoulders, each of which had a bucket hanging down on either end.

'Ah great, I'm dying of thirst,' he said and jogged over.

'Wait.' Hong raised his palm and waved at a pile of firewood that had been collected on the west side of the clearing. A minute later, he trundled back over to where Hong and Minh were sitting and dropped an armful of sticks beside them.

'Can I have some water now please?' Peter said using the most polite words he knew.

'No,' Hong snapped, 'this is mine.' He pointed a length of bamboo at the two youths. 'Yours is at the bottom of the steps. Fetch it before the food is cooked and there may be some left for you.' A smile spread across his wrinkled face.

'That's not fair!' said Minh, 'I caught it-'

'-life is not fair.' Hong pointed towards the poles he had carried up, 'I borrowed these from the tea farmers, take them both and make sure your buckets are full, it will be good for your balance and strength.'

As they set off grumbling and moaning, the logic for the old man's instructions became clear. With the poles sitting on their shoulders, they needed to rotate between the narrow sections of the staircase and overhanging trees every few steps. Within minutes Peter was panting and breathless, his leg and stomach muscles were burning, but hunger and thirst meant they kept the pace quick.

'It's not right. We should have refused,' Peter said.

'Yeah but you saw what he can do, he's got a temper as well, he'd have beaten us up for even trying,' Minh answered.

'No, he doesn't like violence-'

'-he doesn't like killing. I think he'd be fine with giving us both a beating.'

The walk back was easier when they weren't so dehydrated, but the water was still heavy. As they approached the top Hong was stood, leaning casually against a tree.

'You took too long,' he called, 'you're going to have to earn your meal.'

Peter was burning with anger. 'What the-'

'-I have the high ground, get past me and you can eat.'

Minh's face flared with rage, he placed his buckets down being careful not to spill a drop and sprinted straight at him. 'You cruel bastard!' he yelled and dived to tackle the old man.

Hong stepped back just a few inches and Minh crashed into the top step, again and again he swiped at his tormentor's legs, but each attempt was avoided or kicked away with ease. Peter's fists clenched watching his friend's humiliation. *How is this fair?*

He picked up one of the buckets and tried to sneak up behind Minh, getting as close as he could to the top. He flung the container forwards with all his remaining strength. Just like his friend's attacks, the water fell short. Instead of hitting his opponent it covered the top of the steps, turning the dry ground to mud beneath Hong's feet and forcing him to retreat. Peter charged past him on one side and Minh on the other.

'Ha-ha very good,' said Hong, strolling over to the pair, sitting by the fire. 'This is an important lesson for you both.'

'What lesson? I just see you being cruel for no reason,' Minh called back over his shoulder still scowling.

'When facing a powerful opponent, strength will not be enough, you need to have intelligence and flexibility to overcome them.' Hong cleared his throat, 'the man looking to fight has a chance to win or lose, the man who does not *need* to fight has already won.'

Peter glared, 'why didn't you just tell us that then?'

He ignored the question. 'Eat quickly, training begins now.'

They spent as long as possible picking at the meagre meal while the old master was rummaging through his equipment in the hut.

'I'm exhausted... I don't want to do anymore of his stupid tests,' Peter said.

'I'm tired too, but don't you want to learn to fight like he can?'

'Not really.'

'Come on, how are you going to rescue your sister or even survive a day out there if you can't protect yourself?'

'I suppose,' Peter grumbled 'but how long is that going to take? He's been doing this for decades.' Almost on cue, Hong's voice echoed across the clearing.

'Get up and come with me. If we are expecting either of you to become proficient quickly, you will need to do exactly as I say...' Peter sighed. '...and if you fail to follow my orders,

I will be enforcing them with this,' Hong raised a six-foot length of bamboo.

'You mean you're going to beat us with that stick?' Minh said.

'Those were your words not mine.'

Hong stood on the tiled path in the centre of the clearing, the sun was behind him and the new students in front. 'Our first lesson is strength. If your body is weak your mind will be weak too. Now, copy me.'

Hong demonstrated what he called the 'Horse-riding stance'. He squatted low, with his legs placed wide, and toes pointed forwards as if sitting over an animal's back. His arms were outstretched with the first finger of each hand extended, pointing to the sky. On Peter's first attempt he lasted just a few seconds before giving in to the stress and collapsing into a heap.

'It's so uncomfortable...'

'Of course, if it was easy what would you be learning? Nothing!' Hong snapped, appearing to grow stricter by the minute. Next he demonstrated the 'mountain stance', it was a long and wide step as if were ascending a slope, and the 'hunter stance', crouching almost on one knee with hands extended forwards as though waiting to spear an animal.

When they had exhausted themselves holding each position, Hong introduced their second lesson, flexibility. Peter lay flat on the grass while the old man wrenched one of his legs up towards his head, then both as wide as they could go, the pain was so intense it felt like his muscles were tearing at the seams. As the day progressed, physical practice was broken up with meditation.

The pair were instructed to sit cross-legged, eyes closed and try to focus on their breathing and stillness.

'Just like the pain of holding a stance or stretching,' Hong said, 'you need to relax. Do not let your mind burden you. Allow your thoughts to flow free and naturally like water, you can't fight the current of a river, yet equally you do not let it pull you down.'

'When are we going to actually learn how to defend ourselves? All I'm doing here is making myself sore,' Peter moaned, shaking the stiffness out of his legs whilst Minh struggled to keep a straight face.

It had been more than a week of strength, flexibility, and meditation training, now his frustrations were mounting. Without so much as a word Hong whipped his staff behind Peter, sweeping his heels out from beneath him. He lay on the ground staring up at his master's wrinkled face with a bitter look on his own.

'When you can overcome your pain without fear or aggression, we can continue. Remember the steps? You weren't worried about getting hurt were you? Your hunger was what drove you on.'

'It's impossible. How can I not care about pain?'

'Practice.' Hong's frown shown that his patience was wearing thin. 'Now, horse-riding stance ten minutes,' he said pointing at Minh. Not wanting to meet the same reprimands he immediately squatted, and Hong pushed on his head forcing him down further.

'Peter, horse-riding stance, twenty minutes.'

'Ha-ha, ow, ow, ow.' Minh laughed, wincing in pain.

CHAPTER TWENTY-THREE

'YOU FOOL!' Tan screamed with such fury his eyes almost popped out of his head. General Khang turned his gaze away from Song, one of the youngest soldiers in his command, and to the floor. Song was shaking violently as he kneeled in front of the throne, taking the brunt of Lord Tan's wrath as honourably as he could. *Have a heart, please,* Khang thought, *he made a mistake, he doesn't deserve to die.*

'If our men are missing why would you wait EIGHT DAYS to tell me?'

Song started to speak 'I...I'm sorry sir, they were a few days' ride out, I assumed they were caught in the storm but-'

'-but nothing. You were wrong!' Tan's voice echoed through the empty corridors of the castle. 'If their horses were found unsaddled and without any riders, someone must have deliberately stripped them of their load and set them free am I correct?'

'Yes.'

'It was a wonder anyone came across them at all. What would we have done if they didn't? WAITED SOME MORE?'

'I cannot apologise enough sir, but-'

Tan's knee flew from where he stood in a horizontal crescent, meeting Song's head with a sickening crack. He may not have intended to kill the soldier but his combination of rage and skill left little room for any other outcome. Khang's eyes stayed fixed on the floor, his teeth ground and his knuckles turned white, but anger gave way to guilt seconds later. *Why didn't you do something? You coward.*

Khang oversaw the removal of the corpse, still seething. *How did we get here? Lord Tan was never a good man, but he was fair. In all of the battles and campaigns I fought alongside him, he never acted so inhumanely...*

That night he visited Song's widow, he broke the news to her and comforted his children as they mourned. Khang arranged the funeral himself, including a full ritual of Buddhist prayers and veneration of his ancestors. The next afternoon he was stood in the rain, staring towards the sky and trying to focus on the dissonant wail of the two-stringed violin that marked every funeral. It was easier to hear than sounds of Song's grieving family by his side. *It's only a matter of time until Lord Tan's actions catch up with him.*

CHAPTER TWENTY-FOUR

Sophie awoke to the sound of bickering from the far side of the room as the grey, morning light spilled through the windows.

'If she's too ill to go, then it's bad luck for her,' Lanky-Hao said.

'I still think we should wait and see, but okay. Let's get her to do it,' Yen waved over at where Sophie was pretending to sleep, 'they're close enough in size'.

She rolled over and rubbed her eyes, 'What am I doing?'

'Nung is ill,' Lanky-Hao said, 'so you'll be coming with us to the town.'

Sophie gasped. *Don't sound too excited,* she scolded herself.

'Oh, okay, where?' she said feigning weariness.

'The tailor's. Two days from now is the death-anniversary of Tan's father, there are hundreds of guests coming to pay their respects, so we need to get dresses made.'

Finally! Sophie forced herself to stifle the excitement. More than two months had passed since she had found her blade in the tailor's box. She had gone about her business as usual, pretending to be broken-spirited and resigned to life in the castle, but that was anything but true. With each passing day she was observing routines, people, habits, searching for any opportunity or weakness that could be exploited. *Today might finally be the day.*

The three wives were carried into the streets of the citadel in an open carriage, two of Tan's personal castle guards pulled the poles that extended out in front. Their robes were a lighter shade than the brown colour regular soldiers wore, almost red. Everyone in the town seemed to recognise them and bowed as the carriage passed.

The area was much bigger than Sophie had predicted, maybe half a mile across, but she was determined to note with care every door and gate, every hiding place, and every soldier standing guard. The outer wall was vast; grey stone blocks seemed to run endlessly ahead, casting half of the street into shadow. The moist air in the town smelt dank, it was thick with the scent of manure and smoke. Sophie could see grey plumes reaching over the top of the citadel walls, and guessed they were burning off the old rice plants following the recent harvest.

She made small talk with the wives, only half-concentrating as she tried to detail her surroundings. Luckily, Yen would talk with anyone about anything, they discussed how cold it was getting, the approaching Lunar New Year, and the preparations for Tan's father's memorial. When they stopped outside the tailor's shop, which appeared to be nothing more than a shack filled from floor to ceiling with embroidered silk and fabrics, Sophie had mentally mapped out half of the town.

The three women were measured and tried on sample dresses for nearly an hour. Sophie hated the way they were expected to cook, clean, and still somehow appear beautiful and immaculately dressed. *This is so stupid. We're so much more than this,* she thought watching the other two wives getting excited over fabric patterns.

Although today, their distraction worked to her advantage, she focused out on the street watching for any patrolling guards or soldiers and tried to ignore the tailor who continued tightening her dress ever further.

By sheer luck they set off in the opposite direction home, the citadel was horseshoe shaped around the central castle, so she guessed they were near the front of the structure. Sophie ran her eyes across the wall as they bumped up and down on the cobbled street, they had only moved a few yards when something caught her gaze. In a quiet corner of the wall a narrow beam of daylight shone through the shadows. Sophie strained to see clearly. *That's it. What is it? A drain?* There was no grate covering it, but it seemed too small for a person to fit through. She thought back to wriggling through hollow oak trees in the woods as a child. *I can make that. If I can clear enough of the dirt at the base of the wall away, I'll make it.*

As the cart trundled under the curved roof of the castle gates, Sophie glanced towards the inner wall, and her joy wavered. The drop on the outside was high, at least twenty-five feet. *This could be a problem.*

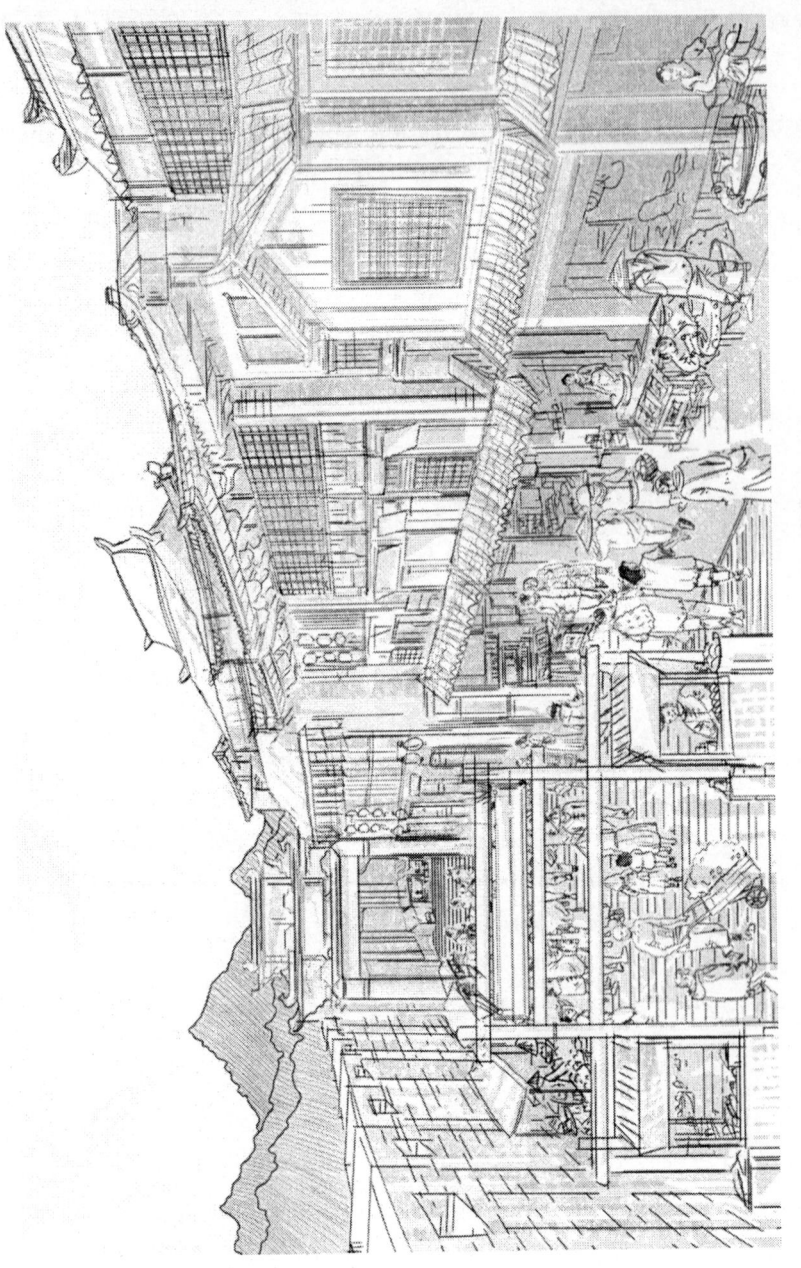

104

The wives' quarters had a sickly aroma to them when they returned. Sophie was shocked to see Beautiful-Nung lying on the mats, she was stick-thin and deathly-pale, looking very unwell indeed. *I don't care,* Sophie thought struggling to swallow her excitement. But she felt a pang of guilt for being so harsh and tried to make herself look busy cleaning the sleeping area. When night fell, she worked through her usual list of chores, washing the dishes, hanging out clothes to dry, then finally sweeping the courtyard and wives quarters. *It's too humid, everything's damp,* she thought looking down at the stone tiles as she swept.

I can't risk climbing that wall unless it's dry... Each day is getting colder, it must *dry out soon.*

Sophie was torn. Waiting was the only way to increase her chances, but she knew also that with each day the likelihood of ever finding her brother, or whoever it was Chi had been talking about grew less and less.

'What are you doing?' Beautiful-Nung's sickly voice questioned.

Sophie jumped, 'I was, err, just thinking,' she replied stumbling to think of a reason why she had been staring into space for goodness knows how long.

'Well, you shouldn't. It'll get you in trouble. A wife should know her place,' Beautiful-Nung said, although it was clear even *she* didn't believe that.

Apparently you're not sick enough to stop being a malicious witch, Sophie thought, angry at herself for the sympathy she had felt a few minutes earlier. *A week. I'll wait one week. Then whatever happens I'm going for it.*

CHAPTER TWENTY-FIVE

Hong walked over to the mattress of bundled branches on the floor of the hut. 'Today is the last full moon of autumn,' he announced, waking Peter and Minh in the process, 'it is an auspicious day. We are ready to begin training for battle.'

Minh smothered a yawn, 'what have we been doing for the last month then?' he said, almost as though reading Peter's mind, 'no way. I'm going back to sleep.' Hong flicked out the end of his bamboo staff cracking Minh on the top of his head. 'Ow, okay I'm up, I'm up.' Peter let out a laugh as he climbed to his feet, but it was quickly stifled by Hong's stern gaze. The pair followed him out into the sunshine and paced over to the west side of the clearing.

'Peter, you punch. Minh, you block.' His first attempt overshot the mark and smashed his friend right between the eyes.

'Owww.'

'Sorry, sorry, it was an accide-'.

'-don't apologise,' Hong said cringing, 'you did exactly what you intended, besides you've taught him two valuable lessons. One, learning to take a hit is important and two, learning to block it is even more so.'

As Minh sat under a tree sulking for the next twenty minutes, Hong demonstrated the body mechanics with Peter alone.

'Make a fist, tightly. Look where you are hitting and throw your weight behind it, drawing the energy from the floor and up through your hips.' He tried a few times, but it felt like there was no power behind his strikes at all.

'Stop over-extending, it will just throw you off balance,' Hong said, 'here, try it on me.' Peter lunged, but the master needed to rotate his body just a fraction to avoid it. The punch slid straight past him and the attacker followed it to the ground with a clunk. He took a deep breath, just as they had practiced, and tried not to let his frustration get the better of him as he clambered back to his feet. 'How can I-.

'-just copy me,' Hong said almost revealing a smile, 'be patient and you'll get it eventually.'

When Minh's pride had finally recovered, he joined back in and they began to work on strikes and blocks one a time. 'Don't be so tense,' Hong said, 'Minh you need to flow, first yield to his attack then strike back—picture a tree.'

'A tree? How's that going to help?'

'The tree bends and sways under the strength of the wind rather than trying to remain stiff and snapping under the pressure. Remember in the village? I could never beat those soldiers with force, I flowed with their movement, remaining calm, using their own aggression against them and BANG!' Hong's rocked forwards his fist burst with speed that cracked the air.

As they rested that evening, bruised and sore, the old man explained, 'the last few weeks I have been testing you. I was hoping for more, but today you have both displayed *some* ability and determination. I have decided to teach you *true* martial arts.'

'What were we doing today then?' Minh said.

'Ha! That was nothing,' Hong laughed, 'practice routines we might give a child.' Both Peter and Minh's smiles dropped. 'Normally I would not take students of your ages; however, as this is a special circumstance I will make an exception. You will each learn an individual style suited to your strengths. I have consulted with the spirits of the mountain to decide the most appropriate for each of you to study.'

Peter stared back, excited to hear what Hong would say. The idea of martial arts had seemed ridiculous at first, he wasn't the least bit athletic or even interested in sports, but day by day he found himself growing more enthusiastic. The repetition of techniques as he tried to perfect them gave him a goal to work towards and making a little progress with each attempt was encouraging. *Maybe I* will *be able to fight? Maybe I* will *be able to rescue my sister after all?*

'Peter, you are intelligent and agile. You will learn the Crane Style. Minh, you are powerful and honourable I will teach you the Tiger Style.' Hong looked at their beaming faces, 'but apparently neither of you are modest,' he added. 'The ultimate goal of these martial arts is peace. You must be one with nature, with life and with death, using force *only* when needed to better the world or the Karma of those within it.' Hong stressed his last sentence, apparently aware that the thought of revenge had been festering in Peter's mind since day one. 'Training is one thing, but ending a life is not something one should take lightly.'

The following morning training began as usual. Hong ordered the pair to the bottom of the steps to collect water.

As they stumbled back into the clearing panting but happy, and put down their buckets, a smile spread across the old master's face.

'Come here,' he said, 'I will demonstrate your *forms*, they are sets of movements that allow you to capture the identity of your style.' Trying to move as though he were a bird sounded like a terrible fighting strategy to Peter, but he was willing to try anything that could improve his chances.

'But how can-' he started.

'-the Crane floats on the wind, fluid and invisible.' Hong answered without even needing to hear his question, 'you try to stab it and you will hit nothing but air. Meanwhile the Tiger strikes fear into its enemies' hearts and tears through them with equal ferocity.'

The master stood up and walked several paces to the centre of the clearing. He gazed into the distance with his palms together raised to his forehead in prayer for more than a minute. In a flash, he exploded into action, leaping up high into the air with a kick. He circled, with deep steps, and his hands sweeping and whipping like wings, while kicks and knees exploded from beneath. The Crane. A moment of stillness passed then his mannerisms transitioned again, one palm slid forward with his fingers pointed, while the other stayed by its elbow. Hong's body coiled low, then lunged ahead, his stabbing through the air with his open hands as though they were spitting venom. The Snake, Peter realised. Finally, he crouched low, the look in his eyes was one of a predator, pure animalism. He pounced forwards with ferocity, ripping and tearing through the air with his clawed hands.

In another moment, Hong seemed to revert back to the old man that had been standing in front of them a few moments before. Both Peter and Minh were left wide-eyed at the display they had witnessed.

'I get it, I understand,' Peter laughed at himself for being so cynical, 'it's like a tactic, we need to be wild and instinctual, like the animals?'

'Yes, but more than that,' Hong said, 'if you can tap into this energy you will be not just powerful, but free from your feelings and concerns. Battles are lost and won long before any sword is drawn or fist is thrown, the man who fights for pride, anger or fear will defeat only himself.' Peter nodded, Hong's words struck a chord with him. All of his life he had been so worried about everything, making friends, looking stupid, moving around, he had sabotaged his own happiness, *he* had defeated himself.

'Solid footing and a powerful core are the key to a Tiger's strength and speed,' he said leading Minh across the clearing to a series of six-inch-high cylindrical logs laid flat on the grass. Peter watched with intrigue as he ordered, 'stand up on the logs, hold your balance and I will attack.' Minh had to move from one to the other in wide steps, avoiding the floor while Hong threw hits and kicks being at his legs and torso.

'Tigers have thick skin, but they are not impenetrable. You must learn to use your hands and feet to catch and redirect my strikes. Over time your bones will become like iron and your ferocity will match.' Hong swung again allowing Minh to block and counter as he moved over the logs. The strikes grew more severe until one kick blasted his leg with such power it buckled and he crashed to the ground.

'Not bad,' Hong murmured. Peter, who seemed to be enjoying the spectacle a little too much, was shown to a patch of trees a few yards away from where Minh had been training. Hong had stripped back the bark on five of them, revealing soft sapwood beneath. Lengths of bamboo had been loosely-tied horizontal to each tree so that they protruded out like hands and feet.

'The Crane circles its enemies and diverts their power with its wings and footwork, each strike must also be a block and each block a strike,' Hong explained. He demonstrated taking wide steps between the obstacles with his palms raised one in front of the other. He shot from low to high deflecting the bamboo poles and snapping kicks, punches, and stabs with his balled fingers. 'This style relies on intelligence, if you pick your attacks wisely you will be able to defeat those much stronger than you. Now try blocking to the left and striking to the right.'

Peter did as he was ordered and Hong cringed at his first strike which was nowhere near his target. 'If you lack accuracy you will shatter your fingers on the trees. I learned this the hard way and if you do too then that is what must come from your training.'

Peter nodded, 'I'll be careful.' He glanced down at Hong's fingers.

'Don't look at me, worry about yourself,' he snapped, 'when Tan's men find you my hands are going to be the last thing you need to care about.'

The old master sat down in the clearing, watching his new students practise. He had considered teaching Peter from the first day they met. He could sense there was something important in his future, but at the same time feared the anger in his heart was too great. Lord Tan was a direct example of where martial arts training without cultivation of the spirit could lead. Hong knew that if he released another man like that into the world his forty-year search for enlightenment would have amounted to nothing.

CHAPTER TWENTY-SIX

Eventually all of the lanterns surrounding the courtyard had been extinguished; the only noise was the far off croak of cicadas in the forest that lay to the west. Sophie was too excited to sleep. She ran through her plan again and again, certain that if she visualised it clearly enough it would work. *It must work.*

As the darkest point of the night approached, she was sure the other wives were sound asleep. She peered over at Yen on the closest mat. *I might actually miss you.* Chi was sleeping on the next one over. *You not so much.* Sophie waited what she thought was another half-hour for good measure, but the seconds seemed to tick by like minutes, and in the darkness and near-silence of the room all concept of time was lost. *Across the courtyard, past the guest quarters, through the garden to the guard tower, then over and down the wall. Simple,* she thought, *then I'm into the citadel, and I dig my way to freedom.*

In theory, the castle was designed to keep enemies out rather than to contain prisoners, so escape from within didn't seem that difficult, it was just the fall from the outer wall that was uncertain. *I'll have to hang by my hands and drop,* Sophie had decided, *but if I get injured I'm done for.* She thought about the razor-sharp knife that lay under the mat and swore an oath to herself. *Whatever happens, I'm not coming back.*

A mixture of fear and excitement gripped Sophie and adrenaline pumped through her veins. In absolute silence, her fingers crept under the mat and removed the blade that was wrapped in a length of cloth. She tucked the knife into her waistband. *Idiot,* she scolded, realising she would impale her own leg if she fell, then turned the blade sideways and crept towards the door. She took one last look to make sure she was not being followed and stepped out of the door into the moonlight. *Bye.*

Sophie took three steps into the courtyard and almost walked straight into a sentry who was turning out of the kitchen. She gasped and her gut reaction was to put her palms out which pushed against his chest. The soldier glanced down at her hands, looking confused, and then straight into her eyes. *Move, say something… come on,* she willed herself, virtually paralysed. Her body finally responded and she nodded at the sentry. He lifted the lantern in his hand and the light blinded Sophie for a moment as he stared into her face.

'Hello,' the young man smiled, he looked happy rather than suspicious. Then dropped his gaze downwards, as though he suddenly remembered his place. 'Ma'am,' he nodded as a guard would to a lord's wife. She smiled back and pretended she was heading towards the toilet on the far side of the courtyard. The sentry strolled off seeming pleased with his late-night encounter and rounded the corner to the servants' quarters, the moment he did, Sophie's false smile dropped. She spun on the spot, paced over to the north of the courtyard and dashed through the narrow corridor that ran by the empty guest quarters and out into the gardens.

Usually she was met with the sight of ponds covered in lotus flowers and trees filled with fragrant, pink, cherry blossom. But tonight she could see nothing in the darkness other than the vague outline of the structure a further thirty yards in front of her.

She crept along the path, judging her position by the feel of stone beneath her feet. Sophie knew the watchtowers along the northern wall of the castle had two guards in them at all times, but they were some distance up and she was counting on them not hearing her over the wind. She moved silently with her hands outstretched, after a few moments they came into contact with the rough texture of the wooden beam at the foot of the tower. She edged around the base of the tower with her back pressed against it until she reached the front. Sophie hoisted herself up onto the wall that sat plush against the beams and rolled over onto her chest being careful not to put her weight on the blade in her waistband. She laid her palms on the smooth stone. It was dry. *Thank the Lord.*

Wrapping her fingers over the far edge, Sophie began to lower her body down inch by inch. Several bricks were sticking out of the wall just far enough for her to put her feet on. As she stretched her body out, extending her arms fully, her foot missed its mark. Sophie fought the instinct to shout as she scrambled for a foothold. Her grip gave way and she scraped her front against the rough stone, but her fingertips caught the closest lip of the block. She had slid only a couple of feet, but was now left hanging a good ten feet from the floor with, her face burning with pain and brushing against the cold stone as she tried to calm herself.

'What was that?' a muffled voice came from the top of the tower.

'Damn rats, they're not stupid. They know we have food up here. Best go and take a look anyway,' one of the soldiers said. Sophie heard the tower guard's footsteps at the top of the ladder just a few feet above her.

If he looks over the edge, I'm finished. There was no choice, she bit her lip, closed her eyes, and released her fingers.

Sophie landed on her feet but her legs buckled, sending her sideways onto her elbow, pain shot through her body as her arm made contact with a sharp piece of stone. The muffled shout and the noise of her fall were drowned out by the guard's descent on the creaky wooden ladder above. A warm trickle was making its way down to her arm and into her palm. It was hard to tell the extent of her wound in the darkness, Sophie's heart was pounding so fast that adrenaline quickly masked the stinging sensation. *I'm bleeding, but I'm out.*

She skidded down the embankment outside the castle and into the darkness of the town's streets; a sliver of moonlight was all she had to follow. *I made it, I'm so close.* Even the air tasted sweeter as she ran blindly towards the few lights still burning in the town. *Please just no one recognise me,* she prayed. Sophie slowed to a walk, not wanting to attract attention even though the town was deserted. *Calm and casual.*

Her thoughts turned to the outer wall, *a couple of hundred yards and I'm there.* She scanned around for any sign of movement or pursuers, nothing. As Sophie rounded the final corner before the tailor's, she walked face first into an old farm-worker, and bounced off his shoulder, yelping in surprise. For the second time that night she froze. The man stared straight into her eyes, she had imagined every scenario and run through every problem a thousand times, she was prepared for soldiers, but coming face to face with this normal-looking old man was something she couldn't have planned for.

'I know you. You're Lord Tan's wife... the foreigner,' he sounded almost as shocked as she was. Sophie's mind raced but no answer came. After what seemed an age of silence, the farmer reached out and grabbed her tightly by the wrist. 'You shouldn't be out here alone at this time.' He yanked her towards him, still in shock she went with his motion, even though it hurt her arm. Suddenly, she was angry at the old man. *How dare he touch me?*

Sophie's fingers found the cold steel. The man began to open his mouth to speak again, but in a flash of rage she tugged the knife from her waistband and with all the force she could muster plunged it into his thigh. The farmer's grip released as both hands went to his leg. A blood-curdling scream split the night. The expression of pain on the old man's face was horrific, but there was no time to care about him. In an all-out sprint, she took the final corner. *They'll be here any second, Oh God please don't let them catch me.*

Sophie sprinted to where she had seen the drain. *Where is it?* Everything was so different at night. She ran up the length of the wall with her hands against it searching frantically but everything was just black. *There.* A tiny change in the depth of the darkness revealed her salvation.

She skidded onto her knees, tearing them to shreds on the gravel and stones that lined the wall, but barely even noticed. The drain was smaller than she remembered. Much smaller. Sophie scratched and grabbed at the soil beneath the hole with her fingertips, but it was dusty and dry, sheltered from rain by the wall. Her fingers were tearing at the floor, but making no progress at all. *That was horses leaving the castle.*

Sophie heard the slamming gate and the sound of hooves echoing through the streets. A bell started to ring and within moments torches were in windows and doorways illuminating half the town.

'Come on, come on, I need just two minutes, please...' Sophie screamed silently at the ground 'WHY WON'T YOU COME UP?!' A second later, her hand grasped something in the soil. *A root.* She tore it from the ground and a fist-sized chunk off earth came with it. She started to dig deeper opening up a hole, but shouts were approaching. *They're getting close.*

Like a dog using its paws to kick up dirt Sophie scratched at the earth. Soldiers were rounding the corner where the farmer still lay bleeding. 'This must be enough, it must be.' She dived down forcing herself into the hole, almost defying possibility her head and left shoulder were pushed out the other side. Her blood on the stone was slippery, it helped as she managed to get her arm to follow, but her second shoulder was still trapped by her body. She kicked off the ground and it nearly popped from its socket. Sophie screamed in pain, but her torso was through. *That's it, they're here!*

Footsteps were beating the earth just yards behind her. She was through up to her hips, when a vice-like grip tightened around her ankle and tore her body backwards through the wall. Sophie shouted, as her spine smashed against the top of the drain, but she caught herself with her elbows flat on the stone. She threw every muscle in her body into a kick behind her, furious at the hand holding her back.

Her heel connected with something soft and a yell rang out sounding almost distant on the far side. Her legs were free. She pushed against the wall and wriggled frantically.

I'm out! Sophie was reborn. She slid face first into a shallow ditch, screaming and almost losing consciousness from the pain as she tried to push herself up with her injured shoulder. She dragged herself to her feet and broke into a run towards the tree line. She clutched her arm with one hand to hold off the pain as it bounced up and down while drops of blood spattered the floor. *Get to the forest.*

As the infantry sped towards the nearest gate almost half a mile away, and other soldiers tried to squeeze through the drain without success, the few remaining white patches of Sophie's dress were swallowed by the darkness of the forest.

CHAPTER TWENTY-SEVEN

Sophie's lungs burned from the cold night air as she ran further into the depths of the forest. No light penetrated the canopy above, and as her adrenaline began to fade the surroundings seemed to grow taller and darker around her. There was silence, only disturbed occasionally by the odd insect or rodent rustling in the undergrowth. *It's so cold. At least I'm out of danger for now,* she thought, wrongly assuming there was nothing deadly in the forest.

Where am I even going? Sophie had no plan, she had been so fixated on escape, what would happen next had become an afterthought. It seemed like a lifetime since she and her family had travelled through the country, and although the pain and anger still felt fresh, she struggled to recall any details of their journey. *We went west for several days through a valley. If I keep heading that way, eventually I'm bound to come across people, a village, or something.* Sophie had no idea how far north or south they had ventured, and now somehow she was trying to navigate from memory alone *and* in total darkness.

What has my life become? Her pace slowed to a walk. *I lost my parents and brother, I was raped, married, and stabbed a man in the street... what if he died?* A pang of guilt struck her as she remembered the look of agony and fear in the old farmer's eyes. *It was his own fault, he shouldn't have interfered.* Sophie gritted her teeth, angry at the old man for forcing her to hurt him and marched on. Her thoughts turned to Peter, she smiled remembering how badly they had wound each other up as they travelled.

"Your friends", that's what Chi said, it must be Peter. You have to find him. A howl in the distance interrupted Sophie's thoughts, her eyes widened and she quickened her pace. Another rang through the trees. Closer this time. She broke into a run. *Please don't be chasing me with dogs.*

As dawn approached, the trees ahead were starting to thin and the noise of nocturnal creatures faded. The sun finally peeked over the horizon bathing the forest in a brilliant red sunrise. *At least it's warm.* Sophie had been shivering for the last few hours. The dew that covered every single branch and leaf of the forest had soaked her clothes, and the beauty of the sight in front of her was all but forgotten compared to the life-giving heat that followed. The fear that had kept her moving all night had dwindled and now every inch of Sophie's body hurt. Her shoulder was throbbing, her legs ached and her walk had slowed to a stumble; now despite the cold, she was desperately thirsty.

A tree ahead, larger and more ancient than the others, split the glow of the sunrise and stretched high into the canopy. When Sophie got closer she could see its base was a hollow cavern, protected by a layer of dead wood and dried leaves that had fallen from the branches above. *I'll rest here. Just an hour, then I can really cover some distance*, she thought, hoping her body could convince her mind to let her sleep. She brushed away the cobwebs, climbed down into the shade, and curled up into a ball, trying her best to become invisible.

Her semi-conscious slumber was twisted, filled with dreams that merged reality and imagination. There were dogs hunting her, they were foaming at the mouth and their teeth were dripping with blood. They chased Sophie, tearing at her

121

ankles as she ran. All of a sudden she was sprinting towards her family, but as she got close something was wrong. They weren't her parents, their eyes were missing, and their mouths. In fact they had no faces at all. Just blank skin.

'Where have you been?' Peter asked, 'we were waiting for you.' Sophie was desperate to explain but couldn't force her mouth open, just as she managed to the snarling pack of hounds descended on her.

Sophie jolted, she was in limbo somewhere between asleep and awake, while anxiety and a cold sweat kept the rest she so desperately needed a fraction out of reach. *Where am I? How long-was I caught?* It took a few minutes for her feverish brain to recall the events that had left her lying in the grave-like hollows of the tree. *I need water.* Sophie tried to pull herself up but could barely move, her arms and legs were like lead. All she could do was lie curled up and wait out the phases of cramping pain in her stomach and chest.

The leaves rustled, brushing her face as a breeze wafted through a gap in the roots. Sophie saw herself lying there as though she was floating above her body looking down. A pathetic sight was beneath, a child, shaking, weak, and vulnerable. *NO,* she tried to shout but nothing came out.
You haven't come this far to die here. Get up, she ordered. Nothing. *GET UP NOW! Or the only thing anyone will ever know of you again will be when they come across a rotting body in a ditch.*

Every ounce of energy Sophie could muster was thrown into clawing herself inch by inch from the grave and forcing her battered body to its feet. Her mind barely registered the sound of barking dogs growing louder with each step. As it finally clicked, she decided, *I'd rather be torn apart by hounds than die there.*

The sun hit her face as she emerged from the forest and stumbled towards the figures in the distance. There were people, and a hut raised on stilts just a short way away. *Maybe they can help me.* She knew it was a long shot, but it was her only option. In open space for the first time, Sophie scanned around for the hounds that were chasing her, but the barking had stopped.

This is why I wasn't caught. It felt like she had been stabbed in the stomach, as only a few miles to her right, without a shadow of a doubt lay the dark stone walls of the citadel. *How? I must have been walking in circles all night.* Sophie tried to hold back the tears that were welling up inside her. She took a deep breath, but the pounding of her own heartbeat was deafening and her vision started to blur. She dropped to the ground. *Shut up! Stop crying you stupid girl.*

In a daze of sickness and despair, she crawled on her hands and knees through the dirt, over the branches and stones that littered the muddy floor and towards the bottom of the hill, towards people. *Why aren't they moving?* She strained to focus on the figures in the paddy below. *Scarecrows.*

Sophie pulled her knees to her body in hope of blocking out the searing pain in her stomach that had returned. She prayed for the swirling darkness to come quickly but it stayed sickeningly out of reach. Then the barking began again, *just a few yards away.*

CHAPTER TWENTY-EIGHT

What's got them so riled up? Tai could hear barking from the far side of field. *Probably another snake.* The yellow-banded kraits often came to lie on the warm, dry land beneath his hut and soak up the sun. They were timid creatures, but still managed to work his dogs into a frenzy almost daily.

Tai continued working for the best part of an hour. It was nearing spring and the final ploughing and irrigation had to be done soon to ensure his rice yield was successful. He was lucky to have made it through the last winter. Having no one to rely on was difficult, but as he often said 'fewer mouths to feed.' Tai's friends from the village had managed to spare enough to see him through, they helped him this year, and knew he'd do the same for them when it was needed.

As he strolled back across the narrow path that separated his waterlogged fields, the dogs began to bark again. *What on earth?* There was something on the ground twenty or thirty yards from his hut. Tai squinted through the glare of the setting sun and something light-coloured caught his eye. *Is that another dog?* He swung his wicker backpack from his hands onto his shoulder and jogged over to get a closer look.

Just a dozen or so feet away he figured it out. *It's a body. A girl... a foreign girl?*

'What in the name of Buddha are you doing here?' he asked in surprise and reached out to roll her over. Tai jumped back upon seeing her face, it looked like death. Her skin was white as a ghost, but smeared with dirt and blood. Her arm was twisted disgustingly behind her body as though it had just stayed still as she turned. He put his ear close to her face. *She's breathing.* Tai threw his backpack down and lifted her over his shoulders. *She weighs nothing... must be on the brink of death.*

As soon as he had the girl lying on the wooden panels of his floor, Tai went outside to boil a fresh batch of drinking water over a fire. While she mumbled and writhed in her sleep, he took the opportunity to drip water into her mouth. As it grew later, she continued to sweat and her cheeks flushed red, contrasting with her pale, sickly skin. Tai found himself studying her face as the glow from the oil lamps reflected off her features. *Even like this she's beautiful,* he thought. *She must be the one, Lord Tan's wife. Why on earth would she give up the luxurious life of a concubine to be out here? I don't understand women,* he thought, reflecting on his daily struggle to survive.

Throughout the night, he checked her breathing as it cycled from rapid pants to slow, deep breaths. *She'll live,* he told himself. *As long as she's not found here anyway.*

As dawn broke, Tai watched the fog rising off the mountains in the distance, *Feels like spring already.* He was tired, he had only slept for an hour or two, but his mind was still too restless to try. After sometime, the girl stirred and briefly opened her eyes, she glanced around looking confused, and then without even focusing on him, she returned to sleep. *Poor girl. The fever will do that to you.* He dripped some more water into her mouth and headed out to finish his work.

After an hour of looking over his shoulder and worrying about the consequences of a royal concubine being found in his home, Tai decided he wasn't going to get much work done anyway and ventured back towards the hut.

It's two days till the market, he thought as he walked. *If I'm not there, people are going to know something's wrong. I've got two days to get her out of here.*

CHAPTER TWENTY-NINE

'*Zay Di*-Wake up, you need to eat.'

Sophie snapped awake. Her clothes were drenched with sweat but she was shivering and covered in goose bumps. It was dark outside. *Where am I? Who are you?* She tried to ask but struggled to get the sound out from her lips. The man staring back at her smiled and his face lit up. 'My name is Tai, can you understand me?'

Sophie moved her head very slightly forwards, unable to manage any more. Her mouth was still desperately dry and her body was crying in pain. *I'm still alive,* she realised half-thankful and half-disappointed that her ordeal wasn't yet over.

Tai held up a small bowl of rice soup, offering it to her. She nodded and tilted her head forwards as he poured a spoonful into her mouth. *It's incredible,* she thought. The warmth washed away the feeling of swallowing broken glass in her throat, and the salt seemed to electrify her brain, allowing it to make semi-coherent thoughts from the mad swirling she had felt before. Sophie hadn't eaten or drunk anything properly for two days and her body was on the verge of giving up. Suddenly she realised how desperate for water she was. 'Water...*Sui,*' she croaked remembering what language she needed to speak. Tai brought over a brown lacquered jar filled with water and held it to her lips as she drained the entire thing. She lay her head back down on the floor, and fell asleep again almost instantly.

The next time her eyes opened, Sophie felt much more awake, her hazy memories of running, graves, dogs, and scarecrows seemed as though they had been nothing but dreams.

Tai looked like he was fixing something on the far side of the room with his back facing her. When he noticed she was awake he walked over and gently sat down in a hammock beside the mat she was sleeping on.

'What's your name?'

'Sophie,' she croaked.

'That's a strange name,' he said smiling, trying to lighten the mood. 'You are one of Lord Tan's wives aren't' you?' Sophie shook her head viciously and her eyes flared with anger. Tai flinched, obviously uncomfortable at the fury his question had triggered.

'Your arm was dislocated,' he said, 'I put it back in when I first found you.'

Sophie nodded.

'There were soldiers nearby last night, looking for you I assume. I could hear them from the forest, but don't worry, nobody knows you're here.'

He stood up and wandered back over to the other side of the hut, stopping to stir a pot that was cooling in the corner of the room. *Nobody* does *know I'm here*, a wave of anxiety hit her. *Why's he being so nice to me?* Sophie calmed herself, trying to weigh the pros and cons of being stuck in Tai's hut. *I was a prisoner before... he's already saved my life and is certainly risking his own looking after me.* It seemed obvious that he was trying to help her, but it was hard for her to comprehend the fact that she might actually be being treated as a person and not just someone's property.

In the following few hours as Sophie drifted through stages of being asleep and awake, she thought on her dilemma. *Should I try to make a run for it?* She wondered, knowing she wouldn't get far. *Besides anywhere is better than the castle and that pig.*

Her concerns had managed to distract her from a splitting headache that now returned with a vengeance, and she closed her eyes in an attempt to block out the pain. When she opened them again, Tai outstretched his hand showing he wanted to feel her head, she nodded in agreement. His palm was rough and calloused, but felt warm as he placed it on her forehead with care. After a second he pulled his hand away fast as though it was burning, Sophie managed a weak smile.

'It's the mosquitoes,' he said, 'when the weather's wet they can make you ill.'

She examined her ankles, they had been shredded by bites and itched mercilessly. As she lay staring up at the thatched banana leaf roof, a forgotten memory resurfaced. The crew aboard *The Princess Helena* were sitting around a long table one evening sharing stories of their travels. It had soon become a contest of one-upmanship of their dangerous exploits, so Sophie's father had regaled the crew with a tale from Algeria. 'My guide and I were caught in a sandstorm, three days out from the city. We had to cut open the belly of a camel and spent the night inside to avoid being torn to shreds. The stink, I'll never forget it!' One of the older sailors countered with his own.

'I was heading for Singapore when I came down with break-bone fever, it came from mosquitoes that had been feeding on the blood of the dead, I wouldn't wish it on my worst enemy.'

All of the listeners sat in silence, as he ran through the different symptoms he had suffered. Unquenchable thirst, bones that felt shattered, no concept of time, and a swelling in his throat that nearly choked him to death as he lay alone in a dank Singaporean hotel room.

It must be that, Sophie thought. Her limbs felt like the muscles had been torn apart inside, her head was pounding, and everything she tasted was like ash in her mouth.

'How long will it last?' she asked.

'Two or three weeks.' Tai sighed and bit his lip. 'I suppose I can help until you get better, but if anyone comes you need to climb out of this gap and hide at the back of the house, okay?' Tai pointed towards an opening in the wall of the hut, was covered by a blind made of strung-together sticks. 'If they find you here, I'm dead. Probably the rest of the village too,' he continued sounding glum.

'Thank you,' Sophie answered, doing her best to produce a smile.

She thought about his words, watching as he softly rocked from side to side in the hammock. *There's no way I can stay here two or three weeks… but I'll get nowhere, at least until I'm well enough to run.* She looked around the room, which was illuminated by a lamp dangling in the corner. It was only about twenty-five feet long, but seemed to be backed onto a hill, meaning if she was to climb out from the gap in the wall it probably wouldn't be a big drop. The brief excitement of being free from the castle had faded and the despair that she had harboured for the best part of a year returned.

This isn't what I planned, Sophie sighed. *But what was I expecting? The British Army to come rolling in and take me home?* She buried her face in the wicker mat, ashamed at how naive she had been. *I have to run*

CHAPTER THIRTY

Winter nights on the mountain were bitterly cold and seemed a world away from the heat and humidity of the village. Each evening the group huddled around a fire built on the doorstep of the stone hut. They ate whatever food they had managed to hunt or scavenge, whilst Peter and Minh nursed their bruised and aching bodies. The fear that any day they would be tracked down and killed drove Peter to train hard and push through the pain. *You need to be ready,* he told himself over and over again.

As training consumed nearly every waking minute, the days all began to blend into one. After what must have been weeks, the clearing was filled with the scents and colours of blooming flowers and budding leaves. As the new season approached, their training ramped up to a level that Peter hadn't thought possible. The practice equipment had been replaced with Hong's own hands and feet, because as he stated with an unhinged half-smile, 'bamboo doesn't hit back.' He would release barrages of strikes, throws, and locks upon the pair, which often came too close for comfort. Both of his students were being pushed to their physical and mental limits and beyond, every single day, and once again Peter's routine became his way of life. Meditation, form training, food, sparring, and sleep.

As their Crane and Tiger forms progressed, Hong introduced weapons to supplement the styles. Minh was given a staff to practise with, around six feet in length, carved from one of the rattan trees that lay in the forest, and hardened over a fire. His stocky build and the low, grounded, style of the Tiger perfectly offset the range of his weapon. Peter used a shorter stick, it was easily hidden tucked in his waistband, and his longer reach coupled with the high jumps and low swoops of the Crane style allowed him surprising angles of attack.

Even though there were near-constant black eyes, cuts, and bruises from near misses with Hong's blade and fists, the pair were becoming stronger and each day was a small triumph as the reluctant beginners became solid students. Despite their progress, both Peter and Minh's frustrations were beginning to grow, they had been on the mountain for less than half a year but the isolation, knowing they were trapped, all the while dealing with their own physical and mental changes was tough.

'The old man has gone crazy,' Minh said wincing as he rubbed the disinfecting sap from a banyan tree over a gash in his thigh. He and Peter were resting under the shaded border of the clearing through the midday heat, whilst Hong lay in the sun just ten or fifteen yards away.

'He's pushing us too far, he's going to kill us before we even get close to seeing an enemy.'

'I hate it too,' Peter whispered, glancing over to see if he had heard them, 'but if we run into Tan's men, they aren't going to go easy on us—this is the only way we can train for it.' Minh knew his friend was right but it still made him grimace in distaste.

'Look at me though, I'm wasting away up here,' he said, his tone growing softer, 'you're okay you've always been skinny.' Peter looked at the man in front of him, it was true Minh had virtually no fat on his body, now he had just bulked out with muscle, and with his dark matted hair and beard growing thick he cut an intimidating figure. *I wonder how many years Hong stayed here alone? It's not surprising he's a bit mad.*

As time passed, Peter found himself thinking more and more about the night his whole life had changed and how different he had been before. *I was so selfish and immature*, he realised. Coming to terms with his new life and living in constant fear of death had taught him modesty, whilst training in martial arts had taught him patience and strength. Now more than anything he only wished he could apologise to his parents for how he had been and tell them he loved them. He wished he could see Sophie again even just once to let he know how much he missed her. *I will.*

CHAPTER THIRTY-ONE

It was almost three weeks before Sophie was well enough to move around freely. *What was I thinking? I'd have barely got out the door if I tried to run before,* she scolded herself for being so unreasonable.

As time passed she got familiar with the routine of Tai's daily life. He was always up at dawn, feeding the chickens and dogs that lived on the dry ground beneath the hut and occasionally chased away vermin. He would head out to the fields for several hours digging, planting, and tending to his crops, while Sophie was left to rest and recover from injury and illness. Tai's hut was simple but comfortable; one side was set against a hill in which he had built a toilet, a small doorway with nothing more than a hole in the ground and a bucket of rainwater, while all of the cooking and farm work was done outside under the shade of the building. Even in early spring, the heat of the sun was strong, but Sophie still felt a sickly chill in her bones. *If he hadn't helped me, I'd be dead, or at the very least trapped back in that hell-hole,* she thought peering through the cracks on the wooden panels to see the shadow of the citadel walls that lay only a few miles away to the east.

As the sun rose on the twenty-first morning Sophie was awoken by the call of a rooster. The pain in her head, arms and legs had come and gone every few days, but today felt different. It had faded through the night and she wasn't sweating or cold. Her shoulder was still agony, but keeping her arm bundled against her body helped. As Tai worked out in the fields Sophie found herself growing restless, her energy had returned and not knowing what to do with it she started to look around.

Who are they? She stared at the portraits of an elderly couple that hung over a small altar in the corner. *Parents? Grandparents? Where are his family?* she tried to work out how old Tai was. She guessed he was in his early-twenties but the way he acted was so mature and responsible it was hard to tell. The creak of the wood as someone began climbing the bamboo ladder caught Sophie off guard, she bolted back to her place on the mat pretending she had never moved.

'Ah, you're awake. That's good, you look well today,' Tai said, with a knowing smile on his face.

'Yes, feeling much better thanks,' Sophie answered, her face still tinted red. A moment of silence passed as she worked up the courage to speak, 'Tai, do you have a family?'

'No family.' His lack of emotion seemed odd. 'My parents were quite old when I was born, that's them by the way,' he waved the back of his hand towards the altar. 'I have a brother as well, but I haven't seen him for years.'

'Oh.' a pang of disappointment hit her 'me too.'

'What about a girlfriend?'

'Ha-ha, where do you think she is?' he said laughing, but the flicker of excitement that crossed his face was clear. 'I was almost married last year,' he explained. 'I couldn't afford the dowry in the end. It's okay though, I'm still young!'

'That's a shame,' Sophie realised he had seen the smile on her face and quickly wiped it off. 'Aren't you lonely here?' she said trying to change the subject.

'It's alright, my work keeps me busy and my friends come to visit when they're nearby, but it's nice having some company.'

'Thank you,' she said, 'for everything. I'd be dead by now if it wasn't for you.'

'It's no problem, you're no different from any of us, and when someone is in trouble, we help each other out,' Tai smiled.

'Not what it was like in the castle.' Sophie had decided that she hated everyone and everything in this country a long time ago. She smiled. *Maybe I was wrong.*

CHAPTER THIRTY-TWO

Sergeant Gia waited for the gates to part in front of him. He ran up the path and burst through the doors into the cavernous main hall. It was almost dark inside, blinds that hung from the rafters rolled down to the floor, keeping it cool but casting narrow slits of sunshine across the space. Gia was surprised to find it empty, he turned towards the door and noticed General Khang, not in his usual position alongside the throne but sitting quietly at a table in the corner of the room.

'Sir,' his voice echoed. The general raised his eyes up from the black and white-chequered board on which he was seemingly playing a game of chess by himself.

'What is it?'

'We found them, the men that went missing; they were buried in the forest outside Xa Pan.' Khang's focus shifted fully to the young soldier in front of him and fixed on his face with a suspicious squint.

'Hmm,' he nodded, 'I thought we'd never find them. Send out a squad, I want everyone questioned.'

Gia was ambitious, he was a young man, but determined to prove himself. Often telling his wife how he would become a general one day. A smile spread across his lips.

'I already sent a squad out sir. Two days ago. I apologise for not waiting for your order.'

'No need to apologise, you have done your job well. What of the results?'

'We offered a bounty for any information about the men, it didn't take long for someone to come forward. Just as you said during your address at New Year, "A leader should be slow to punish and quick to reward".

'You were there?' Khang asked, his eyebrows lifted revealing wrinkles across his face, he seemed impressed.

'Of course sir,' the soldier continued not allowing himself to become distracted from his purpose, 'according to our source, there were three men seen travelling south into the highland gates not long after, a young man, a priest, and a foreigner.'

'A foreigner? Was it a man or woman?' The general's expression was one of curiosity rather than the anger Gia had expected to see.

'It was a boy,' he replied. Khang nodded slowly, but his face seemed to grow even more bemused. 'Has Lord Tan been informed?'

'Not yet sir.'

'Good, keep it that way. Our lord is in ill health these days and shouldn't be bothered with the worry. Send a search party. Find them.'

He seemed well enough yesterday... He had seen Lord Tan walking with his son in the castle gardens, but he knew better than to question his superior officer, no matter how unlikely he story may seem.

'I already gave the order sir,' Gia answered, 'they are preparing now. Five riders, with some of our strongest fighters among them. It will take them a few days to reach the highlands, and from then it is impossible to tell without knowing the criminals exact location.'

'Very good captain.'

'It's sergeant sir.'

'No, now it is captain,' Khang corrected with a nod. 'I want you there leading the squad, strength is abundant, but intelligence is rare. You will ride south with your men, prepare yourself immediately.'

Gia bowed deeply and rushed towards the stables. He set about saddling the strongest horse he could find and sharpened the carved blade of his sword with a wide smile across his face. *Now it's my time.*

CHAPTER THIRTY-THREE

As spring took hold, Tai's hut was filled with the sweet scent of young rice growing and the fields were bathed in emerald. Sophie helped with cooking, feeding the animals, cleaning, and burning the rice husks left over from the previous year's harvest.

In the evenings the sunset was brief, flicking from broad daylight to pitch black in only a matter of minutes. The only light inside was from two oil lamps that hung from the walls, casting long shadows that reached into the corners of the hut.

Sophie and Tai spent most evenings talking. It had been hard to communicate at first, but Tai was patient and always helped her when she didn't know a word or didn't understand his questions. They shared stories and discussed life in her country and within the castle walls. She eventually found herself comparing living with Tai to with her brother when they had shared a room, the siblings used to argue relentlessly but now she missed him more than anyone. The way he always thought he knew better, and how she teased him into such a rage, brought a smile to her face.

One evening the conversation led to the night Sophie had been caught. 'I woke up to the sound of an army, horses, and shouting. The tent lit up orange as the fire surrounded us. I didn't know what to do. I was terrified...' Her voice cracked and she took a breath to try and compose herself. 'My father was pinned down, like an animal. He was screaming "Run, run" so I did. I got thirty or forty yards through the camp before one of them caught me by the hair.

He was so strong there was nothing I could do. He dragged me to the ground and they kicked me while I struggled for breath. I was a coward, I could've helped or at least tried to. But instead I ran.' Tears welled up in Sophie's eyes as she spoke. Racked with guilt, her lip quivering, she finally said the words she had kept inside all this time. 'It's my fault they're dead.'

'There was nothing you could-' words were no use. Tai put his arm around her. She leaned into him as he pulled her head to his chest. It seemed like an eternity since she had felt the warmth of a human being, one she didn't despise at least. Sophie took a deep breath, savouring the moment. Finally, everything that had built up over the past year burst forth, she cried, like she hadn't since she was a child. Together they sat in the faint glow of the lantern until the oil burned off and darkness fell.

I hadn't spoken about it to anyone, Sophie realised as she watched the dawn light spread over distant mountain tops. A sense of freedom washed over her, it was as though a huge weight had been lifted from her mind, and for the first time in longer than she could remember Sophie felt a glimmer of happiness.

They finished their breakfast of rice and vegetables while Sophie listened to the gentle sound of the crickets buzzing outside. Her thoughts strayed off on a strange tangent, as she wondered about Tai and why she seemed to feel so settled here. The more she focused on it the more she began to realise, *If I don't do it now, I'll never escape. Never find my brother, never see my home again, never even speak English again.*

'They must've given up on looking for me by now,' she said. Tai sat up from where he lay gazing out over the fields. 'Yes, I think so,' he nodded, 'If they haven't come here already I don't think they ever will.'

'Next week I should leave.'

His face dropped. They both knew it was only a matter of time, but had somehow avoided discussing it until now. The sadness in his eyes stung Sophie, more than it should. Ashamed, she looked to the floor. After some minutes of silence Tai spoke.

'I'll help you prepare all that I can.'

Sophie smiled at him, she knew she had to face reality, even if it meant letting this brief period of happiness in her miserable life draw to a close. *No more hiding.*

CHAPTER THIRTY-FOUR

Under overcast skies, training on the mountain had been comfortable. Now the spring showers had passed while heat and humidity that rose hour upon hour had replaced them. By late afternoon the suffocating weight in the air would reach breaking point and a furious burst of rain and lightning would restore equilibrium. It reminded Peter of his early days in the village, and how he would lay and listen to the rain pounding on the thatched roof of Yai's hut.

As the first of the summer deluges began to flow, the clearing was swamped. Even knee deep in flood waters, Hong's lessons verged on being purely sadistic, but Peter and Minh had both learned to accept the pain, showing respect and humility to their master. The suffering they shared was what made them a team. Just like with Sophie, he and Minh didn't always get on, but he knew if the time came, they would defend each other to the death.

Peter began to find it amusing at how terrified and frustrated he had been waiting for the soldiers to come crashing through the trees in the first few months. Now he was almost hoping they would be found, life or death was fine, but the fear that he would fall at the first hurdle was what truly worried him. He knew what Hong expected of them both, they were meant to be warriors, but a voice at the back his head still whispered doubts. *What if I freeze? What if I can't bring myself to fight? What if I let them all down?*

One evening, the traps Minh had laid managed to snare a wild pig. The group enjoyed a feast, and probably because of his good mood, Hong revealed the final part of his plan whilst Peter and Minh listened with diligence. The fire crackled and the old master's voice echoed through the clearing, 'We have been here for a long time. You have both made good progress physically and spiritually. I am proud of you.'

Did he really just say that? Peter thought. Hong acted as though nothing they could do was ever good enough, hearing he felt proud was almost unbelievable.

'We still have much to do, but as we come towards summer, the days will be getting longer and the weather will be cool enough to travel long distances. When we are ready, you will head east. Five days ride by horse but probably twenty on foot and you will arrive at the coast. There is a large port and many foreigners there. Peter, you can find refuge and escape by boat. Minh you will return to your uncle's house, we will pass close to your village on the journey and if all goes well your friendship with Peter and absence will go unnoticed. You can take a wife and live a peaceful life. I will venture east then travel north to the great river.'

'I can't go back to the village,' Minh said, his voice sounding equally hurt and surprised, 'not after this...'

Peter was silent for some time. When he finally spoke, the voice that rang through the trees was deep and confident, a far cry from the boy that had arrived at the mountain.

'I can't leave, not without my sister, not without taking revenge on the rat that killed my parents.'

Hong smacked him across the face with the back of his hand and the slap echoed out into the night. 'You fool! Do you remember nothing of what I have taught you? If you go looking for a vengeance you will achieve nothing. The greatest enemy you have to defeat is your own arrogance.' The old man's eyes were filled with fire. Peter twitched in pain as Minh gazed silently to the floor. 'You are obviously not ready.'

'I'm sorry master. I remember.' Peter said, feeling ashamed, he thought he had confronted his anger and let it go, but from somewhere deep down it had risen up and shown its ugly head. He sighed. 'I can't leave without my sister. Tan means nothing to me I swear, but I need to find her.' Hong stared into the flames, the anger on his face faded and an expression of sympathy took its place.

'Very well. There is not much in this life worth dying for, but if you are willing to risk your life for a noble cause, I will support it. However, you must know, Lord Tan has an army and is himself a skilled warrior. It is unlikely that you'll survive.'

'I know,' he answered, 'but if I don't try to save her who will? I'm the only family she has.' The master nodded, there was a distant look in his eyes Peter had never seen before, and for a moment he found himself wondering about the old man's past. *Did he ever have a family? What drove him to the life of a drifter?*

'If you are truly committed to this fate,' Hong continued, 'you must use your intelligence, strength alone is not enough. You will need to play on your enemy's weaknesses, appeal to his fears and ego and you may have a chance. The summer will be arriving soon. We must train harder, and not delay your journey.'

'You won't come with me?' Peter said, a stab of doubt shooting through him.

'No. This is your fight and like any true warrior you must walk the path alone'.

'He's not alone,' Minh said and turned to his friend, his face lit up with a grin. 'I'm going with him.' Peter smiled back, but his heart was pounding and there were butterflies in his stomach. *I can't believe we're really going to do this.*

CHAPTER THIRTY-FIVE

The newly-promoted captain peered up through the cracks in the leaves that lined the staircase. Without a shadow of a doubt, the red glow of embers smouldered against the background of grey early-morning light.

Captain Gia glanced back over his shoulder. *More than enough,* he thought, as the five men crept over the moss ridden steps behind him, silent as ghosts. They weren't just any soldiers, they were the best of the best, war heroes and mercenaries recruited from all over the kingdom for one purpose, quashing rebellion and destroying all opposition.

Gia had been brought up in the citadel; they had lived in a modest house even though his father was as a captain in the Lord's personal guard. His family were never rich, but there was always enough food on their table and his father's red robes had commanded respect. Gia had been proud to be the son of an honourable man and now he wanted the same for his family. He had studied the classics on strategy and warfare, all of them. Countless hours had been whittled away in dark rooms, whilst his friends had been outside wasting their time. Today the merits of his study would be repaid. Gia smiled, thinking back to his favourite passage from *The Art of War,* "Mystify, mislead and surprise."

He was first into the clearing, the gentle breeze of an early summer morning sighed through the grass. There was silence. His men followed, keeping low in a single line with towards the altar that lay in the centre.

The captain glanced around, there was only one place to hide. A decrepit stone hut that lay on the far side.

His soldiers fanned out, circling the shack, until they were spread equally around it. With swords and spears drawn, and a rifle aimed at the doorway, they began to edge forward. One step at a time, like a noose around the neck, they closed in for the kill.

CHAPTER THIRTY-SIX

It was pitch black when Peter woke up. Minh was shaking him by the shoulder.

'What is it?'

'It's Hong,' he said, 'I think he's leaving.'

'What?' Peter bolted upright, 'why?'

'I don't know, I woke up a while ago, he's over there now getting rid of everything, making it look like we were never here.'

'No way, he's not going anywhere without telling us, he owes us that much at least,' Peter said, shocked by how cheated he felt. He jogged over to where Hong was deconstructing their training equipment.

'Hey! What are you doing?' Hong turned towards the pair, his face looked like stone, expressionless, and still under the moonlight.

'They're here,' he murmured.

'What? Who-' Peter realised instantly and cut himself off, '-how do you know?'

The old man raised his hand, far off over the trees and barely visible in moonlight, a wisp of smoke could be seen fluttering skywards.

'That's miles away, plus we don't know it's them,' Peter protested.

'It's not that far,' Minh said squinting at the plume, 'a mile or two at most.'

'I can feel it,' Hong said, 'they are closer than they seem, many of them. You two must leave, immediately.'

'Us leave?' Peter asked.

'Yes. It's the only way. You have your mission and I have mine.'

'So what's yours then?' Minh said.

'To buy you some time.'

Peter was stunned, '...but we're not ready,'

'And you never will be, not until you leave…' The old man cleared his throat, and placed his hands on his hips, standing proud beneath the moonlight. 'I have given you the tools to defend yourselves, and now you will have the chance to repay me.' He looked at Peter. 'My life has been dedicated to creating a better world, one without suffering or tyranny, now this task falls to you. You must not fear violence, nor death, but remember peace *always* is the ultimate goal.' Peter nodded. 'As for tonight, we have our backs to the walls, I may not survive, but you still have a chance.'

Peter was choked up. He couldn't believe it. *Not like this.*

'I understand,' Minh said bowing almost to the ground. Peter just watched, he knew there was point protesting, Hong wouldn't stand for it. Even in the face of death he was hard and stubborn as ever.

'There is only one way up remember, you need to be quick. When you reach the pool, look in the trees, I left you something. Then turn west and pray you do not meet our enemies along the path.' Hong let out a high-pitched chuckle, that if Peter didn't know better he would say sounded almost nervous.

He glanced around at the clearing he had called home for the best part of a year. Sadness, fear, and excitement swelled up simultaneously. He turned back towards his master and their eyes met. A silent moment of mutual respect between two warriors, said more than words ever could. In that instant it struck Peter just how deeply Hong must believe in their mission, so much so, that he was willing to risk his own life just to offer them a possibility of escape. Peter smiled, 'Thank you.' Hong bowed his head in return.

'Good luck.'

CHAPTER THIRTY-SEVEN

They must be in here. Gia smiled, his mind was fixed on the future as his men closed in.

He approached the front of the hut, and whipped his hand down signalling the attack. The squad stormed through the door, and a break in the wall on the far side. Gia was first inside, he scanned the building, every corner, every shadow. *Damn it. Nothing.*

'There's nobody here,' his rifleman replied, 'maybe th-' BANG. A rock smashed into the side of the soldier's head causing his eyes to roll back mid-sentence and he lurched forwards and into the ground.

'AMBUSH,' Gia screamed, 'GET OUT!' He fled the building, his eyes searching frantically for an enemy in the rafters then moving to scan the treeline, but he saw nothing. The clearing was calm, peaceful, and silent. His confused gaze returned to the altar. Now just forty yards before them a man stood in waiting. He was old, frail almost, yet had a quiet confidence about him. His dress was that of a priest, one Gia recognised as belonging to a cult of Taoists that lived in the southern mountains. The captain knew looks could be deceiving, but the old man was also alone and appeared to be unarmed.

'Surrender priest,' he called, 'you had your fun with the rocks, now give it up or we'll take your head.' His men edged forward, now only five.

'No,' the old man said sounding calm and barely even bothering to look at them.

'There are five of us and only one of you, this is not a negotiation.' Gia kept him talking as they edged closer step by step, 'we know you were here with the foreigner and the others. We are to arrest you on order of the general.' The captain's tone changed, it became friendly, 'you must have some family or friends you wish to see again one day don't you? Surrender now and you may do so.'

'No,' came the answer. 'Oh, and one more thing,' the old man said, 'you've got it wrong. There is one of me, there are *only* five of you,' he smiled. 'If *you* surrender now, I'll let *you* walk away.'

Who does this old fool think he is? Rage was bubbling up inside, his heart pounded and his face flushed red. 'KILL HIM.'

Five men charged. As the first approached the priest leapt from the floor, his knee smashed into the soldier's jaw shattering it on impact. He ducked under the lunge of a spear, curling around the shaft and his fingertips stabbed into the attacker's throat dropping him to the ground choking. *Three men.* Gia could hardly believe his eyes, but he knew now was not the time to lose his head. He and the two men to his left charged simultaneously. The first lunged with his spear, the priest rocked back on his heels, the tip of the weapon passed his shoulder and as his body rolled forwards the old man's palms thundered into the soldier's chest, launching him as though he had been kicked by a horse. The captain's sword fell inches from the priests' back. Gia felt its tip lodge into the earth. A deafening roar shook his mind, as the back of a fist connected with his temple.

The scene pulsed before his eyes just long enough to see the point of a sword plunge into the old man's chest, his hands clasped together in a prayer position around the blade trying to hold it from taking his life.

Captain Gia felt his body start to topple as the words escaped his mouth, 'Finish him.'

CHAPTER THIRTY-EIGHT

Energised by their master's words, the pair belted down the steps two at a time.

'Over here,' Minh called. A long package wrapped in brown linen lay just past the treeline where Hong had first revealed the hidden staircase. *There's only one thing it can be*, Peter thought. His friend picked up the item, tore at the knots holding the fabric shut, and unbundled its precious contents with great care. Minh raised his arms to shoulder height, the sword lying flat across his open palms and turned to Peter.

'It's for you.'

'We don't know that,' he answered, even though he knew it was true.

'You realise he was training you to fight with a sword right? Besides you heard what Master Hong said he wants you to continue his work, make the world a better place... I've got my staff anyway,' Minh grinned and tapped the wooden pole that he had strung over his shoulder, his expression was sincere, 'this is *your* mission. Now take it.'

Peter clutched the worn leather of the grip that had been smoothed over the years. The weight was perfect. Every movement he had practiced in training—the vital points, the sweeping and circling blocks, the high and low lunges—were almost made for the blade, something he had never noticed before. 'It would be too small for you anyway,' Peter smiled. 'Thank you, you're a good friend.' He re-wrapped the sword and slid it blade first into the wicker backpack that Minh had taken with some food and water from the clearing.

The pair turned west, picking a more challenging, but better hidden route through the dense forest on the far side of the mountain and down into the valley below.

This is it, we're really doing it, Peter kept thinking. He had been consumed by the idea of striking out, finding his sister, and making it home since the first day he had arrived at the village, almost a year and half ago. But leaving Hong behind, it didn't feel like victory, there was no sense of relief, just angst, softened only by a faint glimmer of hope.

In the forest there were no paths or tracks, and in the dim morning light, keeping their sense of direction was nearly impossible. They used a technique Minh had picked up when hunting as a child. They would pick the furthest recognisable landmark and fix their gaze on it until they were there, then repeat the process again and again, checking their direction against the sun. As they walked, Peter's thoughts wandered back to his soft bed, in their small house, in their quiet street. *Would it even feel like home anymore? I was so different then, so unhappy, and ungrateful. I guess you never realise what you have until it's too late.*

'Do you think Hong is okay?' he said, feeling a familiar stab of guilt.

'I think so,' Minh answered, 'you know as well as I do what he is capable of. Besides it's not like we had a choice is it?' He was obviously struggling with a similar sense of remorse.

'No. I just hope he was right about us and he hasn't risked his life for nothing... I don't feel ready.'

'Me neither.'

The next few nights were spent sleeping rough. They were too caught up with distancing themselves from the soldiers and the mountain to think about making a proper shelter.

'This is killing my neck,' Minh said as he clambered down from the nest-like structure they had built by weaving vines together with the flexible branches of a sapling.

'It'll be better for sleeping than getting shredded by the creatures on the forest floor, trust me,' Minh had told Peter. But after several uncomfortable nights his confidence was waning. To make matters worse, they were covering much less ground than they expected.

As dusk began to roll in on their sixth day of walking, the animal track they had been following wound down into a valley. As they left the highlands, the air became more thick and humid with each step. Normal breathing had become heavy, and the lack of food and water as they rationed their dwindling supplies was taking its toll on both their strength and spirits. Just like their throats, conversation between the two had begun to run dry.

'Let's find somewhere to stop. I don't think we can go much further today. I'm exhausted,'

Minh grunted in response and soon enough dropped his wicker backpack on the damp floor. 'This spot is good enough, we can get off the ground and start a fire to keep the insects away.'

He looks terrible, Peter thought, watching the physically-drained man dragging his legs around the forest floor looking for firewood, *I can't be much better.*

Peter started to search for deadwood to make a platform to sleep on, he snapped off some of the lower-hanging nearby branches and grabbed a few damp pieces from the floor.

'Everything's too wet,' Minh called, his voice was hoarse and tired, 'It's going to be another long night.' All of the normal cheeriness was absent from his words. As Peter eyed the pile of sticks they were planning to sleep on, he grimaced. *I don't know how long we can go on like this.*

Minh boosted him towards the lowest branch, he pulled his torso up so he was sitting on the branch and dangled a leg down for his friend to grab. They started to break off more low hanging branches and tied them in for stability. By the time they were done preparing a rough platform, night was falling fast and within seconds the red glow of the twilight had turned pitch black. Nocturnal insects and animals filled the forest with clicks, rustles, and calls as they went about their business. Peter was shattered, but tonight his brain didn't want to switch off and insisted on conjuring up scenarios to distract him. *What if we don't make it? What if Sophie is dead? What if Hong is dead?* As his thoughts finally slowed, the noise of the forest dropped down to a whisper and his eyes closed.

'What was that?' Peter hissed, suddenly wide awake but unsure why. He scanned all around, straining to see anything in the black of the forest. His movement disturbed Minh who rolled over.

'Eh? What is i-'

'-A noise, walking, I think,' Peter whispered. Minh bolted upright staring into the darkness as another crunch of leaves some way away caught his attention.

There's definitely someone there, Peter thought, his chest was pounding as he fought to hear anything over the volume of his own breaths. Every few seconds a faint crunch of leaves indicated another cautious step. *They're close...*

'Here,' he whispered, he could make out only a shadow. The pair were in absolute silence, not daring to turn to follow it or even breathe. Peter waited for another footstep or the scratch of a sword being drawn. But a sound far more terrifying rippled through the trees. The snarl was unmistakable.

A blur of colour shot out of the darkness of the trees. It froze just inches away, and locked on them with a gaze of curiosity.

'Tiger...' Minh's voice quivered as Peter found himself staring directly into the illuminated yellow eyes of a predator. *It's enormous.* He was paralysed with fear, unable even to hear his friend's shouts right beside him, instead the voice sounded faint and distant. As the hunter's hypnotic stare pulled him in deeper, it crouched, ears pulled back and teeth bared, ready to pounce.

'CLIMB NOW!' Minh's voice cracked as he screamed, tearing Peter's brain back into action. He scrambled for the nearest branches but they were too high, he jumped and finally managed grasp something solid above. A moment later knife-like claws tore through the platform where Peter had just been. He shimmied up part of the trunk, his palms gripping so tightly against the bark that they started to bleed.

The animal scratched frantically trying to pull itself up, while Peter did the same just inches ahead. Adrenaline was bursting through his veins, his heart was firing like a canon and his vision narrowed only onto his target. Within seconds he was near the top limbs of the tree and hugging them for dear life.

The trunk Minh was climbing had tapered out to just a thin branch and he was left hanging on with his arms and knees as it swayed back and forth under his weight. *He's got nowhere to go.* The look in Minh's eyes was one of sheer terror as his gaze caught Peter's just a few feet away.

'Help me! Please?' he was inches from the swiping claws of the tiger that was now up on its hind legs on their platform. Its hungry mouth was snarling and salivating at the anticipation of a meal. *It's going to get him any second. You owe Minh your life don't you?*

'PETER?!' Minh screamed over the deafening roar and splitting wood as the animal tried to claw its way up the tree. *Oh God, oh God, what can I do?*

'HELP ME!' Blind panic raged, Peter was operating in a world of milliseconds; he calmed his racing thoughts just as they had practised and his rational brain responded. *The sword is in the backpack.*

He squeezed his eyes shut and prepared to release his grip. *Here we go.*

Peter slid down almost thirty feet, bouncing off the remains of the platform, and crashing onto the leaves and debris of the forest floor. The noise shifted the tiger's attention towards him. Now the beast stared down through the cracks in the tangle of branches above his head and its eyes narrowed. His enemy circled, waiting for its moment to strike.

Peter dived the few yards across the floor for the backpack, it was just out of reach. His fingers scraped the wet vines as he struggled to move over the sodden floor. Almost hyper-extending his arm in desperation, Peter stretched and as one finger caught the edge of the backpack it skidded towards him. He whipped the sword from within, slid off the protective cloth on its blade, and stabbed up through the gaps of the platform at the tiger's paws. The first few lunges hit nothing. The beast moved like Hong had, composed, watching each strike as it came with complete confidence and control. On his fifth attempt, Peter finally felt the steel meet the creature's soft underbelly, a thundering roar of shock and pain rattled the branches of the trees. The tiger lowered its head and bared its teeth as if it was trying to warn him, 'you don't want to fight me.' It edged closer and Peter's grip tightened, the warm leather-wrapped hilt resting in his hand. *You're ready for this.* He crouched low with his blade extended, but the animal stood its ground, as if it was toying with him.

'COME ON THEN?! WHAT ARE YOU WAITING FOR?!'

In a flash of fury, the beast leapt. Peter shot backwards, his rear foot dug deep into the dirt. Knife-like claws slashed the air, missing his face by fractions of an inch. The outstretched blade arched up catching the tiger's front leg mid-lunge and it landed with a howl that split the night. The animal glanced over its shoulder at Minh and turned back to Peter, snarling, it limped backwards, one step at a time, and sunk down, preparing to pounce again. Then as though it had reconsidered, turned and fled back into the darkness as quickly as it had arrived.

Peter collapsed into a heap where he stood, panting and shaking whilst Minh shimmied down from his perch and joined him on the damp forest floor. They lay beneath the tree and as their adrenaline faded away and exhaustion took over there was total silence, not even an insect. *It's as if they knew.*

'Thank you,' Minh said after what seemed like an age.

'You saved my life remember? I owed you.'

'I remember. I would do it again too,' he paused in thought. 'But maybe not a third time, we're even now,' he grinned. Peter chuckled and this set them both off, nearly an hour went by with the pair lying in the darkness of the forest wiping back their tears of laughter.

CHAPTER THIRTY-NINE

Sophie was awake long before the sun climbed over the peaks that lay in the distance. She put it down to the nerves of venturing out alone again, but there was a nagging sensation in the back of her mind that troubled her equally. She just didn't know why.

As she and Tai had eaten their final meal together in the warmth of the summer evening, Sophie had explained the dilemma she'd been wrestling with for the past few weeks.

'It's been more than a year and even if my brother's still alive, I think it's unlikely I'll ever see him again. I need to travel east to the coast,' she sighed. There had always been a lingering trace of hope that she'd find Peter, but she knew now it was now a choice between getting captured again, and dragging Tai down with her, or making a break for it alone.

'I'll try to talk my way onto a boat, then maybe I can get to Hong Kong and notify the authorities, they could search for him, or at least arrest Tan for murdering my family.' In her heart Sophie knew it would never happen, but she needed a goal, something to push for.

'I could come with you, until you reach the coast at least, what do you think?' Tai said. 'I know the region-'

'-No. You've done enough already,' Sophie said forcefully, 'I'd never have survived without your help.' She looked away, 'I'm sorry Tai, I want what's best for you, and coming with me would be a death sentence.' He sighed.

'I'll take you to the edge of the forest. I can show you the best route to get through the valley and to the coast,' Tai said, obviously trying to hide how he really felt.

The next morning he wrapped some balls of sticky rice in banana leaves, and loaded them into one of his weaved crop-carrying backpacks. Sophie stitched up the holes in the sandals she was provided with the day she had arrived at the castle. They were worn and on the verge of falling apart, but comfortable, now shaped around her feet and she had given them a new lease of life using braided vine to re-tie the straps.

A crash broke the silence outside the house. She glanced at Tai and the look of surprise on his face told her all she needed to know. The dogs started barking followed by the sound of footsteps speeding off down the path. He leapt towards the entrance and was just in time to see the back of a man sprinting away along the dusty track. One of the water jugs had been knocked over beneath the hut.

'He must have been watching us,' Tai said frowning as though he'd been betrayed. 'He was dressed like a farmer, I don't know who it was, but they must know you're here.'

'What should we do?' Sophie searched his face for guidance.

'We need to go, now. A friend would never have run.'

They frantically loaded everything up. Water, food and a machete were all thrown into the wicker backpack.

'I'm sorry, that's all I've got...' he said staring down at the half empty bag, 'hopefully it'll be enough.' Tai slung it across his shoulders and Sophie followed him out of the door and down the ladder.

Knowing that time was against them the pair moved with purpose, away from Tai's land and out the track that led the opposite direction from the citadel.

'Isn't this the way they ran?' Sophie asked.

'Yes, but it's the only path that leads east, we'll follow it for a little while only and then get into the cover of the forest before anyone knows we're here.'

I really hope so, she thought.

They kept up a quick pace for nearly an hour in the mid-morning heat. As the sun climbed higher and beat down on them, they were forced to slow to a more manageable speed.

'Thanks for everything you've done for me,' she said, glad she finally had the chance to talk. 'You're so generous... it's amazing.'

'It's nothing. I don't have much to give anyway, so it's my pleasure to share it with someone so kind and beautiful.'

Sophie didn't know how to respond. She couldn't tell if she felt flattered or guilty.

'I'll miss you. You know that don't you?'

'You don't need to,' he laughed 'I'm just a farmer, really nothing special.' But she could see from his face that he felt just as awful as she did. Tai whipped his head round as a noise caught his attention.

'Over there.' He pointed down the straight path ahead, just as the outline of a group of men on horseback emerged from the blurred horizon.

'It's a trap. They must've been waiting for us. Why else would they be here?' Sophie said.

'Don't worry. It's not a trap.' Tai spoke softly, trying to be the voice of reason. 'They don't know we're here or they wouldn't have waited somewhere so easy to see. Into the trees now, they might not have seen you. I'll distract them.'

'No. No way.' Sophie's voice turned sharp and stubborn. 'They'll know you were helping me, they must have known I was here. Go home Tai, pretend you've never met me and play innocent.'

'It doesn't matter, they were bound to find out sooner or later. Get into the treeline quickly,' he ordered. Sophie glanced forwards at the blurs of soldiers on the horizon growing larger with each passing second, then backwards at the path that led towards Tai's hut.

I don't have a choice, do I? Sophie's teeth gritted in frustration. She grabbed Tai with both arms around the back of his neck and pulled him in as tightly as she could, pressing her head onto his chest. After a moment, she raised herself up onto her toes and she leaned her face towards his. Sophie kissed Tai softly on the cheek and whispered into his ear, 'Goodbye. Thank you.'

She fled into the trees as fast as she could. Tears were streaming down her face and by the time she hit the depths of the forest, the realisation of what she had done stopped her like a brick wall. *I've just left him to die. After he saved my life* this *is how I repay him?* The thought brought her to her knees, Sophie struggled to breathe through her sobbing and attempted in vain to shake off the cowardice and disappointment she felt.

Over more than a year, her body had pushed beyond the level of pain she thought she could endure, but neither the illness, forced marriage, nor fear of death compared to how she felt now. It took her back to the night her family was taken from her, and there was only guilt. For her parents and for the life they had given her, they had shown her the world and all that was good in it whilst all she did in return was make things hard for them. For her brother, who she loved but never told, and wished she had treated better. And for Tai, who had almost certainly given his life for nothing. *To protect a foolish girl, who he had known for just a few months.*

Sophie didn't know how long had passed, but as the minutes ticked by she managed to calm herself taking long and slow breaths that helped to shake her panic. Finally she mustered enough strength to wipe the tears from her eyes and find her way to her feet. *They're coming. You can't let Tai's sacrifice have been for nothing.* She reached into the backpack for the machete and using her uninjured arm hacked deeper into the wilderness while the voices of soldiers behind her grew louder.

CHAPTER FORTY

Every single muscle in Peter's body felt like it had been stretched to breaking point. It was like nothing he had ever experienced, but despite the pain, they pushed on making steady progress in the few days following their encounter. The pair had wound down from the forests of the highlands, through the depths of "Tiger Valley"—as it was now known—and out through the other side.

The land began to flatten and the trees thinned, finally giving way to a series of marshes and wetlands. Each step had to be calculated and observed to make sure it wasn't about to get lost in the quicksand-like mud that covered every inch of the ground. Tree roots jutted out in a tangled mess from all directions. They were stained with the horizontal markings of flood waters, but now after more than two weeks without rain, the roots formed a path that could be used to clamber through the marshes and swamps. Peter remembered descriptions of the Indian mangrove forests he had read about in books, the way these adventures were told sounded beautiful and romantic. But the thick, putrid air, insect bites, and mud caked all over them made the reality much less entertaining.

Climbing through the knotted terrain made travelling in anything even close to a straight line impossible, and anxiety soon started to set in as Peter realised they had no way of knowing which direction they were heading. Finally, after a full day of scrambling they emerged into an open valley covered in grasslands and fields.

Peter felt like he had been reborn. Lying on the dry, soft ground with a cool summer breeze running over him was paradise.

'I've never been as far east as the citadel,' Minh said as they lay gazing up at the stars in the cloudless sky, 'how will we get in?'

The same question had been at the back of his friend's mind for some time.

'I don't know.'

'What if we attack some soldiers and take their horses? They could lead us there and we could sneak in?'

'Let's just head east for now.' The more Peter thought about it, the more he worried, but he knew that sooner or later they were going to come face to face with Tan's men. If it wasn't for the skills he'd learned from Hong they'd never have escaped "Tiger valley". Even though soldiers were no comparison to the ferocity or strength of an innate predator, they were no less daunting. *I've never even been in a real fight… we have to train more.*

The next morning, they practised their forms, weapons, and meditated as they had done each day on the mountain. As they were preparing to leave, Peter surprised his partner with something new, throwing an attack out of the blue. Minh saw his punch coming a mile off and ducked under his arm, frustrated at how easily it was avoided he threw three more in quick succession, clipping his friends around the ear with the final strike. Muscle-memory took over and they found themselves sparring. As Minh struck back, Peter dodged and ducked, then leapt in closing the distance. Minh tackled his legs and they scrambled on the ground for a few minutes before Peter was overpowered and made to submit by having his head and shoulders pushed into the floor and his arm wrenched upwards.

'Okay okay, you win.'

'Ha-ha, you almost got me with one kick,' Minh said and 'I'll hold back a little less next time then.'

Each new morning as they trained, one would attack the other without warning and they would spar until either a clear strike or escape marked victory. On the second day, Peter side-kicked Minh down a hill as he chased after him. On the third he was choked to the floor as his friend caught him from behind while packing. Their fights were taken seriously, but with good spirits, they both knew it was providing them with real practice, how they would have to survive against soldiers' tricks and cheap shots. As Hong had taught them, 'Your enemies will always fight from the high ground—you must make his advantage a disadvantage.'

Slowly the foothills began to lead back into the highlands and across small mountains.

'This is good,' Minh said as they reached the first plateau since the dried-up river bed.

'We're definitely on the right path, we must come across some villages soon.'

It had been more than a week since they had seen a soul. Whatever food they could catch or gather from the trees had served well enough, but now despite the safety of isolation, Peter was missing the sounds, sights, and even smells of other humans. He could only imagine how Minh must have felt all that time on the mountain. He was always the social one,

173

talking about how he wanted to meet new people and find a girlfriend. *Not at all like me.*

Eventually, man-made paths started to replace the animal trails. Within a few miles the wild bushes and patches of bamboo that lined either side had grown more and more ordered until they were among cultivated fields. The occasional stilt house elevated over rice paddies began to pop up and after just two more hours the pair passed through the bamboo walls surrounding a hamlet. Meandering through the small collection of farm huts, they were met with shocked expressions. Peter didn't care, they strolled confidently along with Minh grinning and waving.

'Who are you?' 'Why are you here?' were some of the questions called out to them from the windows of huts. 'We're travellers,' or 'we're visiting friends,' Minh called back, but Peter could see from the expressions on their faces that nobody believed a word he said.

Within the next week, the pair found themselves strolling through several other villages. Most of the time people would pour out to see them and curious as to who they were. Some days the pair were welcomed in as other travellers might be, offered food or a place to sleep in exchange for odd-jobs like building or ploughing. At other times people just pretended not to see the odd party that was roaming past their doors.

The head of the fifth village they came across greeted them personally, as though they were old friends. Toc, invited Peter and Minh into his hut to rest.

'The women are preparing a meal,' Toc said entering the hut the door, 'please help yourself to some tea, and if there is anything you need I am more than happy to help.'

'Thank you for your hospitality,' Peter replied.

Toc smiled, obviously impressed, 'Do you mind me asking how you came to speak our language so well?' Peter grinned back.

'I spent a long time in Minh's village and then in the mountains, I had to learn if I wanted to talk with anyone other than him,' Peter smiled and slapped his friend on the back.

The pair continued to make small talk for some time, until the conversation turned to where they were headed.

'Tan's castle is located in a district called *Ta Ram*,' Toc explained, 'but his reach stretches nearly to the coast. His army numbers more than five thousand men.'

This news sent a shudder down Peter's spine, it was not unexpected, but intimidating nonetheless. *Just don't think about it... one thing at a time,* he told himself.

'Tan's men patrol the main roads in groups, normally one or two officers on horseback and a foot soldier keeping an eye on the equipment,' Toc continued, sounding almost excited to help. He rustled around in a corner of the hut among a stack of boxes for a few minutes before presenting a paper tube which he unrolled to reveal what looked like a very old map. It showed exactly where they were, along with trade routes through the district, and most importantly pointed them in the direction of the citadel.

As the conversation progressed, another of the village elders who Peter learned, had been a diplomat some years ago explained further, 'since the death of the last Emperor, the government has controlled all the central ports and rivers, but they see little value in the land Tan rules over. They allow him to hold on to power and keep things in check, just like his father and grandfather did before him and they expect his heir to do after.'

All of a sudden it became to Peter clear why Lord Tan was so aggressive and power hungry. 'It's obvious,' he said sighing with a mixture of relief and irritation at his own stupidity for not realising sooner. 'He's scared. Tan I mean. The world is changing and he's trying to his hardest to cling onto his power through fear.'

'Exactly. Toc nodded. 'He is the last of a dying breed. He thinks it is still the age of battles and warlords, he is blinded by his own ego and ignorance.'

'I thought it was just the people in my village that hated him,' said Minh as he listened to the stories spilling from Toc's mouth.

'It is only a matter of time before there is rebellion, then he'll be slaughtered like the animal he is,' Toc continued, 'but for now, us farmers just try to get along peacefully, a simple life with our families is all we desire.' The sadness on his face melted away to a smile.

'If you keep heading west for a day's walk you will come across *Xa Phi* village. My brother lives there, they are richer and better supplied than us, please tell him I sent you and you'll receive a warm welcome.'

'Thank you,' Peter replied, although a voice in the back of his mind questioned why they were so willing to help. There was something disconcerting about the whole situation.

CHAPTER FORTY-ONE

Half a day had gone by before *Xa Phi* appeared engraved ornately onto a horseshoe-shaped stone about knee-height by the side of the road. 'We made good time,' Minh said.

'Yeah, we did.' Peter wondered how Toc's estimates could be so off. 'He made it sound like this was a busy route, don't you think it's a little too quiet? I mean I had expected to see some people or something'.

'He's an old man,' Minh said, 'plus he was probably thinking about pushing a cart of vegetables along.' He chuckled to himself, but Peter wasn't convinced. The mud and gravel path beneath their feet was well worn, tracks of wheels, footsteps and horses were scattered all over it and it was wide, *it's definitely a busy route*.

After another hour or so, the path led them around the foot of an enormous natural limestone pillar. Peter squinted up towards the top through the bright sunlight. The wind was shaking the trees that perched on its peak and eagles circled above, darting in and out of caves hollowed out from the rock. The only sounds were the occasional call of a bird and trickle of the stream that had carved out the valley over millions of years. Peter licked his dry lips, there was a bitter taste in the air, one that felt strangely familiar.

As they followed the path round the base the towering stone, a plume of black smoke could be seen billowing into the sky just a mile or so ahead.

'What do you think it is?' Minh said.

'I don't know, it could be them burning crops?' Peter answered hoping he was right.

'I doubt it, the smoke wouldn't be thick like that.'

Peter shuddered as his thoughts returned to the blackened ruin and toxic air that surrounded his family's campsite.

'Let's check it out.'

'Ha-ha, okay.' Peter's forced laugh sounded worried, rather than the confident image he had hoped to project. His palms were sweaty and shaking as they rounded the final edge of the limestone pillar and the path in front opened up.

Oh my God. Peter stared open mouthed at the destruction. The fields in front of them were black with ash and smoking piles of debris lay where houses once stood.

'There must have been hundreds of people living here,' he said, 'where are they all?' his eyes darted around, scanning for movement. *Please,* he prayed. *Let there be someone, anyone.*

The pungent stench of burning hair stung his nostrils first. Then cloth. Then flesh. The pair broke into a run, belting down the path that weaved through wreckage where the village square had once been. Like a scene from a nightmare, a smouldering stack of bodies loomed into view. They had been piled up in the centre of the square almost ten feet high. Arms and legs stuck out from the heap dangling down and blackened by the smoke. It was like the descriptions of hell Peter had read in the Bible, only infinitely worse. The acrid stink of burning flesh hung like poison in the air. *They're all dead. Women. Children. Everyone.*

As the reality of what he was seeing hit, Peter dropped to his knees and forced his face into the ground desperate to wipe the vision from his mind.

In a daze, Minh pulled his staff and backpack off and they clattered to the floor. He slumped over, burying his head in his knees and choking through tears. The wind whistled through the empty fields, and only the occasional crackle of a fire still burning broke the silence. Neither could make any sense of what they had seen and Peter didn't know how long they spent speechless before Minh finally broke the silence.

'Wh..why would anyone do this?' he said his eyes still streaming with tears.

'I don't know. Who could be this...vile?' Peter's words shook.

There was a voice coming from the distance. *People? Survivors?* Clearer now, the sound of a conversation echoed through the empty streets. They were both on their feet in seconds, desperate to find anyone alive. Minh grabbed his staff and shot towards the north side of the square trying not to glimpse the corpses as he passed, he ran straight down the opposite path towards the voices with Peter just a second behind. Minh turned a corner by the collapsed remains of a smoking hut. Four soldiers were loading tools, swords, and jewellery onto horses, chatting away, seemingly unaware of the men sprinting towards them just a few dozen yards away.

'YOU DOGS!' Minh screamed. The volume and fury of his booming voice brought instant panic to the faces of the soldiers and froze Peter in his tracks. Two men at the rear, lifting a case up onto the cart dropped their load and it crashed to the ground.

'WAIT!' Peter shouted but it was too late. Minh was thundering towards them like an unstoppable juggernaut of fury.

The front two soldiers' eyes almost popped out of their heads as they fumbled to draw the swords from their sheaths. It was pointless.

The end of the hardwood staff plunged directly into the face of the first soldier shattering every tooth from his mouth and launching him backwards into the cart. The next swung his sword horizontally, badly misjudging the distance between he and his assailant. Minh closed the six feet with lightning speed and barrelled shoulder first into the chest of the second man, lifting him from the floor and throwing him onto his back. He stamped through the soldier's leg with the force of an elephant, folding his knee in half. As he cried out in pain, gripping his crippled limb, a further stamp to his throat silenced him permanently. The third solider had edged in, a few yards from Minh's back. *He's too close.* Peter thought, suddenly realising he was still stuck frozen on the spot. *Move.*

His hand struggled to release the sword that was tucked into his waistband while he ran. Sparks flew from the impact as their blades met. Peter circled his weapon down throwing the soldier off balance and gashing his hand. A left fist followed immediately into his jaw. *A lot softer than a tree.* The soldier's legs buckled, and his eyes rolled back into his head as he hit the floor. The last soldier—who was a barely more than a boy—threw his sword to the ground at his attackers' feet and his hands shot up into the air. Minh turned, meeting his gaze and stepped towards the boy.

'WAIT. Please don't kill me, I'm unarmed, I don't want to die!' he shouted dropping to his knees and clasping his hands together in prayer.

'What about the villagers?! Do you think they wanted to die?' Minh spat.

'It's different, they were traitors they refused to follow the orders of our Lord-'

'-YOUR LORD IS A MONSTER.' He charged smashing his knee into the young soldier's chest. The boy landed hard twisting his arm with a crunch as he fell upon it. Minh raised his staff, blunt end lined up with the soldier's face. He tore it down with all of his strength.

The weapon stabbed into the ground, grazing the boy's tear-stained cheek. It took Minh a second to realise it was Peter that had kicked it off course.

'WAIT. Wait,' Peter said as his friend shot him an icy glance.

'This boy deserves to die. But if we kill him unarmed and in cold-blood then we are no better than them.' his voice fell from a shout to a whisper, 'I have a plan, let him live. He'll call out the guards...' a smile crept onto Peter's face '...and we will be waiting, one by one we'll take them out. We can take their weapons and arm people, at least giving them the chance to defend themselves. We need to show Tan and his dogs that we're not afraid!

Minh's frown softened, he grabbed the young soldier by the leather armour on his chest and pulled him to his feet.

'Run. Now,' Minh snarled. 'Tell them we're coming.'

CHAPTER FORTY-TWO

As they wandered through the cloudless night, the cool air against Minh's face made a welcome change from the stifling heat of summer. Just a few days before he had been chatting with Peter while they walked and found himself perched on the crumbling edge of a ravine. 'From now on I'm going to shut up while we're moving,' he had said with a smile.

Tonight, there just wasn't anything to say. Minh knew they had to get as far away from the burnt remnants of the village as quickly as they could. The horrific image of the bodies stacked high, and the reek of burning flesh had carved itself into his mind. Distraction was all he could hope for as they trudged onwards in silence to the point of exhaustion and beyond.

When the yellow glow of sunrise started to spill over the horizon it reminded Minh of home. *Maybe this is a mistake. Maybe I should give up, go back to the village and become a farmer? It's not too late.* He dismissed the idea as cowardice.

'What now?' he said, shaking Peter from his thoughts.

'I say we stick with the plan, the soldier from the village will be on his way back to the citadel already, then they'll come looking for us. We can keep heading for the castle and take as many of them out as we can along the way. What do you think?'

Minh nodded. 'I say we take revenge, make them suffer!'

'No. No revenge,' Peter replied with a calm firmness in his voice and distant look in his eyes that made Minh wonder if he'd given up completely.

'I need to find my sister, but death and revenge without purpose will make us no different from th-'

'-I don't think so,' snapped Minh, 'they're murdering the innocent—we're protecting them!'

'Yes, but from their perspective aren't we the evil ones? I came to Tan's land uninvited and tried to force religion on his people, *and* we just killed a group of his men.'

'I suppose.' It was frustrating but he knew his friend was right, acting out of anger and vengeance wouldn't bring back his parents, or Peter's, or the villagers. Minh swallowed his rage and let out a slow breath.

'They go in units of three or four right?' Peter asked.

'That's what Toc said. But what are we even going to do if we find them?'

'Well let's lay some traps or something, we'll arm the villagers with their weapons. We can avoid killing unless we have no choice, but giving others the opportunity to defend themselves must be the right thing to do?'

Minh thought for a few seconds, 'I agree.' He felt a lump rise in his throat, 'I never wanted to kill anyone either,' his voice cracked as he fought to hold back tears. 'I know what Hong taught us was true, but when I saw that fire. I don't know what came over me. They needed to pay for what they had done.'

'I know,' Peter placed a hand on his shoulder, 'I felt the same.'

As his emotions began to fade, Minh realised how exhausted he was both physically and mentally. The bags under Peter's eyes showed he was the same, but his face was alight as he stood in silent contemplation.

'If we can surprise the soldiers, cause panic and confusion, they won't know how many of us there are, we could even make Tan think there was a rebellion,' Peter said. 'If word got out that it was happening, people would rise up against him, I'm sure of it.' For the first time that night a smile came to Minh's face.

The pink haze that followed the sunrise signalled that it was going to be a hot day, something Uncle Yai had taught him during his first season working in the rice paddies. Talking about what they had witnessed the day before, had lifted a weight from Minh's mind, it felt as though the air between he and Peter had been cleared.

After just an hour of sleep, the chirping of birds in the tree above and sun beating down through the cracks in the leaves roused him. From the delirious look on his friend's face it seemed as though he hadn't even tried to sleep, maybe he was scared to close his eyes.

As soon as Minh was awake enough to hold a conversation, the subject turned back to their mission and Peter relayed his idea at a thousand words per minute, pointing at the ground with a stick to demonstrate.

'We find an ambush spot on one of the big roads and wait for a squad to come through—as soon as the one we left gets back with his news it'll be a few days at most until they send more and we'll be waiting, we can use your traps! If we get killed trying, at least it will have been for a good cause. Maybe then others will follow our lead.'

For the first time in a long while Minh was thinking clearly. He remembered Toc's words as he described the opium and tobacco trade routes in detail, and the paths they should take to avoid being found by soldiers. 'I've got it,' he said, 'I know where we can set the ambush.'

They won't know what hit them.

CHAPTER FORTY-THREE

It only took an hour of walking to find one of the larger routes. The path was plastered with footprints and hoof-marks that to Peter's untrained eye seemed fresh. Minh eyeballed the tracks for less than a second and looked up smiling.

'A day old at the most, probably less.'

'This is our spot then,' Peter said as the pair approached a bend in the road. 'They won't be able to see far in either direction from here, we've got thick trees and hedges on both sides and the rocky path will make a fast getaway impossible.'

'Good thinking,' Minh replied obviously impressed with his attention to detail, 'but we're going to need to cover our own tracks here.'

I hadn't even considered that, Peter's ego deflated. They started kicking over their own tracks in the dust, trying to jump from one to the other without making any new footprints.

'I think we should hide in the trees on either side, then we can attack from two angles' said Peter, trying to visualise their enemies.

'No,' Minh's face appeared decidedly unimpressed, 'when hunting pack animals, you need to separate them. They're strong as a group but on their own they are weak. You need to stay here and create a panic, this'll drive them forward, the faster ones will charge ahead straight into my staff,' he said whipping it from his back and miming a stab at the soldiers he pictured rounding the corner. 'I'll take one or two of them off their horses at least. Then as the slower ones realise what's happened they'll run back the way they came and you can cut them off.'

Surely they won't be that stupid? Peter thought.

'Trust me,' Minh said noticing the look on his face, 'It works every time.'

'But you were hunting animals before...'

'Still am,' he laughed, 'now they're just bigger.'

They set up camp behind the treeline, just far enough to be hidden, but still within earshot of the path. As night fell, the pair took shifts to stay awake, watching and listening for any sign of enemies. The next two days were spent, training, resting, hunting and eating. There were plenty of fruits in the surrounding trees and a river cut through the forest that was teeming with catfish. Peter felt infinitely better than he had done since they first left the mountain, physically at least. But the nerves and anticipation as they waited for an encounter grew with each passing hour.

Just before dawn on the third day, the sound of slowly clopping hooves echoed through the trees. He was jolted awake by Minh, who had a wild and manic look in his eyes.

'They're coming,' he hissed.

I knew it. Peter shot to his feet and shook out his arms and legs, attempting to wake up his tired limbs. He jogged over to the spot he had carefully planned out and lowered himself face down through the leaves, hiding his whole body in the undergrowth. A pile of rocks he had collected lay to his side and there was just enough of a gap for him to see the path ahead. *What are we doing? We're going to get ourselves killed! Come on,* Peter told himself as the distant clop of hooves grew ever closer. *We've spent more than a year training for this moment, if you aren't ready now. You never will be.*

Minutes later the sound of voices were ringing through the humid, windless air breaking the rhythm of the horses' steps. Peter raised his hand in signal, showing his palm. Minh—who was about thirty yards further on—waved back, retreated into the forest, and seemed to effortlessly ascend into the branches of an overhanging tree that was covered with thick leaves and vines. *He's invisible. This might actually work.* He thought in amazement.

The long dawn shadows of approaching soldiers edged round the first bend in the road. Peter was shaking and sweating, praying that none of them would notice the movement just yards from their feet.

One...two...three...four?! A moment of panic ensued as he counted the men, all armed and mounted on horseback, at the front rode the senior officer, wearing a red-banded wicker hat. *That's not fair.* He felt cheated, they were expecting two or three at most, but it was too late to back out now. Peter tried to fire himself up, he thought back to "Tiger Valley", how he had felt at the burnt village, and the camp in which his own nightmare began. *You can do this.*

As the group passed by, he was close enough to see their faces. They seemed tired, shuffling onwards slowly, with bags of heavy supplies. Peter felt a pang of sympathy for the group. They too were just people, they probably weren't *all* evil.

He took a deep breath, feeling the jagged edges of the rock he had been cradling in his palm, he gritted his teeth, and launched it with all his strength. It struck the rear of the closest horse; the animal shrieked and broke into a gallop.

The two leading soldiers, shocked by the sudden commotion, tugged their reins and sped forwards as though the horse behind was about to career into their own. The second man at the back was slow to move. Peter took his chance and hurled the heaviest stone he had from just a few feet away. It smashed against the side of the soldier's head and as he tumbled sideways, his foot caught in the opposite stirrup flinging him upside down. The soldier's neck buckled with a crunch, he was dead the moment he had hit the floor.

The two front runners kept riding, one glanced back on hearing the sound of their colleague's shout as he fell. The soldier on the panicked horse had overtaken them and as he tried to calm the animal, rounded the bend. Minh leapt from his branch, a good ten feet to the floor. As he dropped, the flat end of his fire-hardened staff pounded into the chest of the rider. He was lifted off this steed as though he had hit a brick wall and crashed to the ground below whilst his horse sprinted off into the distance. The two remaining men rounded the corner half a second later to see Minh standing with a smug grin in the centre of the track next to the unconscious soldier. A brief look was exchanged between them as they sized each other up.

'KILL HIM,' the officer screamed. He drew his sword and dug his boots into the horse's side. Minh ducked under the charging man's swing, but was too slow. The tip of the blade caught his face opening up a deep gash on his cheek and Minh screamed with a mix of anger and surprise. As the second enemy attacked, his staff caught in the horse's reins. The animal reared up and the soldier was tipped backwards, he fell to the ground, rolled over his shoulder and returned straight

189

to his feet. Both men focused on Minh, one behind and one in front spread across the width of the path. They seemed to have forgotten what had started them running in the first place and didn't even hear Peter closing the distance.

He and the officer—still on his horse—were exchanging words, but Peter couldn't make them out. Whilst he was distracted, the standing soldier lunged towards Minh's back. *Coward*.

Peter caught the blade against his own a fraction of a second after the attack began. As it was locked it in place against his opponent's body, Peter's right hand shot out and caught the soldier's lead arm, his fingertips gripping deep into the gap under his bicep. The jolt of pain caused the man to jerk and drop his sword, he spun to escape and swung with his elbow from behind. Peter ducked the strike, and rushed forwards with his shoulder pressed against the soldier's torso. His enemy was flung over his back and landed a few feet behind, breaking a leg on impact with the floor.

The officer charged again and missed with his swing, but the horse collided with Minh and sent him flying. The soldier leapt down and ran over, drawing his sword to deliver the killing strike. Peter ran from the side and jumped, firing his right leg out, his heel caught the officer's head and a spurt of blood shot from his mouth, as both men crashed down to the floor.

'Are you okay?' Peter asked, clambering over to his friend.

'LOOK AT MY FACE! Of course I'm not okay,' Minh screamed back, his expression contorted into a crazed smile.

He scrambled to his feet, scooped up a handful of dirt and rubbed it in his wound to stem the bleeding. Minh winced with pain, picked up his staff, and pointed it to the men on the floor. 'Now, which of you dogs are still alive?'

CHAPTER FORTY-FOUR

The forest had covered Sophie's escape well, the foliage was thick while clusters of bamboo and bushes ensured that horses wouldn't be following her. Despite already having been on the run for three days, she felt a thousand times stronger than she had the last time. Her shoulder still throbbed and seemed to be getting worse, but she could focus through the pain. *Thank goodness it's my left arm*, she thought, keeping it pinned close to her body.

Tai's supplies and directions had helped her to make good progress through the forest, but Sophie's agenda had changed. She had barely travelled a mile during the first day before her mind was made up, *There's no way I'm going to abandon Tai to suffer in my place. I'll get to the coast, find help and come back for him.*

All day and night, her thoughts were consumed by possible scenarios, and in the absence of a realistic plan, she eventually managed to convince herself that that her idea was destined to work. Sophie knew that Tan's power came solely from his ability to line the pockets of any potential threats. *If I can convince any of his enemies that I'm wealthy or powerful enough they'll challenge him. Whatever they want I'll promise it, if they can bring him to trial.*

Nights in the forest had been spent sleeping rough, in whatever makeshift shelter Mother Nature provided. By the morning of the fourth day, the trees that had surrounded her like prison bars were thinning. Sophie pushed on through the muggy heat for several hours, she could taste fresh air before she could feel it, but eventually a breeze whipped through the woods in front and offered her some relief.

As she emerged into the sunshine, a valley lay before her. Brilliant green fields were encircled by towering hills and mountains; the sight first brought back memories of travelling with her family, and then turned her thoughts to Tai.

She crept up to the jagged rock face and peered over the lip. *It's at least seventy-five feet down.* Even though she normally had no trouble with heights, a pang of dizziness come over her as she peered at the boulders crumbling down from where she was perched. A stream cascaded across the rocks a few hundred yards to her right and eventually joined a river, which weaved through the depths of the valley and off far into the distance. There were a handful of huts scattered along a path, and even from here, she could see several tracks that wound up from the lowlands into the surrounding hills.

I'll be a sitting duck down there... but it'll take me days to go around. Each moment she wasted meant the chance of finding help or rescuing Tai grew less likely. She was overwhelmed with a feeling of despair, her breaths became panting, she choked, struggling to get enough air, and her dizziness swelled until she could no longer stand.

Sophie pinned her knees to her chest and took a series of long slow inhalations; trying to focus on the things around her seemed to help. The peak of the mountains in the distance, the sweet scent of young rice wafting up from the valley below, and the sounds of the birds' tuneful whistles that emanated from the forest.

What would Peter do? What would my mother have done? she thought trying to get into a logical mind set.

After wavering for far too long, Sophie made her decision and started to look for a place to scramble down. She was going to follow the path straight through the valley; it was risky but definitely the quickest route east.

She weaved across the ridgeline for nearly an hour, before finding a suitable slope that transitioned into the stepped ground of a rice paddy. *I really hope there's no one here,* Sophie thought, choosing to ignore the fact that the carefully farmed terrace must belong to someone. She scanned around for any signs of movement. *Nothing.*

Each step was knee deep in water making her clamber down slow and difficult, as she got closer to the basin it became apparent just how populated the area was. From above the fields had appeared random and undefined, but at this height she could see they had been ploughed for miles in every direction, while young rice shoots had been planted meticulously with just enough space to grow on either side.

The tips of the plants rippled in the wind like a vast green wave below. *It's beautiful,* she thought. *Shame that the only time I'll ever see this is when I'm running for my life.* Sophie stifled a stab of self-pity and shook it off, determined to keep moving.

As she reached the valley floor, daylight was fading over the mountain tops to the west and bringing darkness fast. Familiar clicking and chirping began, the insects had been all over her on the ground of the forest for the past few nights. The constant itching and discomfort had been agonising, but compared to life as a Tan's prisoner, it was the lesser of two evils by far. Now it was the first time since the castle and Tai's house that she hadn't been hidden in woodlands. Between the water-filled paddies and farmhouses there weren't many options. *Get through the middle of the valley and you can worry about sleep later.*

Sophie found the path in the dimming light. It was rocky and uneven, littered with potholes and debris, but the feeling of the rough ground underfoot helped guide her in the darkness.

'Ouch,' she said, almost tripping as her toes caught on the rim of a pothole. The night was cloudy and the moonlight came from barely a sliver, but as she walked further the path became easier to navigate, better defined from the tracks of the horses, carts, and people. *This can't be good, it's only a matter of time until I'm spotted.* She was barely managing a few steps before giving in to the urge to glance over shoulder. Her imagination played cruel tricks, making every shape or noise seem like a figure about to grab her any moment.

After several hours the road started to thin and a gap in the clouds allowed a fraction more moonlight to filter through. As Sophie passed a farmhouse just a few dozen yards from the path, a dog started to bark. She picked up her pace until it was almost a run, at that moment her foot landed in a pothole and her ankle buckled. A searing pain shot through her body as she crashed to the floor, struggling to suppress a scream. Sophie touched her fingers to the twisted joint and recoiled; it had swollen up almost instantly and burnt with agony. Using her good arm, she pushed herself to her feet and tested to see if she could stand, it would support weight, just.

You've got to rest. Sophie's body was beaten and exhausted, her entire leg was throbbing in pain and her thoughts were dizzy and slow. She scanned the area, there was something in the distance in front of her. *What is it? It's too small for a house...*

she strained to make out the structure. It was about ten by ten feet. *Probably a store or tool shed.*

Limping over, she pushed open the door that was hanging on by a single hinge. *Urgh.* The stink of mould and rat urine made her retch. *At least it's out of use.*

In the corner there was a pile of woven sacks. As she lifted one, an enormous spider fled from the material, and dropped onto her foot before scurrying out the door. Sophie smothered her gasp with a hand over her mouth. *It's still better than being outside.* She shuddered. *It can't be long till dawn, just an hour or two off my feet, and then I'll find somewhere better to hide.*

Trying to get comfortable with her head resting on her arms in the least dirty corner, was nearly impossible and even though she was shattered beyond belief, sleep still didn't come. She pictured Tai being dragged along behind the soldiers, and tried to convince herself they would take him alive. Sophie's thoughts turned to Peter; she just wanted to know what had happened to him. She thought about her family, the people she loved most in the world. All of their arguments, fights and disagreements now seemed to be wonderful memories that brought a smile to her face. At the darkest point of the night, just before dawn beckoned, exhaustion caught up and her eyes closed with echoes of her mother, father, Peter and Tai's voices ringing blissfully in her mind.

CHAPTER FORTY-FIVE

A voice outside jerked Sophie's eyes open. She shot back deeper into the corner and pulled the disgusting sack over her head trying to be as still and silent as possible. *Relax, they won't come in.*

As she tried to control her racing heartbeat, the door swung open hitting the back wall and sending dust showering down from the rafters. Through the weave in the sack she could make out the face of an old farm woman. Without even bothering to look, the woman tossed a stack of wooden buckets into the shack. One of them landed on Sophie's shin causing her to jolt in pain, the movement caught the corner of the old woman's eye just as she was turning to leave.

'HEY. COME HERE,' she yelled across the field behind her. 'There's something in here... hope it's not another damn weasel,' she muttered squinting into the dark corner. A man's voice called back to her, but it was too distant for Sophie to make out any words. The old woman slowly leaned in through the door and in one swift motion whipped the sack away. Sunlight flooded into Sophie's eyes, blinding her for a second before her vision could adjust. The old woman was staring down, her eyes almost popping out of her head in surprise.

'Who are you? What are you doing here?'

'I... err,' she had barely let out a noise when the woman snapped back at her.

'You need to get out of here. I hate to think what would happen to us if they found you here.'

'IT'S THE GIRL THEY WERE SEARCHING FOR' the woman yelled, not realising the man—probably her husband—was just a few steps away.

'Who?'

'The foreigner…Lord what's-his-names wife.' Their reactions caught Sophie off guard. Although the couple weren't friendly, they didn't seem to be hostile either.

'I'm sorry, I was just resting. I'll go now. I promise no one will ever know I was here,' Sophie said as her mouth caught up with her brain.

'Yes, quickly then,' the man said, nodding in agreement. 'There were soldiers here just a couple of days ago inspecting all the houses. Don't go that way though,' he said in a low voice waving vaguely in the direction of the path.

'Ah, yes,' the woman added, 'the soldiers went ahead to the next village didn't they? You'll want to turn off east as soon as you can and get out of the valley.'

'Thank you,' Sophie smiled, her fists unclenched, she had been ready to fight her way out, but the relief that she didn't have to hurt someone innocent again, like the old man in the street, was enormous. Tears of gratitude welled in her eyes. 'I'm going right now.'

'Yes, don't hang around, I don't want anyone to see us talking to you. Come on now.'

The husband tapped the old woman on the shoulder and whispered in her ear. The pair mumbled for a minute, too quietly for Sophie to hear.

'Fine,' the woman said and turned back to her. 'There's some water and a ball of sticky rice in the basket, you look like you could use a meal. Take it and get out of here.'

Sophie thanked them and was quickly hustled off. Fortunately, her swollen ankle had gone down overnight, it hurt, but wasn't damaged as badly as it had seemed. A few hundred yards down the road, she turned off on a narrow path that wound up the side of the valley, exactly as they had told her, and was soon skirting a narrow ledge that weaved up the hillside.

As Sophie edged higher, the landscape became cluttered with trees and bushes that had laid roots in the stable ground. After more than an hour, she hit the crest of the hill and a path opened up. Boot-prints and horse and cart tracks littered the muddy ground, while birdsong and distant monkey chatter echoed up from the valley floor. Sophie glanced up to the morning sun, she was now heading almost directly east. *Finally some luck.*

A few miles down the road, an ancient-looking banyan tree straddled the centre of the path. Enormous vines hung down like tangled braids of hair, which for some unknown reason conjured up memories of her mother. She sighed and licked her cracked lips. *A quick rest only, you have to keep moving.*

Sophie swallowed the last few drops of water from the bamboo tube and ate the ball of rice she had been given. Her throat scratched as she swallowed, she was still desperately thirsty, but the sleep had done her a world of good. Now her target was in sight, she was through the forest, out of the valley and—if her directions were accurate—it would be just a few days east till she hit the coast. *Then I'll get help and come back for Tai.* Sophie forced a smile, as though appearing confident might help her feel that way, but the idea she was being naive tugged at her. *You have to try.*

Sophie continued on for only a few hundred yards before, a breeze swept down the path carrying in voices. She bolted to the side of the track and buried herself in the waist-high bushes that lined the way. Her worst fears were realised, as through the haze of the morning, two soldiers could be seen ambling towards her. As they came into earshot she listened, remaining as still as possible.

'...don't know who you mean, I always thought he was the taller one, uglier as well,' the older man said chuckling as he talked. Sophie recognised the red, sergeant's armband he was wearing; fortunately this officer didn't seem to take his job very seriously, dawdling down the road looking uninterested and lazy. *Not like soldiers at all.*

'Right, once we're done in the valley I reckon we get the horses and ride back west, we'll just tell them there's no sign of foreigners,' the sergeant said.

Foreigners? Are they looking for me? Or someone else? Either way it's good.

As he was passing the spot where she lay hidden, the older man stopped in his tracks.

'Hold on,' he said. Sophie's heart leapt into her mouth. 'I've got to piss,' he told his colleague sounding proud. *Urgh... they never grow up.* The sergeant walked to the side of the road just inches from where she was lying beneath the leaves and started to urinate. Sophie didn't move, she didn't even breathe, she just buried her face in the ground praying not to be seen. A drop of warm liquid splashed on the back of her head. She ignored it. But as the drips became more and more frequent she was grinding her teeth with anger. *Sick, vile, man.*

Even more worrying was the feeling of something beginning to crawl up her leg. Whatever it was, it felt big. Scratching as though it was bristling with hair—she fought every instinct in her body not to brush it away and stayed motionless. A searing pain shot through Sophie's leg as the creature bit and unable to fight it, she twitched.

At the very same moment the sergeant's stream halted and the rustle in the bushes below caught his attention.

'What was that?' he asked himself out loud, 'Bon, bring my sword. We might have lunch here,' he called keeping his eyes on the bush.

He's found me? Really? This disgusting excuse for a soldier. Sophie could make out the shadow of his figure leaning in, cautiously trying to figure out what had moved among the thick leaves.

'Here's your sword,' said his colleague jogging to his side. The sergeant rose up without taking a step back and took the weapon. He turned away for less than a second but Sophie seized her opportunity. She rolled onto her front, propping herself up on her elbows so her hands were held up by her face. The sergeant leaned in using the tip of his sword to brush away the leaves, Sophie held her breath. *Any second now.*

The sunlight rushed through the gap revealing his face just inches away. Sophie stabbed both fingers into his eyes with all her strength.

'AARRGGHH,' the sergeant shrieked in a high-pitched cry dropping his sword into the undergrowth. In the few milliseconds of distraction, Sophie was on her feet, tearing through the trees. Running was almost impossible and she was hurdling over the bushes.

'GET THEM! NOW!' screamed the sergeant still on his knees with hands clasping his eyes. The younger soldier snapped out of his shock and shot off just a second behind her. She could hear his shouts and footsteps, he was gaining ground fast. Sophie's chest burned, she gasped for air, trying to blank out the pain shooting from her ankle. She broke from the trees into a clearing covered with grass so deep she was needed to wade through it. Scanning behind for her pursuer, a hidden tangle of roots wrapped around her foot. Sophie's legs were whipped out from beneath her and she went face down, disappearing into the depths of the foliage. She could hear the soldier stumbling around, scouring the undergrowth where she had fallen, but her vision was covered by the matted grass. Sophie thrashed to get back to her feet dragging herself as if through quicksand, but there was no solid ground beneath her. As the soldier waded closer towards the movement, she prepared herself to fight. When the sound was almost upon her she kicked up from her back, throwing her free foot with full force. It caught him under the jaw with a dull thud. The soldier hobbled backwards clutching his face, but didn't go down.

'YOU BITCH!' he screamed 'I'LL KILL YOU!' and charged again. She kicked up once more, this time hitting him in the groin and dropping the man to his knees. Sophie scrambled to her feet untangling her leg in a desperate rush. *Come on, so close.*

She made it to her feet and had just started to limp away as a deafening metallic bang reverberated in her ears. It took a moment for her to realise she had been hit. As Sophie fell back down towards the grassy pit she didn't feel any pain.

Her vision went grey, the scent of the forest flooded over her bringing flashes of her childhood to her mind. Sophie's hand pinned itself to the side of her head just in time to feel the warm blood dripping into her palm and the world fading into darkness.

CHAPTER FORTY-SIX

After their last attack, Peter and Minh had tied up the three survivors and marched them into the nearest village.

'These men are your property now, do what you will with them,' Minh had announced, 'I'd suggest you set them free in exchange for their silence, or there are other options to make sure they don't talk... I'll leave it to your imagination.'

The senior officer had stood solemn and emotionless, his broken-legged colleague hanging onto him for support, while the third man sobbed like a child as an angry mob formed around them.

Along with food, water, and money the soldiers had carried an old European rifle with dozens of bullets. Minh questioned the injured man, confused why they hadn't tried to use it.

'They rust up and backfire in the humidity,' he explained, 'they aren't accurate either, that's why we barely ever shoot. They're more for show than anything.' His explanation made sense to Peter, the cost and effort of maintaining guns coupled with the lack of open space to fire, made swords seem the better option by far. Years ago he had hunted rabbits with his grandfather back in Britain, he had a good idea of how guns worked mechanically and was glad to get his hands on the rifle.

'The noise and smoke will scare the life out of our enemies,' he said to Minh, 'they won't know if it's just the two of us or an army they're dealing with.'

Peter and Minh rode east for a day before releasing the soldier's horses. They continued on foot, figuring it would be better to draw Tan's men out to them, rather than show up on his doorstep without a decent plan.

Within a few days, they learned from a local farmer that another squad of men had recently travelled through, questioning the villagers about attacks on soldiers in the area. Minh managed to catch the trail they had left and stalked the group for the whole next day. As they approached the spot where the squad had set up camp, it was a pitch black, clouded night. *Perfect,* Peter thought.

He aimed the rusted rifle just above where one of the horses was tied, and squeezed the trigger, praying the rusty weapon wouldn't blow up in his hands. The blast of the gunshot ripped through the forest sending the horses into a frenzy. Realising they were under attack the squad fled to their mounts, finally managing to calm them down, and charged down the path in the darkness. The first two went straight into a rope Minh had tied up at head height between two trees. *They're lucky if they survive that,* Peter thought, hearing the crash as he sprinted from the rear. As the final two soldiers frantically tried to load their downed colleagues onto the back of their own horses, one man turned just in time to see a figure emerge from the darkness and the butt of a rifle streaming into his head. The last man standing surrendered willingly when he realised he was outgunned and outnumbered.

'You might actually hit someone with that thing one day,' Minh laughed, as they searched through the supplies that had been abandoned in panic at the soldiers' camp.

Each group they had encountered so far were carrying plenty of food and water, now after days of being well fed and hydrated Peter was feeling a level strength of energy he hadn't done for a long time.

'I'm not trying to hit them, just scare them,' he said smiling, pleased with their success. 'It worked though didn't it? Fear got them right where we wanted. Just as you said, they were like trapped rats.'

As they passed through the villages that dotted the roads leading east, it was clear the pair's reputation had preceded them. Some onlookers rushed out to praise them for their actions, others shouted insults, while some simply hid, hoping the pair would pass by without incident. Peter and Minh played on the rumours that surrounded them, fanning the flames of confusion whenever they can, saying they were mercenaries or part of a rebellion.

The next squad they encountered seemed much more professional, Minh took down man one with the rope trap and another with a kick to the head shortly after. But the captain engaged in a sword fight with Peter as though it was a matter of pride, he swung fast slicing him across the chest and causing him to drop his sword as he convulsed in pain. An inch higher and his throat would have been slit. From across the path Minh cracked his staff across the captain's hand, shattering his knuckles, whilst Peter struck at the vital points through gaps in his armour, leaving him unmoving on the ground. The fourth man tackled Minh and they grappled on the floor, before the soldier managed to draw his sword Peter smashed him round the side of the head with a back-fist that finished the fight.

'*Namo Amitabha*-Praise to Buddha,' Minh muttered as he lay the corpse of the dead captain down in the trees and covered him with leaves. *It was his Karma, this man's life led him here*, Peter re-told himself. *It is for the greater good.*

'Did you hear what they were saying about us?' Minh asked as they walked away from the remaining men they had left tied up by the side of the road.

'No I didn't catch it,' Peter said. It was hard for him to understand anything much said in the commotion and madness of a fight.

'They were calling us the "Tigers", sounds scary right?'

'They definitely scare the life out of me.' Peter shuddered remembering coming face to face with the predator that roamed "Tiger Valley".

'Let's stick with it then, it can be the title of our rebellion!'

'Yes.' Peter smiled, 'Minh you're a genius.'

CHAPTER FORTY-SEVEN

'I want them dead! Today. Not tomorrow. Not next week. Today. DO YOU UNDERSTAND ME?!' Lord Tan screamed. General Khang was patiently kneeling before him as the summer rains pounded on the tiled roof of the main hall.

'Sir, we are trying our best. We have despatched several units, but unless we are willing to go to war against these outlaws we should just consider them an inconvenience. Until we know exactly how many men we are dealing with and how much power they have we should refrain from making a move. I believe they are trying to lure us out.'

'You fool! Don't you see what they're trying to do? They're dragging my reputation through the mud. They're trying to make *me* look weak, and you think we should just wait it out?'

'With all due respect sir-'

'-don't give me excuses. The *only* reason you're still here is because of my father, don't you forget that.' The general bit his tongue and nodded, Tan's bloodshot eyes continued to stare, bulging out from his haggard face. Khang wondered how long it had been since he had last slept.

'Prepare your men,' Lord Tan continued. 'I want everyone armed, we will burn every tree and village until they show themselves.'

Khang sighed, *It's not them making you look weak; you're doing that all by yourself.* It was depressing to see this once dignified leader spitting and raging over a few small time criminals. Admittedly, the confusing reports Khang had received in the past few weeks had started to ring alarm bells in his mind, something strange *was* going on. One group of soldiers described a pair of young men as their attackers, whilst others reported a whole gang. The troops had started calling them "The Tigers" as rumours of rebellion and treason circulated through the ranks. Tan's insistence on despatching more and more men to hunt them down was just adding fuel to the fire, but the stubborn fool wouldn't listen.

General Khang had questioned the survivors from several squads, and he knew their tactics. *Divide and conquer - simple but effective.* It was a classic play for both hunters and military tacticians, probably because fear always brought out the same foolish instincts in animals and men alike. Regardless, it wasn't long before his men started to make excuses to avoid going out on patrol. Khang considered making an example of the first coward that feigned injury in front of him, but the lesson his father had taught him seemed relevant now more than ever, *"A true leader is the one that chooses mercy over violence."* *If only Lord Tan had such wisdom.*

Later that week, Khang found himself taking a narrow path through the citadel, he didn't normally venture this far east, it was where the farmers lived and it smelt like it too. He covered his face as he arrived at the tea-house, partially for fear of being recognised but also for the unpleasant aroma outside.

As he entered the dimly-lit room, four well-dressed men were sitting on the far side of the room. He cringed at their flamboyant attire, *I thought this was meant to be a secret meeting.* The owner and two young women bowed to Khang, gesturing for him to join the group as though he were any normal customer; but being out of his uniform in public felt disconcerting. The usual pleasantries were exchanged before the topic turned to their purpose of their meeting.

'I fear his own ego and paranoia are getting the better of him,' the general whispered to the envoys, 'If he's not stopped soon, we will have a rebellion on our hands and the government will have to step in and clean up his mess.'

'General, you have already proven yourself as a leader and a soldier,' the oldest of the groups said. 'But unless you can prove that Lord Tan has violated the treaty that was signed with his father, then we have no choice but support him for as long as he lives.'

'I understand,' Khang nodded in agreement. *As long as he lives.*

CHAPTER FORTY-EIGHT

It wasn't long before the locals started hearing the stories of "The Tigers", a group of rebels that fought against Lord Tan's men and shared their wealth. Peter explained to Minh about the legend of Robin Hood, how he stole from the rich to give to the poor, and learned there was an almost identical story in his culture. How their countries could be so different, nearly a world apart, yet still so similar brought a smile to his face.

By utilising intelligence rather than just strength, it had taken only a few weeks for Peter and Minh to convince the enemy soldiers they were up against an entire gang of rebels rather than a couple of inexperienced teenagers. Now their opponents were no longer just fearing "The Tigers", but expecting to lose. Likewise, the pair stared death in the face and learned to respect it without trepidation or fear. By the end of the fifth week Peter had lost track of how many times he'd be rocked by powerful blows and how often he'd almost made fatal mistakes in a battle. Still, as time passed his confidence grew.

'I bet that rat is pissing his pants with all the stories he's hearing about us,' Minh laughed, 'I can't believe our nickname stuck.'

'I hope so,' Peter said, 'it's nearly got to the point where he'll have no choice but to meet us in person or risk losing control of his own men... you know it's only a matter of time until we get caught though?' He was pleased with the progress they had made, but fearful to be too contented.

'Yeah I know,' Minh replied, apparently uncaring about the consequences, 'but we might as well enjoy it now... look how happy people are to see us. We've shown them they don't have to be afraid anymore. This is the beginning of the end. I'm sure of it.'

Peter smiled, *It's a big difference certainly, but the beginning of the end? I doubt it.*

Both men were in good spirits, they had been offered a place to rest in a village that was built upon a sloping hillside. From what Peter could gather, Giang, the old man that had invited them in seemed to despise Lord Tan even more than most. It had been more than a week since they had spent a night out of the daily deluge that mid-summer had brought and being among friends put both Peter and Minh at ease.

They sat and talked under the light of an oil lamp in the communal longhouse while their hosts were finishing up daily chores. As conversation progressed Minh explained how the villagers here were a different tribe from his own people in the west. Although just separated by a number of miles, they spoke a different dialect and had customs that even he found strange. As he spoke, a breeze whipped through the hut carrying in the scent of roasting meat and herbs, and bringing a growl Peter's stomach.

'Sorry to interrupt,' Giang said and ducked through the wooden door followed by two middle-aged men. 'The women have prepared a meal in your honour.' A smile spread across his face, 'it is not often we have guests, let alone ones like yourselves.'

'That's great,' Minh beamed, 'thanks again for your hospitality.'

'Not at all, we are pleased to welcome you into our village. Make yourselves at home for as long as you need.' The old man took a seat on the wicker mat beside them, and an older woman, who Peter guessed was his wife, followed him across the hut carefully carrying a large tin tray of food and several others entered behind her.

'We haven't had a meal like this for long time,' Peter said staring at the plates of roasted pork and vegetables the women were laying out upon the wicker mat that lay between them. Both he and Minh's gazes were fixed on the food in front of them, urging everyone to sit down so that they could eat. As the last woman stepped into the light of the lamp, Peter's gaze was diverted. *Wow, she's beautiful.*

The girl was young, close to his age. Her jet-black hair was pinned on top of her head, contrasting with her pale skin and red lips. She smiled, laying another tray down on the mat and Peter panicked, suddenly aware that he had been staring at her the entire time. He glanced at Minh who appeared equally transfixed. Almost as if by habit Giang cleared his throat. 'This is my daughter Han,' he said, 'she is an excellent cook and will be happy to serve you for as long as you choose to stay.' Han smiled again, catching Peter's gaze for just a split second, before turning down to the ground as if she were shy. The casual smile still on her face showed she was obviously used to this kind of reaction.

The men sitting either side of them handed Peter and Minh glasses of sweet fruit-liquor and toasted the meal. As they ate and drank, the women who all sat opposite, kept filling up their bowls and cups as soon as they ran low.

The pair talked about their journey, where they had come from, where they were going, their encounters with Lord Tan's men, then there was singing and music that lasted late into the night. Peter watched one of the older women as she sang and played a soft melody on a stringed instrument like a small box-shaped guitar. His head was swimming from the liquor as the gentle beat of the music continued. For the second time that evening Han's gaze caught his own, her eyes lit up and a touch of red showed on her cheeks. He couldn't help but grin back.

Something about the whole experience was exciting. Peter rarely even thought about women, he had been so focused on his mission for so long, yet for some reason, tonight things seemed different. For the first time in a long while, he felt relaxed and confident, even though he had no idea how he must look. *I haven't even seen a mirror in over a year,* he realised, *maybe it's just the alcohol?*

As the joviality of the evening finally came to an end, Peter and Minh were back to their usual place, the pair of them alone in the darkness.

'She's beautiful isn't she?' Minh whispered in English, very aware that they lay separated from the family by only a few thin wicker partitions that divided up the rooms.

'Who... Han?' Peter muttered, trying to sound as though the same thought hadn't been on his mind since the moment she had left.

'No, the old women,' his friend hissed, but Peter failed to find his sarcasm funny. 'I thought you had more important things to think about than women anyway?'

'Hmm,' He ignored the question, rolled over and closed his eyes, finding comfort in having something that sent his thoughts off in a happier direction even just for a single night.

CHAPTER FORTY-NINE

A mosquito landing on his arm caused Peter's groggy eyes to open. His mouth was dry and his head was throbbing. *What's wrong with me? Am I ill?* He wondered for a moment until the taste of stale liquor in his mouth reminded brought a reminder of the previous night, and with it a sense of nausea. *I need some water.*

Feeling embarrassed, but uncertain as to why, Peter tiptoed to the stairs of the raised hut and hobbled down them trying not to make any noise. The sun hadn't yet risen and the light outside was murky and blue. *Where was the well?* he thought, trying to recall the hazy memories of their conversation the night before. He followed the path past several huts, before it banked sharply downward towards what sounded like the trickle of a river. The ground was lined with fog, and in the darkness before dawn, seeing more than a few dozen feet was hard. *That must be it,* he thought, trying to focus on a stone structure that sat twenty yards or so in front of him.

As Peter got closer, the outline of the well grew more defined, but there was something black sitting on top of the stone slab that covered it. He stumbled over trying not to lose his footing on the slippery grass of the river bank and picked up the material. *What is that? Clothes?*

A sound to the right snapped Peter's attention away. His hand shot to his side searching for the leather handle of his sword, but found nothing. *Fool.* Peter cursed himself as he tried to focus on the shadow of the figure just thirty or forty yards away.

They weren't moving towards him, but seemed to be in the stream. A splash confirmed his thoughts, but it was too dark to make out who was there. *It could be soldiers, do I run for my weapon or find Minh?*

Peter hunched down by the well, he waited for a few minutes as daylight began to seep through the clouds overhead and it seemed to grow lighter by the second.

'Oh my goodness,' he said out loud as he realised what he was witnessing. The long black hair, now untied, reached all the way down her back, shimmering in the first rays of light as she poured a bucket of water over its length. Han's body looked like something he could only compare to a work of art, in that words couldn't express his sense of awe. Almost on cue she turned and her eyes widened as she caught Peter's gaze. A second of bewilderment passed before he realised he was now hiding behind a well, holding her clothes and staring open mouthed.

Oh no, no, no, no. Peter flung the material forwards onto the stone and every muscle in his body tensed up as he froze like a statue. *Oh God, please don't have seen me.*

'You can bring those over here if you like?' Han said, without even bothering to look his way. *What should I do?* He heard the splashing as she continued to wash, seemingly uncaring. A vague memory sprung up of Minh laughing about getting up early to see the girls bathing in the river, he had assumed it was a joke, it certainly wasn't something he thought was normal. Peter tried to speak but nothing came out of his mouth. 'Yes... ok, I will,' he croaked. *Idiot.*

His body felt like glass on the verge of shattering, as he lifted what was clearly now a black dress and took a timid step forwards. Han stepped out of the stream and started towards him, running her fingers through her hair as she went. She looked right into his eyes and smiled, with the confidence that only a beautiful woman in front of a petrified man would possess. Peter stopped, his gaze fixed on the ground until she was just inches in front him.

'Can I have them please?' Han put her hands out expectantly and Peter passed her the clothes, daring to take only the briefest glimpse at her face, as she stood naked in front of him. In a moment that he had thought couldn't get any more embarrassing, it did. He felt the stir of his trousers tightening around his groin, his eyes flicked down for a fraction of a second, before he turned to look at the river, trying desperately to draw Han's gaze anywhere else but there.

'You don't need to be so shy,' she said, 'you look like you've never seen a woman before. It's quite normal for my people to bathe in the rivers, in case you hadn't noticed?'

'I hadn't,' Peter answered, his face feeling as though it were on fire.

Han took a step forward, and Peter jerked back, immediately realising that she was walking towards the well and not him.

'See you later,' she said with the faintest of smiles breaking through her thin, perfectly-shaped lips. Peter stayed on the spot, not even daring to turn around until he was absolutely certain she had left, although now he was more concerned about her seeing the mile-wide the grin on his face than anything else.

In a daze, he finished collecting the water and returned to the hut. He stoked the clay stove that stood in the corner of the room and waited for the squawking roosters to set about rousing the remainder of the village. Minh awoke shortly after, mumbled something about training and went off to wash his face. When he returned Peter was sitting gazing off into the distance on the far side of the hut.

'What's wrong?' Minh said.

'Oh, nothing. Just thinking,' Peter replied.

'Are we going to practise then or not?'

'What? Errm, yeah sorry.'

'It's the girl isn't it?' Minh asked, catching Peter off guard, his face flushed red.

'Come on, I know how you feel. Believe me, I do, but now is not the time. They could be here at any moment, we need to be ready.'

'Yeah, I know. It's okay, I'm fine. I promise' Peter replied.

'If you say so.'

Most of the day was spent helping out in the fields, lifting heavy bundles of rice plants onto a cart in the sun. As evening came, Han and the other women cooked yet another enormous meal, apparently it was the tradition for when they had guests.

Peter felt awkward seeing her at first, but as it became apparent she was acting perfectly normally, he relaxed a little and they talked over dinner. Following the meal, he, Minh, Giang and the other elders were sitting around a wooden table beneath the hut sipping tea in the fading light, when a man in ragged farming attire approached.

'Apologies, but we need to talk with you,' he said with a hint of worry in his voice, and bowed first towards Giang and then to the guests.

'What is it?' Minh said, apparently noticing the same aura of concern Peter had picked up on.

'We've got some news,' he said, 'a group of farmers have just returned from the road to the north. There's a squad of soldiers heading this way with a prisoner.' Peter bolted up to his feet spilling the tiny porcelain cup that sat on his lap.

'A prisoner? Who is it? Who saw them?'

'One of the farmers, Sun, was trading in the village yesterday morning.'

'Get him, quick,' Giang ordered. Within a few minutes, the group were upstairs with Sun standing by the entryway looking awkward, as though the news was somehow his fault.

'What did you see exactly?' Minh questioned, pacing the hut with a hand on his chin as though he was investigating a crime.

'They were getting ready to leave when I was on my way this morning,' the farmer answered, 'six soldiers, two officers on horses and four on foot. At the back there was a man tied up by his hands and with a bag over his head.'

'Oh' Peter's face dropped and his excitement disappeared. For a moment his thoughts had flicked to Sophie, *Is she still alive? Has she escaped?* before he realised how ridiculous it was to get excited without any evidence.

'Where were they going?' Minh said.

'They were coming this way, but I made good time. They won't be here for a while with all that equipment, you probably have at least three or four hours.'

'What do you think?' Peter asked, already knowing what his friend would answer.

'Easy. We find a good spot to cut them off before they arrive,' Minh said with his usual enthusiasm. 'Sun, are there any points close by where the road narrows?' He turned to Peter and spoke in a lower tone. 'If we funnel them into a bottleneck and they can't back out, there could be a hundred of them for all the difference it'd make...'

'Do you really think we should risk taking on that many of them? What does it matter if they have a prisoner? We'll just have to drag him along or set him free anyway. I say we just hide out in the forest and let them pass.'

'Oh.' Minh's face dropped apparently catching Peter's train of thought. 'You want to stay here don't you? I know that look in your eyes.'

'Maybe, just a few days-'

'-Don't be a fool.' Minh spat, 'We need to move now, and you need to get your head straight and stop thinking about women or you'll get yourself killed.'

'That's not it at all, I know what I'm doing, I just don't think it's worth the risk,' Peter answered, trying his best to sound offended.

'Well I'm going, with or without you. Come and find me when you figure out what's actually important.' Minh stormed off leaving Peter to boil in his anger.

He's just jealous, besides it really isn't *worth the risk.* After more than an hour of grumbling to himself, Peter closed his eyes and drifted off to sleep.

CHAPTER FIFTY

As dawn approached, Minh lay low in the bushes that lined the road.

One girl and forgets who his friends are?! *Idiot!* he thought, stewing with rage. After some time he managed to push his aggravation aside. *Come on, this is more important than any of us. We can't let Lord Tan win.*

Before long, he could make out the long shadows of soldiers on the path as they funnelled deeper towards his trap. *They'll never see me coming.*

A thunderclap and a flash of lightning split the peace and the skies opened up. For as long as Minh could remember, the summer was always like this. Heavy raindrops that stung as they fell, would absorb the heat and humidity, restoring equilibrium. Like Yin and Yang, dark and light, they were counterparts. *Just like them,* he thought, *my mission is the good to Lord Tan's evil.*

In a matter of minutes, the rain had beaten through the leaves overhead and soaked him to the bone. It didn't take long for the track to become a swamp and seeing or hearing more than a few feet was impossible. The soldiers were practically upon him when the squelching of hooves through the thick mud gave Minh his bearings. They were two by two, with the mounted men first, four behind, and one man at the back dragging the prisoner along by a rope around his throat. Exactly as they expected.

Here we go, he thought, *it's just me, honourable and brave, like my parents.*

Minh took a deep breath, pushed the leaves aside with the tip of his hardwood staff and charged.

The closest soldier was slow, the blunt end of Minh's weapon caught him under the ribs and sent him tumbling backwards and hanging upside down tangled in the stirrups, while his horse charging off in panic. The second soldier was much quicker. Minh swivelled sideways, the motion he had practised so many times with his buckets on the steps was automatic, but the blade grazed his shoulder and his weapon clattered to the floor.

He screamed in a combination of pain and panic as the officer turned his horse to swing again. Minh ducked under the blade crouching low and pounced, his fingers wrapped around the officer's leather armour and tore him face first down to the ground. The next two men on foot, apparently not expecting their superiors to fail, were now sprinting forwards. Minh realised for the first time he was now unarmed and facing four men. *Come on Hong, don't let me down.*

Screaming like an animal, he charged straight back at them, with his knees powering into the first soldier's sternum and dropping him to the floor. The next man swung several times, but each of his strikes were redirected. On the fifth attempt Minh pounced straight into him, the grip of his tiger-claw attack caught the soldier around the throat with his fingertips and pinned him to the ground. Out of nowhere, a foot smashed into Minh's chest knocking the wind from his lungs. He gasped for breath as yet more kicks and stamps rained down on him. He caught a glimpse of a sword raised above his head.

He closed his eyes and clenched his teeth. *This can't be it.* Memories of his parents, Yai, Thi, Peter and Hong, flashed through his mind. *It's over.*

CHAPTER FIFTY-ONE

Sophie's eyelids fluttered. A few seconds passed before her brain responded then a searing pain tore her back to reality. Her head was spinning and groggy. *Not again,* she thought, recognising the rhythmic pounding of hooves beneath her. *Please don't be taking me back to the castle.*

This time she was sitting upright, leaning against the rider's back. Her hands were tied in front and a blindfold made of coarse cloth was chafing her face as they bounced. Through a gap in the bottom she could make out the feet of the rider and the horse's hooves which were hitting the ground at speed. *My head is killing me.* Sophie tried to reach up with her hands but they jerked her body forwards where they were tied to the cantle of the saddle.

'What was that? Are you awake?' the voice of the sergeant called back.

'Yes.'

'Good, you can sit up then, it's killing my back having you leaning on it. We'll be at the city in two days if the weather stays good.'

'What city?' she asked, dreading the answer.

'The capital, the citadel. Obviously. I thought you foreigners were supposed to be smart?'

Idiot. His condescending tone angered Sophie, but she knew better than to show it.

'Please don't take me back. I'll do anything you want.'

'Listen you stupid little girl. You're lucky we didn't kill you back there after you attacked us. Besides, we have our orders and they're to bring you back alive.'

The sergeant's tone softened, 'we're going to be rewarded well for finding you. Actually it was pretty lucky for us wasn't it Bon?'

'Yes sir! My wife will be over the moon with the money,' a happy voice shouted back.

Sophie's heart sank, it felt as though her head was splitting with every jolt of the hooves, and a wave of nausea rushed over her. *Come on, you need to see,* she urged herself and tried to lift the blindfold higher by shrugging her shoulders. After more attempts than she could count she got to a position where she could partially see. *Where are we?* They had left the mountain trails and were cutting through rice paddies, the fields were dotted with buffalo pulling farm equipment and snow-white egrets feeding on the crabs and fish that lived in their waters. After hours of the same scenery Sophie's worst fears were realised, the grey of the citadel's stone walls loomed into view on the horizon.

Her head was pounding, the heat, thirst, and her injuries made her weak.

'We need to stop. Please. I need water,' she said.

'Ok, we'll rest, but just for a few minutes' the sergeant replied, 'and don't even think about trying to escape. We're going to be back at the castle tomorrow morning and that's all there is to it.'

Sophie knew it would be foolish even trying to run, she was exhausted, injured, tied up *and* on foot. Although Bon and the sergeant seemed like some of the least capable soldiers on the face of the planet, getting away from even them would be impossible. As their horses slowed and came to a stop, her captor reached back pulling the blindfold from her head. It was late, and the sun was setting to the west. They had stopped in front of what must have been an old temple. Three entrances were cut into the stone of an ornate gateway with its roof carved to resemble the body of a dragon. Sophie admired the structure for a moment, she'd always loved the sense of freedom travelling had given her, seeing new things and visiting new places, but now becoming a prisoner again, her soul felt crushed.

Whilst the soldiers re-tied the loads onto their horses, she scanned the area for anything that could be of use. *A few old buildings, rocks and rice, the same as everywhere.* After a few minutes, Bon untied her wrists from the saddle and with one hand on his sword lowered her down and led her from behind into the courtyard of the temple. Tree roots were bursting through the floor and the moss-covered altar in the centre reminded her of Tai's house. *How will I ever help him now?*

Sophie lay down on the tiles gazing up at the hazy red sky. The warm, flat, ground against on her back helped with the nausea that had been plaguing her all day. She drank some water the sergeant provided and felt a little better. *This is the only chance I'm going to get. What can I do?* She clambered to her feet and walked over to where the two soldiers were sitting on the steps of the temple doorway.

'I'm sorry for hurting you before, I don't remember what I did but I'm sorry.' She recalled the sunlight splitting the leaves in front of her as she hid in the bush, then nothing.

'What do you want?' Bon asked.

'Please let me go… no one knows I'm here, I'll never tell a soul I promise.'

'We can't do that' the sergeant snapped, 'and even if we could, why would we?'

'I can pay! Not now, but if you help me to get to the port, I have friends there and I can give you money, a lot of it.'

'Ha-ha, and what reason would we have to trust you? Anyway, the port's more than five days ride from here, we'd be hunted down as traitors if we went.'

'Think about it though, what has Tan ever done for you? Has he treated you well?'

'Look I feel for you, I really do. Everyone hates Tan, even his own men… but right now he is still our boss and he still pays our salaries.'

'And he'll be giving us our reward,' Bon chimed in.

'Yes that too. Now, back on the horse, let's get this over with,' he said sounding almost sympathetic.

'There must be something I can do to change your mind? Something you want?' Sophie tried her best to look alluring, even though she knew how dirty and battered she was. *Urgh, I can't believe I just said that,* she thought trying to hold back a wince as she eyeballed her captor's disgusting buck-toothed face.

'Not that you're not pretty,' he replied with a chuckle, 'but I think I'd rather have the money.' Sophie gritted her teeth, but buried her face in her arms as it burned with to hide her burning embarrassment.

For the next few minutes, she sat listening to the two colleagues chatting casually about their families and day to day lives, it calmed her down. *They're just normal people.*

She hadn't even thought about the soldiers having lives outside of their work and desire to hunt her down, but their words got her thinking. *I saw them carrying out soldiers' corpses nearly every day... I wonder how many of his men know about their friends and family members dying at Tan's hand? If he's insisting on bringing me back to the castle alive I'm going to make sure it's the worst mistake he's ever made.*

CHAPTER FIFTY-TWO

A slap stung Peter's face.

'You coward!' Han was almost shouting, 'I thought you were meant to be brave. But you left your friend to go out and fight on his own?'

Oh no. Peter felt like he had been punched in the stomach. He hadn't thought for a moment that Minh would actually go on his own. *What have I done?* An overwhelming sense of guilt rushed over him blocking out the burning on his cheek.

'How long since they left?'

'Hours,' Han's tone was grim, but even furious she was stunning, 'I just found out.'

Peter glanced at the door with a second of silent contemplation, it was still dark outside. *Maybe I'm not too late?*

'I need to go after him. I'm sorry,' Peter said, 'we had a fight...' he scrambled for excuses desperately hoping he might even believe them himself.

He had been running as fast as he could manage for nearly an hour when the path finally began to narrow as described. It was barely light enough to see and the ground was swallowed in mist. Rain had started to fall, but the noise up ahead told him he was close. His wet hands fumbled to grip the handle of the rifle; out of nowhere a horse with a rider dangling from its stirrups charged passed almost crashing into him. Peter kept running, his heart was pounding in his ears. *Please God don't let me be too late.*

With just thirty yards to go he thought he saw the outline of Minh pinning a man to the ground. *Twenty yards.*

A torrent of kicks from two soldiers rained down on his friend while, a prisoner and guard stood to their rear. Peter pulled the wooden butt to his shoulder, barely able to see through the rain.

Fifteen yards. A blade glimmered as the soldier raised it above his head, readying for execution.

BANG. The volume of the shot stabbed his eardrums and the smoke blinded him. Peter kept running. He threw the rifle over his back as he approached, neither man was moving.

A body with half of its head missing had spilled a cascade of blood into the puddles of mud and rain. Closing the final few feet, the remaining soldier's sword was shearing through the falling drops towards his face. The tip of the blade sliced his cheek as he tore his own weapon in an upwards arch. It caught the soldier's extended arm and carved it clean off just above the elbow. Still brandishing its weapon, the limb fell to the ground as a shot of blood spurted from the wound.

'YES!' Minh's hoarse voice shouted over the soldier's screams as he fell clutching his bloody stump. 'It's about time!' Peter whispered a silent prayer.

Minh scrambled to his feet, his face bloodied and swollen. The pair both turned to the remaining man, who was standing with his foot on one end of a rope, the other was tied around the prisoner's neck. The soldier had an arrow pulled back in his bow, flicking with uncertainty between his attackers. There was fear in his eyes, he knew that he would only be able to hit one of them before the other got to him. Peter pulled the rifle from his back and pointed it at the man. *I hope he doesn't realise it's not loaded.*

'There's no need for you to die here,' Minh said with his palms raised, 'let's talk about this.' He and Peter stepped simultaneously towards him, the soldier instinctively took a half-step backwards, and the tension fell from the rope. Out of nowhere the prisoner charged, blindly cannonballing into his captor's waist, and launching him five feet into the air as the arrow glided off into the trees. The soldier landed on his head with a crunch and his body slumped onto the rope dragging the prisoner down by the neck.

'Huh? What just happened?!'

'No idea' Minh said, 'but I like it, let's see if he's still alive.'

'Minh I-' Peter started

'-save it, let's get these men tied first.'

They grabbed a length of rope from the saddlebags of the remaining horse that had become tangled around a tree. It quickly became apparent there was not a lot left to tie. The first rider was long gone, the second was pale and unmoving at the bottom of a dirty red pool fuelled by blood and rain. One soldier lay headless, one lay armless and pale. The last man was unconscious, probably, from the terrifying throw of his captive. Peter approached the prisoner who was shaking and jolting on the ground.

'Why's he doing that?'

'I don't know.' Minh stared at the convulsing body for a few moments seemingly deep in thought, the scene reminded him of the way the animals would shake in traps, as they gasped for air.

'He's suffocating. Get the rope now!' Minh struggled to hold him down whilst Peter carefully used the point of his blade to cut his throat free.

The prisoner gasped like it was his first breath, several longer and slower gasps followed before he seemed to return to normal breathing. Minh stepped in close, leaning down with caution and reached for the sack, as his fingers found the neck of the thick linen he whipped it from the prisoner's head and stared into his eyes.

His face meant nothing to Peter, it was tired, bruised, and dirty, but he was a young man, maybe just a few years older than himself. Minh leaned appearing equally confused.

'Who *are* you?'

The man's eyes flickered for a moment, his mouth opened as though he was desperate to speak, then silence.

CHAPTER FIFTY-THREE

'I'm so sorry, I don't know what I was thinking.' Peter knew there were no excuses good enough for how he'd acted. They continued rooting through the bags of goods that had been scattered around in the fight for several minutes, throwing anything unessential into the undergrowth to hide their tracks.

'You weren't thinking! That's the problem.' Minh finally boiled over. 'That's what beautiful women do you fool. Next time how about you listen to someone with experience?'

'Wow,' Peter was impressed more than he was hurt, just when he thought they knew each other, Minh surprised him for the second time that day.

'Either way, what's done is done,' his tone relaxed and he out a sigh. 'Now what shall we do with him?' He said nodding down towards the unconscious, sickly-looking man in front of them.

'I'm not sure,' Peter said, 'should we just leave him?'

'There's got to be a reason why they've bothered dragging him all this way,' Minh said still sounding exasperated at Peter's intelligence. 'They've have been walking for a few days at least.'

'Right,' Peter glanced around at the supplies that had been scattered in the melee, the pots and pans that had fallen a few feet away all seemed well-used. 'I'll try and wake him up,' he said still hoping to make amends.

'Fine, but if he doesn't come round you're carrying him,' Minh grumbled almost sounding like his old self.

Peter took the gourd bottle that was tied onto his waist and dripped some water into the prisoner's mouth. *Maybe he's dead? Or paralysed? He did hit that soldier pretty hard...*

He leaned in to take the man's pulse and just as he reached for the neck, he began coughing and spluttering. The prisoner slowly came round, eventually pulling himself up to a sitting position.

'More water, please?' he croaked. Minh passed him the bottle and both he and Peter watched him suspiciously as the young man drained it in one and lay down flat on his back again for several minutes, as though even that small effort had been too much.

'So who are you then?' Peter asked, unable to wait a moment longer. 'Why are you so important they'd bother dragging you this whole way?'

'I'm only a farmer, they captured me and were taking me to the city, I don't know why.'

He's lying, Peter knew almost instinctively.

'Shall I kill him?' Minh said, trying to sound tough.

'Ha-ha,' the man laughed, not in a spiteful way, but one that sounded relieved.

What? Who does he think he is? Peter's face twisted, angry that this prisoner seemed not to be the slightest bit scared of them.

'How about I wipe that smile off your face?' Minh said squaring up to him.

'Sorry,' he raised his palms looking weak, 'I mean no offence. I just realised, you two are the *gang* all the soldiers are worried about aren't you? "The Tigers?"

What's so funny about that? His amusement drained Peter's confidence, suddenly he felt like a boy again, a far cry from the warrior that had triumphed against his enemies just minutes before.

'Yes, what about it?' he asked trying to fit the part.

'You're Peter aren't you?'

'Right, I'm going to kill this guy unless he starts explaining himself in about three seconds,' Minh spluttered aiming the butt of his staff at the man's head with both hands gripped tightly ready to stab. His friend raised a palm and squatted down staring deep into the prisoner's eyes.

'How do you know who I am?' he asked intrigued by the stranger's knowledge.

'Everyone has heard of you two, all the soldiers are on the lookout for "The Tigers".

'I meant how do you know my name?' he said, starting to lose patience.

'Your sister-' Without even thinking Peter's body fired into action, his foot smashed into the chest of the prisoner and pinned him to the ground while the tip of his blade pressed against the man's jugular. A drop of blood ran down from the point that had nicked his skin and fell into the mud.

'WHERE IS SHE?' Peter screamed through clenched teeth. 'WHAT HAVE YOU DONE TO HER?' His anger even surprised himself. The look of confidence on the stranger's face had turned to sheer panic as he realised he was facing death.

'Wait, wait, wait. You don't understand,' he spluttered. 'She was dying. I saved her life, that's why I'm her-'

'-YOU'RE LYING!'

'I swear, I'm not. I was a prisoner, I'm their enemy, think about it.'

Peter lowered the sword, his brain struggling to make sense of the situation. His tone softened, 'But why would you help her?'

'She needed it. She was really ill and where I'm from when someone needs help, we help them.' He responded as though it was just common sense. Minh stepped forward, placing a hand on Peter's chest and nudging him back a few inches.

'I don't know who this guy is or where he came from,' Minh said holding his gaze, 'but we did the same for you remember? He wouldn't have a reason to lie about it.' He looked solemn, maybe even annoyed that after all this time Peter couldn't believe that his people would do that for a stranger.

'She was heading east to the port,' Tai continued, 'I took her to the forest myself. They caught me, and were taking me to be questioned.' His expression turned glum, 'but then this morning a rider from the castle told us she had already been captured. I couldn't believe it, but now meeting you two, maybe this has all happened for a reason.'

'If she's been caught why would they have kept you alive?' Peter demanded, still not convinced. He wanted to believe the story, but there was no way of knowing if they were walking into a trap.

'I'm not sure, they probably want to question me about you... you're the ones attracting all the attention, they wouldn't have even found us if they weren't patrolling day and night looking for you.'

'Tell us everything you know,' Minh ordered, placing himself between the two men.

As Tai explained about Sophie's escape from the castle, her sickness, and the time they had spent together. Peter listened in disbelief, his sister had always been tough, but he had never imagined just how so. The snarl on his face melted into a grin as the three men sat in the drizzling rain sharing their stories. Finally, the clouds of the dreary morning passed giving way to one of the most beautiful sunrises Peter had ever seen, the sky was painted with streaks of red, yellow, and purple. *This is it, now our path is clear.*

CHAPTER FIFTY-FOUR

Within a day the group found themselves among a cluster of huts nestled high on the ridgeline of a valley. From here they could see the centre of the lowlands, and less than fifty miles away lay the sinister black silhouette of the citadel, standing out through the haze against the green backdrop. It made sense to rest and refuel here as they formulated a plan.

'We're honoured to welcome you to our commune,' one of the elders told Peter as they were handed cups of tea in his stilt house. 'After hearing about your exploits more and more people are being inspired to stand up to Tan and his men,' the old man smiled, 'although I think the villagers were expecting there to be a few more of you.'

'Thank you,' Peter said, unsure if it was complement or an insult. He was grateful to have been invited in, but at the same time was hoping not to get engaged in a lengthy conversation, he and Minh needed to talk strategy.

As the old man left to lock up his animals, Peter waited a few minutes to make sure they were alone before the conversation turned to their plan.

'I have an idea,' he said wincing, 'but it's kind of risky.' *More like suicidal.*

'We want to get in front of Tan right? But if they know that's what we want they'll never take us. I think we need to launch an attack on a squad, make it look like we mess up and get caught, then with any luck they'll bring us to him. Then we can challenge him to a duel for our freedom. If he's as arrogant as everyone says there's no way he could lose face to "The Tigers", it's got to work right?

Peter looked over to Tai, just a few hours of rest had done him well, but there was trepidation in his eyes. 'I can't ask you to come with us, but if you wish to then we would be glad for your help.' He didn't say anything for a few seconds, but slowly nodded his head in agreement.

'One question, how do you know they won't just kill us on the spot?'

'We're relying on our reputations-'

'-And the bounty on our heads,' Minh said, 'apparently Tan is offering a year's wages for each of us that is brought in alive… and half a year for us dead.'

'Yeah, but we're hoping that they'd prefer the extra money and not to have to carry our bodies the whole way there.'

'I hope so too,' Tai said, not looking any more reassured.

'You both should know,' Peter added, 'even if we do make it in, there's a very real chance we won't get back out alive.'

'Ha-ha, it wouldn't be a normal day for us if it didn't endanger all our lives,' Minh said with a grin that almost spread to Peter. *Very true.* 'Besides,' he continued, 'I haven't come this far to back down now. This mission is more important than any one of us, that's why alive or dead, we've got to finish it.'

The swish of the metal sharpening against flint was soothing as Peter ran the stone up and down his blade. He sat on a grassy verge beside the stilt house, to his left Minh was flicking his staff in and out of the flames scorching streaks of black across it as he hardened the wood. Peter tried to quell his worries by focusing on their plan a single step at a time.

He knew it was selfish, but he had to keep reminding himself that their goal was about more than just him and Sophie making it home. Every time he thought back to the sickening scent and image of the piled bodies that had been seared into his brain, he knew it was true.

'Do you think it's a good idea to take him with us?' Peter said in a hushed tone, glancing towards the hut where Tai was still asleep. He wasn't sure if a farmer would have the stomach to fight.

'Yes, I do.' Minh said with a confident nod, 'he's no fighter, but he's tough, plus he's clearly in love with your sister.'

'Really?!' The idea had never even occurred to him.

'Ha-ha of course! You can't tell me you didn't know that?'

'Honestly, I hadn't even thought about it...'

'For someone so smart you really don't know the first thing about people do you?' Minh said mockingly. Peter felt his cheeks glow as a wave of embarrassment washed over him.
I only knew Han a day. Did I love her? He'd thought about what had happened back at her village so much he didn't even know what was real and what he'd imagined any more.

'I'm all set,' said Minh, snapping Peter from his trance, 'but let's get Tai one of the swords from the soldiers too. He'll need it.'

The summer sun was beating down hard as the group descended the steep paths towards the sea of emerald below. They made good progress alongside a fast-flowing river that weaved like a serpent through the fields, and as the day flicked to night in an instant, the men found a quiet place to rest under a patch of trees.

A breeze swept through the valley floor, it was cool and comfortable, but the absolute silence around them felt to Peter like the calm before the storm. He couldn't shake a sense of dread, the stillness of the night reminded him a little too much of "Tiger Valley".

As the sun dawned over the mountain tops that surrounded them, the landscape was illuminated in an orange glow. The call of roosters and dogs barking in the distance brought a nostalgic feeling for civilisation, that had become a rare luxury since before his time on the mountain with Master Hong.

Peter had barely slept, he was too on edge. Instead he meditated and practiced his martial arts. *Calm and composed, like the Crane, like Hong.* He pictured the serenity on the old master's face when he first saw him fight back in the village all that time ago, *I need to be like that.* Eventually, Minh and Tai joined him. Together they taught their newest recruit the basics of sword usage, and as the sun rose higher they gathered water from the stream to replace the lost torrents of sweat.

A strange mix of apprehension and excitement filled Peter as the three men then started down the road deeper towards the citadel. Soon they arrived at the outskirts of a village built up on the banks of the river.

'It's quiet here, too quiet...' *Please don't all be dead,* he prayed.

'People are here,' Tai answered, as if reading his mind, 'the fire over there is still burning.' He pointed towards a metal stove smouldering beside the riverbank. They kept walking, but the only sounds they heard were those of animals.

Eventually Minh came across an old woman working in the fields.

'What's going on? Where is everyone?' he called.

'Hiding from the likes of you obviously,' the old woman shouted back. 'Now get out of here, they patrol the road constantly.'

The group paced straight on through the village and out onto the path ahead. It was much larger than the others, obviously a well-used route, but within just a few miles it had become steep and rocky as it led back uphill towards the edge of the valley.

'This is great,' Peter said, 'we're not too close to the citadel, and here we can come from the low ground here and fight straight on like we did that first day carrying our water up the stairs, remember Minh?'

'How could I forget—that old bastard Hong made me so angry,' he grinned, but his eyes held a hint of sadness as if remembering how they had left Hong alone on the mountain. The group planned their hiding places in the bushes to make it seem like a legitimate attack. Minh and Tai were on the left and Peter was on the right, the trees lining each side of the path weren't thick like the forests in the highlands, but there was enough that they could hope to go unnoticed.

The next hours were spent in shifts, taking turns as lookouts around a bend in the road ahead to ensure they had sufficient warning. As expected, it was less than a day before Tai came sprinting back through the trees.

'They're coming' he panted, glancing around for the spot where his partners were lying relaxed in the early afternoon sun.

'Loads of them, at least six, all on horses, they'll be here in minutes.'

'Get to your positions,' Peter commanded with almost over the top confidence.

As he lay in wait, a rustling nearby caught his attention, it took Peter a moment to realise it was the shaking of his own hands. It had been a long time since he'd felt like this, it cast his memories back to hiding beneath the crates in the village while Yai distracted the soldiers. Only now the stakes were infinitely higher, it was no longer just his life in the balance, virtually everyone he loved was counting on him to make it into the castle and somehow, against all odds, take Lord Tan down. *It all comes down to this*, Peter prayed, *Please don't let me mess it up*.

CHAPTER FIFTY-FIVE

The gates in front of Sophie stood shadowed from the early-morning sun. After what seemed like an eternity, the black, tombstone-shapes parted, inviting her inside. She shuddered, knowing whatever awaited her was surely worse than death.

As they arrived at the castle walls, she was lifted from the horse, heavy iron shackles were clamped around her wrists, and she was led like an animal on a chain out of the morning sun and into the cool shade of the castle entryway.

Thank God. She was flooded with relief as they led her past the main chamber. Her happiness was short lived as it occurred to Sophie that without seeing Tan she wouldn't be able to find out about Tai. *Please let him be alive.*

They didn't cross the courtyard to the wives' quarters as she was expecting, but instead the castle guards led her to the top of a winding stone staircase behind the kitchens, somewhere she had never been before. Sophie contemplated what lay behind the door of the dark basement corridor ahead. *This can't be good.*

She became a deadweight, her wrists were already bloody and sore, and she didn't have the energy to fight, but there was no way she was going to make it easy for them. The two soldiers dragged her down the stairs and pushed her towards the wooden door at the end. As it swung open the putrid, mouldy air wafted out almost causing Sophie to vomit. The room was large, probably twenty yards across, piles of boxes, ropes, and weapons were scattered around, making it immediately clear that the store doubled as an interrogation room.

Sophie wasn't surprised or scared, now only crushing guilt and sorrow remained. *Tai is probably dead, you're next, it's all your fault and you can do nothing about it. You deserve this.*

Finally, she found herself alone sitting on the damp floor and as the door swung shut virtually all light was lost. A vent in one corner allowed in a trickle of fresh air and just enough of a glow for Sophie to make out the shadows of the rats scurrying around in the corners.

It was several hours before the sound of footsteps echoed down the corridor. The clunk of a heavy bolt being pulled across the latch reverberated off the stone walls and the door creaked open. Without even looking at her, a guard laid down a tray in the corner with a tin cup of water and a handful of plain white rice.

'Leave me alone you pig, I want nothing from you!' Sophie spat.

The guard, shocked by her reaction, hurried back out of the room and bolted the door behind him. The moment she was alone thirst and hunger overwhelmed all other thoughts and with both hands still shackled Sophie ate ravenously. *I need more*, she thought as the last drop of water fell through her cracked lips. *I've barely eaten or drunk anything for the last two days*, she realised, wondering why her body suddenly felt so weak and tired.

It's impossible. How can I get through this? she thought lying with the side of her face pressed against the cold stone floor. *How can I stop ruining people's lives?*

Sophie's eyes followed the narrow ray of light that cut through the darkness of the room and as if to answer her prayers, something on the far side glimmered back at her.

She crawled towards the crates and using her feet as levers managed to heave them apart, she reached both hands in to retrieve the item nestled in between. It was a hook-shaped tool, about six inches long with a sharpened tip—obviously used for opening crates—but there was no straight edge on it.

For the next hour Sophie's thoughts turned away from her spiral of depression as she once again had a goal, figuring out how to use it. The hook would never be able to separate the iron shackles that locked her arms together, but Sophie had another idea. *If I get the angle right, I'll die quickly,* she thought lining the point up to the arteries in her wrist. *But one mistake and I'll lie here for hours, bleeding to death drip by drip.*

Her thoughts had become delirious, probably from the lack of water. She talked to herself, a conversation ran back and forth for hours as though two people were in her mind. Her head throbbed and as she sat cross-legged staring at the hook on the floor, time began to lose all meaning. The sound of footsteps in the corridor outside snapped Sophie's mind back to reality. She kicked her tool over to the crates and scrambled to the far side of the room nearest the light.

The door bolt clunked open and Lord Tan swaggered into the room followed moments later by Chi, General Khang, and two of his personal guards. Sophie did her best to appear composed, but, her own cowardly escape plan made her so angry and ashamed all she could do was stare at the ground. *Don't give them the satisfaction. You'll be done with all of them soon enough.*

'So, this is how you repay me?'

Silence.

'I give you everything, food, clothes, a place to live, the honour of being my wife. Everything. And you run from me? Your disrespect sickens me.'

'YOU SICKEN ME!' Sophie exploded, pulling up her last reserves of energy. 'You murdered my parents and forced me to live here! You did nothing for me...' She tried to spit at him but her mouth was parched and dry. The smirk on Tan's face, turned to an expression of surprise, taken aback by the power in her voice. Chi simply shook her head in disbelief, whilst Khang stood gazing off into space as though distanced from the scene playing out before him.

'Don't shake your head at me.' Sophie climbed to her feet and stood swaying for a moment before advancing towards Chi. 'You're no better. The only reason you're here is because you gave this dog a son. One of these days you'll see how worthless you really are.'

Tan's hand caught Sophie's face with an ear-splitting slap as the back of his knuckles crashed across her cheek. It stung for just a second until her face hit the floor with a dull thud and pain disappeared. Instead she felt warmth. The wound already on her head started to trickle, in the shadowy room the blood seemed to run black into her blond hair.

'You fool,' Tan's words echoed in her ears as though they were miles away. 'Until you decide to show your gratitude, you will live here with the rats.' She could see his scowling red face and his eyes bulging as she gathered the strength to speak.

'Then you might as well kill me,' she croaked, struggling to get the words from her mouth. Tan flew into a fit of rage punching and kicking, whilst Sophie instinctively curled up to protect herself from the blows. Everyone else in the room stood in silence, flinching with each hit as Tan tired himself, seemingly determined to take her life.

Khang grabbed Tan's hand as he tried to lift Sophie's head by a fistful of hair ready to drive it into the wall.

'Sir, she has had enough, do you mean to kill her?'

'What if I do?' he spat, 'Kill her or not, my decision is none of your concern.'

Tan released his grip and she slumped down to the floor. As the door slammed shut, an indescribable pain pinned Sophie to the ground, it was like a thousand knives stabbing all over her body. Happy memories of Tai, Peter, and her parents returned, and with them a feeling of peaceful warmth spread across her body, calling her, begging her, to follow it towards relief. Sophie's panting breaths slowed to a crawl. In, out, then nothing.

CHAPTER FIFTY-SIX

'She's dead.' Khang was kneeling on the damp floor of the basement with his fingers to her neck, watching and listening, hoping for some sign of life. It had been only minutes since Tan had stormed out leaving him and Chi standing over the mangled body, but already her spirit seemed to have slipped away.

'Stupid girl, brought it on herself,' Chi said.

You heartless whore, Khang thought, glaring up at her. *All you care about is gaining more power for your own despicable family.* She caught his gaze and her cold eyes stared back as though she had heard his thoughts. Chi turned on her heels and bustled out of the door, leaving him alone in the dark room.

Khang found an old wicker mat in the corner. *I suppose that'll have to do.* He unrolled it with care and flapped it out, for a moment it's dusty scent reminded him of his own childhood. He would prepare the mats before the altar for his father and mother to complete their prayers each morning.

The mouldy mat in his hands was now a world apart from those kept in the government official's house where he had grown up. They were useful, cared for, even respected. *I know how they feel.* Like them he was verging on becoming a festered relic, simply taking up space within the castle walls, while the chances of him doing anything meaningful with his remaining years seemed to be slipping further away each day.

A cloud of dust billowed from the mat, catching the narrow shaft of light in the darkened room. It fell down to the ground, coming to rest gently over the body of the young girl in front of him. *Such a waste of life.*

CHAPTER FIFTY-SEVEN

The shadows of the squad stretched out along the path; they seemed to be moving with purpose. Exactly as Tai had described, there were half a dozen men on horseback.

The moment the leaders reached his spot, Minh sprung out. He played the part perfectly, stumbling into a clumsy charge, face on with the soldier on the right, whose decorative stars emblazoned on his leather armour marked his status. Tai ran, sword in hand at the man on the left. Minh's staff shot out towards the officer. *He's too close,* Peter winced in anticipation as he watched from the treeline. *Come on, they'll have to kill us if you get him.*

With a fraction of an inch to spare his friend's staff fell short, exactly as his fists had done swinging at Hong on the highest step. The officer's sword whipped down gashing Minh's forearm, he recoiled and fell to the floor, gripping his arm tightly to stem the bleeding. Meanwhile, Tai's inexperience worked in his favour, as his opponent's sword met his own there was enough force to knock it clean from his hand, and the soldier kicked him in the face dropping him down beside his colleague. Peter belted forwards directly between them, two men from the rear had dismounted and were charging with swords drawn, the front soldier arrived first stabbing directly at Minh, who barely managed to scramble back from his position on the floor.

'DON'T KILL THEM!' The officer's scream ripped through the trees, but the second soldier had already lunged.

Peter caught the sword with his own blade a fraction of a second after and circled the strike downwards wedging the blade's tip into the ground, he leapt up kicking the soldier with both feet in the chest before falling to the floor. He made a convincing play of losing his weapon as he fell and began to scurry towards it, just then the officer's boot came down on his hand and he yelled in pain.

The soldiers—all now dismounted—surrounded their defeated enemies with a circle of steel, glinting at them under the afternoon sun. Peter glanced at Minh and Tai to his side, *No way out now.*

'It's you isn't it? "The Tigers?" the man with the stars questioned, 'Ha-ha, it's almost disappointing. I was expecting more from you. I really was…' he smiled cockily and looked back towards his men, 'I mean, I *knew* we'd get you, but this was a truly feeble attempt.'
The soldiers sniggered at their commander's taunts obviously pleased with themselves. *Perfect.*

'Give me one good reason why we shouldn't kill you right here?' he sneered, and the faces of all his men dropped.

'You want the money don't you?' Minh said, feigning fear.

'Hmm, that I do, but the reward is for the gang members, we all know of the big guy and the foreigner, I don't think I'll get much for this amateur here without the rest of the gang,' he locked eyes with Tai.

Oh God. Peter's face was stunned, *Is he serious? Does he know it was only us?* He peered over to where Tai and Minh knelt, they were both wearing the same expression.

'He's part of our team…' Minh stuttered, still gripping his injured arm to his chest. 'He helped Tan's wife to escape and should be brought in too.'

'Fine,' the commander's gritty voice switched from sounding pleased to deadly serious.

'But the slightest word out of any of you and I slit his throat immediately.'

They all nodded. 'You three,' he waved towards his men not even bothering to look at them, 'get a rope around these warrior-frauds.'

Each of their hands were bound tightly behind their backs and roped to the leather pommel of one horse's saddle. Tai struggled as they did it, just enough to make it seem convincing, and Peter followed his lead.

'It'll take at least three days to reach the castle, I expect all three of you to keep pace, if anyone slows down you die. If anyone so much as thinks of escape you die. Got it?'

'Yes,' they all answered in unison trying to appear as glum as possible. Peter sneaked a look at Minh's arm, he was bleeding, but there was still colour in his cheeks. *Thank God, they must have missed a major blood vessel or he'd be dead already.*

Up until now he had been distracted by the success of their plan, but as their caravan of soldiers and prisoners began to move, a terrifying realisation dawned on him. *Sophie is caught, Tai can't fight, Minh is out of action, now I really am on my own.*

CHAPTER FIFTY-EIGHT

'Guards,' Khang called out, 'we need a corpse removed.'

Namo Amitabha. He bowed saying a silent prayer to the dead as he always did. As Khang walked towards the door a faint rustle caught his attention. *Did she just move?*

He rushed over and pulled the mat from Sophie's face, hoping for a sign of life. *No breath, no pulse… must have been the rats.* He scolded himself for being so soft hearted.

Several minutes later two guards entered the room with the stretcher they had managed to manoeuvre down the narrow staircase that led to the basement. Khang's fingers were still on her neck as he squatted down beside the corpse, he turned his head to see the men behind and sighed. 'Find a good burial spot for her'

A tremble ran through his fingers. It was virtually nothing, Khang dismissed it as his imagination.
Again. There was a heartbeat. Clearer now. *How did I miss that?* He pressed his ear to her chest waving for the other men to be silent. 'She's not dead!' he said in disbelief, *Looks like you have some fight in you.*

The guards approached his rear, the first man recoiled on seeing the girl's bloody, swollen face. In that moment it dawned on Khang that he was now trapped, facing a dilemma. *If I say nothing I'm a traitor, if I do he'll leave her to die.*

'Wait.' He raised his hand to the guards, his chest clamped up as he stared into the green eyes of the young girl barely clinging to life. Khang knew what he needed to do

CHAPTER FIFTY-NINE

A bang on the door woke Giap. *What do they want at this hour?* He climbed to his feet and stumbled over as the knocking continued. 'Wait a minute, wait a minute, I'm coming,' he called. *So impatient.*

The old man fumbled for the handle, it took a few seconds for him to find it in the dark of the room. He swung the door open to see a young soldier standing on his doorstep. Giap pushed his glasses up from his nose and stared at the man's face.

'I'm an elderly man you know, you shouldn't interrupt my rest.'

'I'm sorry,' he replied, 'General Khang asked me to come immediately, a patient is dying.'

Doctor Giap was Lord Tan's personal physician, he had trained in the French colony to the south for years, before finding a comfortable home within the citadel. He rarely dealt with serious injuries anymore, but plenty of Tan's paranoid ramblings about the latest life-threatening problem he or his precious son were allegedly suffering from. Giap had seen it before, this kind of anxiety was common among the powerful. Tan, like the others needed to turn his fears and problems into something physical, something that could be controlled or fought. It was the first step on a slippery slope that descended only into madness.

He had hoped for the peaceful retirement that was promised when he entered the citadel as a retainer. *Not tonight apparently.*

Giap sighed, grabbing the coat and bag that stayed on a table by the door, he was on standby to attend to Lord Tan day or night and knew better than to keep him waiting.

The doctor followed the young soldier west from his small residence towards the looming walls of the castle, that stood out even blacker than the night sky. The gates parted and Giap was led through the maze of corridors into the guest quarters of Tan's octagonal castle.

'What happened to her?' he questioned, contemplating the fate of the bloody wreck that lay on a wooden-slatted bed in the modest guest room.

'Lord Tan,' General Khang said from where he stood, inconspicuous in the corner of the room, 'she ran away and he beat her as punishment... he thinks she's dead.'

'Probably for the best, looks like she pretty much is,' said the doctor as he pressed his ear against her chest listening for a heartbeat. *Despicable.*

He had seen many battles, some of the worst injuries people could sustain. *But war is war, to do this to an innocent person, one little more than a child no less, is unforgivable.* He sighed long and deep, *I had so hoped to be done with this.*

'We can treat some of her injuries with proper cleaning and medicine, but if her organs are ruptured she will not survive.'

The doctor set about his work, he disinfected the wounds all over her body and stitched shut the laceration on her head. 'If she wakes up, tell me and me immediately.'

Khang nodded, and summoned in an older women who worked alongside the wives.

'You heard the doctor, not a word,' he muttered to the maid, seeming to be almost as exhausted as the old man felt.

Giap clicked his tongue, shaking his head, and wearily shuffled towards the door.

CHAPTER SIXTY

It was two days before Sophie opened her eyes, although the pain that coursed through every inch of her body made her wish she hadn't.

The room was darkened and unfamiliar, judging by the sounds of guards and servants chatting outside and birds chirping in the gardens behind the wooden shutters, she knew she somewhere in the west wing of the castle. Sophie was lying on a bed made of wooden slats, with a hollow wicker case as a pillow. She ran her hand across her head and felt stitches where it hurt; on a table by the door there were several bottles of clear liquid that looked medicinal. *Someone must have summoned a doctor.* Even more curiously there was fruit and water sitting beside them. *Who's been looking after me? and why?* Sophie wondered, *Yen is the only one that didn't hate me, but I doubt she even knows I'm here.*

As Sophie faded in and out of sleep, she recognised the friendly face of a house maid who checked in on her from time to time. On the third day the wooden panelled door slid open and instead of the woman, General Khang strolled in with a tray of rice and vegetables, clattering it down on the table.

Why would he be here? She had only met him a handful of times, and other than overhearing his frustrated arguments with Chi, she had never seen him show any hint of emotion. Khang stood by the door in silence for what seemed like forever. He was older than Tan, maybe his late fifties or sixties, his face seemed stern but there was a hint of warmth in his eyes.

'That was pretty stupid what you did.' His gruff voice broke the silence and he stared down at her with the kind of look a disappointed father would give his child. 'I just came to make sure you were still alive.'

'I'm alive…' Sophie squeezed her eyes shut as a wave of pain ran over her, '…but why do you care?'

He sighed. 'I felt sorry for you. I know the pain of losing loved ones,' he said, gazing up at the corner of the room.

It had been nearly four years since Khang had lost his daughter. He was proud when she had married, and supported her when she moved to live with her husband's family west of the citadel. After returning from a months-long diplomatic mission, he learned how a drought had hit the province and that the order had been given to appropriate supplies from surrounding villages. People outside the citadel were left with almost nothing. Between the lack of water and hunger many lives were lost.

'I fear he's losing his mind,' Khang said, 'he was never a good man like his father, but at least his decisions as a ruler made sense, now it seems he cannot even control himself.'

'So why don't you do something about it?' Sophie said, struggling to get the words from her mouth. 'You're the general aren't you? You control his army.'

'I can't go against our lord. I would be branded a traitor, convicted of inciting rebellion, and put to death.'

'Fine, but you know as well as I do what happens outside the castle walls,' her weak voice croaked. 'Your men are killing innocent people under his orders, there is only so long this can last until they rise up against him, and you.'

'I know,' the general replied, looking to the floor. A wave of sympathy came over Sophie, it was clear he was a good man, she could see the guilt in his eyes at very mention of the lives lost. *Maybe he is actually on my side?*

'Do you know any information about a man called Tai? He was taken prisoner just a few days before me.' Khang adjusted his robe, looking glad for the distraction. 'No, we haven't had any new prisoners arrive in weeks, except for you of course. If he was captured, he hasn't been brought in.'

For a moment Sophie's pain almost vanished and her face beamed at the thought that maybe he had somehow escaped.

'I'm going to have to tell Lord Tan that you're alive,' Khang said. Sophie's happiness was gone in a flash.

'He doesn't know?'

'Not yet. With any luck, if you apologise he will request you return to the wives' quarters.'

'No.'

'Listen,' he sighed, 'I have risked many of my men's heads keeping you here. Maybe it was a mistake, if so I will pay with my life as may you. But those that stood guard, the doctor, the servants, they all knew you were here. Do not make them pay our debts.'

Sophie hadn't even realised how many people must be involved, and deliberately keeping that from their leader seemed to be a huge risk.

'I'll apologise.'

In the past she would have fought tooth and nail against orders like this, now she just didn't want to be responsible for any more suffering. 'I'll do whatever he asks, just don't let anyone else take the blame for me.' Khang nodded.

'Do you really think he'll have us executed?' She asked.

'If it is our fate, then we will accept it with dignity.'

The general bowed and stepped out of the door, gently sliding it shut behind him.

CHAPTER SIXTY-ONE

She's right, Khang thought. He ran his hand through his hair, staring up at the glistening statue of Amitabha Buddha in front of him. *Whether it comes by revolution, invasion, or the government, our time is nearly up. The world has changed around us, while we have not.*

He prostrated three more times and chanted in prayer to the figure, 'Om Mani Padme Hum,' before quietly picking up his sword and exiting the pagoda that lay just south of the castle walls.

General Khang walked slowly through the gardens towards the main hall, making sure he savoured the chirping of the birds, the gentle fragrance of the flowers, and the cool summer breeze for what may well be the last time. All too soon his moment of peace had passed, he wrapped his fingers around the wooden handles of the main hall's door and pushed.

Lord Tan was on sitting upon his throne at the far end of the room. On the dais beside him, Lord Cau kneeled practicing calligraphy while his father watched with a smile on his face and his hand gently resting on the boy's head.

'I'm sorry, to interrupt sir,' Khang said, taken aback by the almost touching moment between father and son. 'It is your wife sir, I found her still breathing and took her for treatment. I apologise for acting without your orders.' He bowed.

'She's alive? Some of your soldiers couldn't even take a beating like that!' There was no trace of shame or remorse in his voice, instead his demeanour seemed strangely happy. *Not the reaction I was expecting.*

'Why did you bother to save her?' Khang could see suspicion rousing on Tan's face.

'Sir, you beat her to within an inch of her life...' he could tell this was not going to be a satisfactory excuse and decided to appeal to the only human part of his lord that still remained.

'...as you know. I have, had, a daughter. They would have been around the same age now. Your wife reminds me of her, stubborn and outspoken...'

'You're getting sentimental in your old age,' he sneered, his face displeased, 'a warrior can't show mercy-'

'-but a leader should.'

A frown crossed Tan's brow. 'You have two days, I want her back here doing her duties or I will give her another beating. And this one she won't recover from.'

'Thank you sir.'

Lord Tan nodded.

'Now we just have to take care of the *other* traitors around here,' he growled and narrowed his eyes, scanning the room. A servant was cleaning in the corner. A gentle breeze was whistling through the eaves of the roof. That was all. General Khang bowed once more and slipped out as silently as possible. With the doors closed behind him he broke into a jog. *How could he know?*

CHAPTER SIXTY-TWO

Sophie awoke to a commotion out in the courtyard, the sun had not yet risen but a warm pre-dawn breeze whistled down the corridor and into the wives' quarters. Instinctively she knew something big was happening. Sophie pulled her aching body towards the door and hung back just out of sight, listening to the conversation outside with excitement.

She had been back among the wives for only two days, but had already decided on a new plan for escape. As Beautiful-Nung, and Yen had helped her change her clothes, they talked, curious about where she had been and how she had survived. The two women seemed shocked to learn how life was outside the castle walls, they'd both come from rich families and were married off to Tan while still young girls. Sophie gradually came to realise that voicing some of the unspoken truths, how he had executed whole villages, starved his people and killed his own men, would grow disdain like a delicate seed that she could nurture and water each day. Then it wouldn't be long before roots took hold and the shoots of distrust and resentment showed themselves. *It'll own be a matter of time before someone takes him out.*

Sophie leaned up against the coarse wooden frame of the door, taking the weight off her aching stomach and legs, and focused on the words of the two soldiers that had just arrived and were now speaking to Khang rapidly.

Chi's voice cut across through, stopping the speaking soldier mid-sentence as she bustled out into the courtyard from the corridor that ran between the main hall and Tan's private quarters.

'What's going on here? Why are you making such a noise? Our lord is sleeping, have you no manners?'

'I'm sorry Ma'am,' the soldier bowed, 'it's just that we've got some important news, our party have apprehended several of "The Tigers". They are on the way now with the criminals in tow. We were ordered to ride ahead and present Lord Tan with this excellent news.'

Criminals? Surely they don't mean Tai? A burst of excitement shot through Sophie's body. At the same time smile broke out on Chi's cold face. 'That *is* good news,' she said, 'I'll inform his Lordship. Khang, when will they arrive?'

'I'm not sure Ma'am, but I should present the news to our Lord, it is my duty after all-'

'-Your duty!? You old fool, you don't even know where your own men are!'

I hate her, Sophie thought picturing Chi's bitter face twisting as she spoke. Even the other wives, as stuck-up and spiteful as some of them had been, were nothing compared to her.

The general took a deep breath and turned towards his men, 'How far ahead were you?'

'We rode from a day out sir, they'll be here by the afternoon.'

'Excellent,' Chi said before Khang had a chance to respond, 'make sure no one knows about this least of all that insolent little girl.'

Sophie gasped and all eyes shot to the door. She dived back down towards the mat just a moment before Chi peered in through the door. Even with her eyes tight shut, Sophie could feel the older wife's stony gaze on her face. A few seconds later, she turned around and paced back out to the courtyard before leading the group further into the interior of Tan's quarters. *It must be Tai, or Peter, why else would they need not to tell me? What did they call them? "The Tigers"?*

As first light broke over the limestone peaks that peered over the wall, Sophie almost looked forward to the day of painful work that lay ahead of her. She lay face down trying her best to make sure no one could see her smiling. *Today a change is coming, I can feel it. Just one more job to do,* she thought, *I need to make sure Tan dies.*

CHAPTER SIXTY-THREE

We must be nearly there, Minh thought as they trundled onwards into their third day of walking. They had spent a few hours of the night sleeping, tied up with their backs to a tree while a pair of soldiers took turns to guard them. Minh was sore and stiff, his arm throbbed, but they were forced to push on several hours before dawn. A full day of walking in the heat of the unshaded lowlands could kill.

Minh let his mind wander trying to ignore the pain. The chirping of birds before dawn conjured up memories of the cages that dangled in their cages from the roofs of his village. Each morning he would wake to the calls of his family's songbird just outside the window of their hut. He and his father had caught it themselves, it was something that Minh was always immensely proud of, he had always considered it the most beautiful in the village.

Poor Uncle Yai and Aunt Thi, he thought, realising that just like the bird he had never heard or seen them again. *They must have no idea what happened to me. I need to survive this, at least just to let them know I'm alive.* The last thing he had said to them was, 'I'm going to see if they need any help,' as he jogged off down the path when Hong had led Peter away from their village.

'Not long now,' Minh whispered to Peter who was trudging alongside him, 'I'm scared.'

'Me too.'

Rays of red sunshine lapped over the rice fields. For the first time since Peter travelled through in the carriage, they were truly in the lowlands. Mountains spread out in the far distance, but now just a few paddies and dirt paths were all that lay between them and the outline of the city walls, that loomed larger with each step towards the horizon. *Whatever happens, today is the day,* he thought, *one way or another by the time the sun sets tonight everything will be different.*

'Are you okay there?' Peter asked Tai, realising he had barely said a word all morning.

He smiled back, 'Just making sure I remember the route. The fastest way in will be the fastest way out too.'

'Good idea,' Peter replied, not daring to voice his thoughts. *There's no way we'll be leaving there alive.*

In the farmlands surrounding the citadel, progress was slow, there were checkpoints every few miles, farmers leading trails of buffalos and cows that took up the entire track, and every one of their party was exhausted. As the sun began to climb higher into the sky, they closed the final few hundred yards between the green farmlands and dusty lifeless soil that had been worn down by the endless stream of farmers, soldiers, and traders visiting the city.

The group were cast under the shadows of the colossal stone walls as they approached. The captain banged the hilt of his sword against the iron bars that lined the gate, echoing with a metallic ring. As Peter's gaze ran up to the towering battlements above, a shiver ran down his spine, for the first time the scale of what they were attempting truly sunk in.

'Who are you?' a voice called down from the watchtower.

'I'm Captain Yot. We have three prisoners with us. "The Tigers". Lord Tan is expecting us this afternoon, we've made good time.'

After what seemed like an endless wait, the rattling of chains and banging of bolts gave way to the creak of the heavy gates parting. Rows of guards came into view, nervously gripping spears and holding rifles trained on the group. They walked behind the horses, each man astounded at what they had managed to achieve through spreading fear and confusion. From behind the front line, shouts and cheers rang out, Captain Yot, waved at the crowd looking extremely pleased with himself.

'They obviously heard we were coming,' Minh said smiling and Tai let out a nervous laugh that startled some of the forward-most soldiers. The captain was presented with a large leather book and signed his name, which was then stamped with a bright red seal, officially confirming their arrival. Peter tried to imagine how things might play out as the group began to wind their way up through the narrow streets of the citadel.

This may well be the last morning I ever see, he thought enjoying the warmth of the sun on his face. He watched the mad rush of farmers and market vendors running around setting up their stalls and a nostalgic memory of the docks surfaced making him smile. As they pushed further through the town, more and more people poured out of the narrow, stone walled houses and gawped at the group being led behind the horses. *I'm used to being stared at, but this is ridiculous.*

Despite his obvious pain and exhaustion, Minh was wearing a great big smile. *At least someone's enjoying their celebrity status,* he thought, then looked to Tai who seemed unsure how to react to the onlookers. Three symmetrical gateways adorned with curved roofs marked the entrance of the castle, looming over the centre of the citadel and casting a menacing shadow against the morning light.

They were led through the smallest of the entrances and greeted by yet more guards. These ones wore red silk robes embellished with gold trim, rather than the plain brown material and leather armour that the soldiers they had met outside the castle walls all wore. With spears and rifles extended, they stood along the length of the tree-lined pathway that ran towards the main gate.

'Looks like someone is a little paranoid,' Minh whispered, bringing a smile to Peter's face as they walked the gauntlet of swords and guns, that followed them with each step. Judging by the disappointed expressions on their faces, Lord Tan's elite were expecting a more fearful reaction at their display of strength than the one they received from the unperplexed young men strolling past.

Once they reached the entrance, they were circled, before being led through a garden behind the walls, and down a short corridor that opened up into a courtyard. The ropes that bound their wrists were cut free; Peter could feel the blood returning to his fingers, preparing them to ball into fists at a moment's notice.

Captain Yot led a small group of guards and the prisoners through a passageway enclosed by hundreds of red archways, each decorated with gold text and intricate patterns. At the end of the corridor a set of doors opened into a cavernous hall. Peter's eyes were immediately drawn to the throne, which was raised several feet from the ground by a stepped dais. There was tea sitting on a table beside it and smoke wisping from an altar in the farthest corner. Several women in silk robes were preparing vases of flowers and plates of fruit, their footsteps echoing off the octagonal tiles that covered the floor of the chamber. Around the borders of the room were statues of Buddhist and Taoist deities, Peter recognised the patron saint of martial arts from Hong's descriptions—a fierce looking demigod with a long beard, gripping a sword and sceptre—while others were different in style as though coming from further afield.

The three prisoners were marched into the centre of the room. A guard behind Peter gripped his shoulders and kicked the back of his knees forcing him to kneel on the cold tiles whilst he waited in silence, hoping to finally come face to face with his enemy. He looked over to Minh on his left who gave him a nod, then to Tai, who offered a nervous smile. *This is it.*

CHAPTER SIXTY-FOUR

'I've waited a long time for you to be kneeling in front of me,' a booming voice echoed from down the corridor. Moments later Lord Tan swaggered out of an entrance adjacent to the throne, followed by several feet of sapphire-blue robe and two beautiful women.

He strode towards the throne with an air of arrogance and seated himself casually. Everyone in the room bowed their heads low and without even realising the three prisoners followed their lead. It took Peter a moment to realise what had happened and he sat back up straight, studying the face of the man that had killed his family. Tan was certainly getting older, but he was a far cry from the deranged, old man Peter had visualised. He was tall and well-built, but that wasn't worrying compared to the glint of madness in his eyes.

Tension seemed to hang thick in the air, as though the guards to his rear and even the women that were pouring tea seemed uncomfortable in Lord Tan's presence. An older soldier, with stars emblazoned on the collar of his robe, along with an attractive middle-aged woman entered the room a few moments later, the soldier walked over to Captain Yot and shook his hand bowing, 'Excellent job,' he said.

'Thank you General,' the captain answered with a smile, and the older soldier moved to stand by his side.

'So, we meet at last, "The Tigers", Tan sneered. His eyes bulged as they moved over the group, scrutinising their faces one by one, weighing them up.

'Is this it? I was expecting so much more, both in size and number,' Tan laughed, amused by his own joke. 'Now,' he shifted to an official tone. 'You've caused me and my men many problems. What do you have to say for your crimes?'

'Where's my sister?' Peter said, not showing even a flicker of emotion.

'Your sister? Ah you mean my wife? Khang bring her in, let's show this boy that just like the animals all people can be trained too.'

Focus, Peter ordered himself, *be like Hong, live in the moment, no fear, no anger.* He closed his eyes and exhaled, focusing on the world around him, the sounds of birds chirping in the gardens, the cold tiles pressing on his knees, and dusty scent of the hall. The flood of emotion washed over him rather than sweeping him up in its current, even if Hong was gone, his teachings and spirit lived on with them. The older soldier nodded and paced through the exit beside Tan's throne.

'Murder, theft, sabotage, treason...' Tan listed their crimes as though the idea was boring him. 'These are the charges of which you are accused. Naturally the penalty is death...'

CHAPTER SIXTY-FIVE

Sophie had heard nothing since before dawn. As the day wore on there was definite unrest among the soldiers and castle staff, but she had been confined to the wives' quarters and watched over by several guards. Now General Khang entered the room, bowing as was customary, much to her frustration his face revealed nothing.

'Come with me,' he said waving Sophie to her feet from the mats in the corner. *Why are we going here?* she shuddered remembering the night of her marriage, as Khang led her across the courtyard, now filled with guards, and towards the main hall.

Please let it be good news, she prayed. The sound of her footsteps reverberated through the empty corridor that ran from Tan's quarters towards his throne at the far end of the room. With every step her angst grew, the short walk seemed to last forever.

Oh thank you God, he's alive! Sophie's heart leapt into her throat as Tai's face came into view. He was kneeling on the floor, looking worn and tired. Several feet to his left kneeled another man, *Who-* her thoughts were interrupted as a third person, came into view. It took her several moments before she could even recognise the bushy-haired, unkempt man, kneeling in the centre of the immaculate room. There was no trace of the weak and uneasy boy she had known growing up, even surrounded by soldiers an aura of strength and confidence filled the room. *He's alive! I can't believe it!*

Tears were streaming down Sophie's cheeks before she even made it to the entrance of the hall. Her face was lit up with joy, but her thoughts were swallowed in a maelstrom of happiness and fear. Everything good in her life had been taken away from her one way or another. *Is this just a trick? Am I going to lose it all again?* The wooden heels of her sandals hitting the stone echoed throughout the hall. All eyes were upon her.

CHAPTER SIXTY-SIX

Oh my goodness. Peter recoiled at out how weak and thin she looked. Sophie's face was swollen and bruised, her long blonde hair was pinned up tightly to her head and she was dressed in a white silk robe adorned with green stitched flowers. A world apart from the tomboy that had been playing shuttlecock with the deckhands on *The Princess Helena* all that time ago. A grin spread across his face as their eyes met and through tears she smiled back.

'Well isn't this touching?' Tan interrupted with a smirk on his face. He turned to Sophie, whose face dropped into the cold stubborn expression that Peter had known so well.

'Now, who would you like to see die first?'

'YOU,' she spat. The back of Lord Tan's hand struck her across the face and dropped her to the floor. All three men shot to their feet, but were immediately forced back down by the soldiers pressing on their shoulders and stamping on the backs of their knees while they struggled and shouted.

'TAN, LISTEN TO ME,' Peter boomed over the ruckus. The room fell silent, his face burned as every single gaze fixed upon it. 'I want to make you an offer.'

'An offer?!' Tan's face broke into a smile, making him almost seem human. 'What do you think you could possibly have that I want? You are a penniless, worthless child.' Tan spat on the ground in front of him.

'Me,' he said, 'I heard you were once a skilled warrior. I want to know if you were actually any good, or just a spoilt child who got told everything he wanted to hear. Now you have the chance to prove yourself.' Lord Tan's face dropped.

'I fought battles for twenty years before you were even born boy, what makes you think you have the right to challenge me?'

'Nothing. I have no right to challenge you. But I know a man that isn't scared doesn't need to hide behind guards.' Peter's voice and body were trembling, but his enemy's twisted visage only spurred him on. *I really hope I'm not that transparent*, he thought, trying to cull the shaking and sweating that was almost out of control.

Peter felt as though he had transcended rational thought and just let go in. 'You know I'm better than you ever were don't you?! That's why you had all these soldiers here waiting for us. We managed to take out entire squads of your men with no more than a few sticks... honestly it's embarrassing...' He laughed, forcing a mocking tone and spat a string of insults in English that just seemed to confuse and enrage Tan further. His was face twitching, teeth clenched, and growing redder by the second. *Come on, it's all or nothing now.*

'You really think you can take us on? The Tigers? You're past it, a pathetic, weak old man... you're a joke!'

Causing him to lose face in front of his men, his wives and his people was a big risk. Whatever the outcome now, he knew the streets would be filled with talk of what happened within the castle. Tan glanced around the room for a moment at his men. Every single pair of eyes were fixed firmly on the floor. No one dared to meet his gaze. Tan looked over to Sophie who was now standing silently by the entrance to the corridor with a hand on her bruised cheek, then at the older woman who was standing by her side.

'Sorry, do you have to ask your wife first?' Peter mocked. He could see the fire burning in the woman's eyes, she nodded at Tan as if to say 'go on then.'

'Fine,' he said, 'but if...*when* I win, you will watch as I personally skin your sister and friends alive. Then you will be cursed to spend all eternity starving in the realm of hungry ghosts.'

'And what if I win?' Peter said, 'I want all of us to go free.'

'Ha, don't be a fool. If by some miracle you manage to best me, I'll let this harpy go free.' He waved vaguely in Sophie's direction. 'I find her tiresome anyway... you "Tigers" will die, but it will be with honour. A warrior's death.'

For a fleeting moment Peter had allowed himself to wonder if he might survive. But if the cost of taking a stand against tyranny, was his life, it was one he would gladly pay. Peter turned to Minh, there were no words needed. The smile on his face said it all. *Make this bastard pay...'*

'You have a deal.'

CHAPTER SIXTY-SEVEN

'General Khang prepare the room. This will not last long,' Tan said.

'But Sir-'.

'-PREPARE THE ROOM,' Tan thundered with an outburst that shook the ground.

It took just a few minutes for the hall to be cleared. General Khang, Captain Yot and two guards remained by the entrance, while Sophie and Chi knelt to the right of the throne. The tables that ran along the outside of the hall had been pushed back, leaving a circle of around twenty feet in the centre. Thin rays of light pierced through the wooden slats of hanging blinds and illuminated their makeshift arena, while Peter stood facing Minh and Tai on the far side. He circled his head and swung his arms back and forth, making sure he was warm and loose.

'Are you sure you want to do this?' Minh said.

'We've haven't come this far to give up now. Besides, if I don't fight we're dead anyway, what choice do I have?'

He placed a hand on Peter's shoulder and pulled his head in close. 'You can do this,' he growled low, 'remember what Hong taught us, this is your karma, it is your chance to create a better world. Do it for him, do it for all of us... Now take this bastard down.'

Tai grasped his hand and shook it hard, 'Good luck, I know you can do it.'

I hope you're right.

Peter could hear his opponent's footsteps as he entered the circle to his rear, he took a deep breath in, spun on the spot and took two steps into the centre of the room. Tan was waiting, standing wide with his hands on his hips.

'What weapon do you choose boy?'

'My sword of course.'

'Very well. Captain, return his pile of rust and bring me my halberd.' Tan waved over to a rack of weapons at the rear of the hall, in the centre sat a six-foot wooden staff with a jagged sword blade mounted on top.

In silence, their gazes met. Tan was trying to intimidate him, but Peter could see right through it. *You're not fooling me. You're afraid.* He stared back past his enemy's eyes, into his soul. They both knew there was no way out now, the build-up had been too great. *Before this can end, one of us needs to die.*

Captain Yot returned moments later and handed him Hong's sword. It felt alive in his hands—natural and clean—like an extension of his own body. Peter focused on the leather grip against his fingers and listened the weight of the weapon. He could almost feel Hong's energy emitting from within. He pictured his master, weaponless on the mountain, fending off the attackers, all for one purpose, to give him a single chance. This chance. *Yes.*

Kneeling, the captain raised his outstretched palms and offered Lord Tan his halberd. Its blade gleamed under the rays of light that spotted the room, the dark-wood handle was inlaid with figures of serpents and demons, it was a fearsome weapon, but Peter knew the outcome of this fight would come down to will alone.

The two men gave each other the slightest of nods, a tradition among warriors that showed mutual respect of the each man's bravery. Neither Peter nor Tan dared break eye contact for even a fraction of a second, both started to circle with weapons extended, Tan stepping purposefully to the left and Peter edging to the right. Slowly. Feeling their opponent out, waiting for the other to make a move. For what seemed like an age there was absolute silence in the hall, not even a breath.

Tan's impatience got the better of him first, he shot forwards with both hands lunging the jagged blade at his enemy's chest. Peter skipped backwards dodging the strike with ease. In frustration he lunged again, this time with a warrior's roar of 'KIAI,' and three quick stabs towards his face. The first he dodged, the second was swept aside as the blades of the two weapons clashed, and as the third came in, Peter caught the wooden handle with the hilt of his sword and slid it down the length of the carved staff towards his opponent's torso with lightning speed. Tan released one hand from the weapon saving his fingers at the final second, and as Peter slid closer he twisted the wooden butt of the handle, cracking it into his face. The strength of the hit sent him stumbling back while warm, metallic blood dripped from his nose and down the back of his throat.

Tan saw his opportunity to finish the fight and leapt forwards thrusting the halberd at arm's length. A heartbeat away from death Peter swung his sword in an arc upwards smashing through the wooden shaft and severing it in two, the blade-end went flying and Tan was left with only a stick to defend himself.

'YES!' Minh's voice roared with excitement. Fired with adrenaline Peter lunged, instantly realising he had neglected Hong's first lesson and charged straight on, sacrificing his speed and balance, while simultaneously pitting strength against strength. Tan sidestepped the attack with the speed and agility a warrior, half his age would be hard pressed to match. As Peter tumbled forwards he whipped the short stick cracking his arm, face and hand with a combination of strikes. One. Two. Three. Tan's final hit crushed his fingers with a snap, blinding pain shot throughout his body and Hong's sword rattled to the ground at the edge of the arena.

Tan threw his stick to the floor beside the weapon.

'Now we'll see who is truly the superior warrior. Fist versus fist.'

His knuckles cracked as his fingers balled and clenched tightly beside his face. Tan stepped wide and low, his right palm slid outstretched towards his enemy's eyes, as he assumed the spirit of a serpent.

Snake style, makes sense, Peter thought finding a new sense of concern. With terrifying speed Tan launched venomous stabs towards his throat and stomach, followed with a leaping scissor-kick at his head. Peter's conscious mind switched off and the energy of his training began to find itself, remaining calm and composed he blocked the stabs, pushing them aside with his palms and circled out of range from the kicks. He followed with five rapid strikes to Tan's vital targets. Left of the neck with his fingertips clenched into a ball, right of the neck with a chop, two knuckle strikes to the abdomen and one towards the eyes. Tan's body twitched as the pain from the attacks sent his nerves into overload; he toppled onto his back with a panicked look in his eyes. *Maybe I can actually win?* Now it was Peter's turn to attack.

What's he doing? Minh thought as Tan tumbled back and immediately began fumbling with one hand inside his robe. Peter started to run, ready to finish the fight. A glint of light caught Minh's eye as Tan removed the hidden blade from his waistband. *He's going to go straight onto it.*

'STOP!' screamed Minh at the top of his lungs. Peter's head turned, the shout had caught his attention but he was already mid-sprint only yards away. Minh was belting forwards when Tan noticed his thundering steps approaching. The guards were just the blink of an eye behind, but they were too slow. On impulse Tan spun on his back towards him.

Minh landed catching Tan's arm mid-lunge. He tried to force the blade from his grip but a fraction of a second later Peter's body careened into his own and sent him lurching forwards.

A white-hot pain coursed through Minh's body. Suddenly, he was aware of how cold the blade felt in his stomach. A drop of blood fell onto his hand as he held himself up, hunched over his knees. The falling droplets became a trickle. Pooling on the floor around his fingertips, its heat was strangely soothing.

You'll die like this, get on your back, he thought, unable to process if his logic was nonsense or genius. The first attempt almost made him black out from the pain. Minh gritted his teeth and screaming forced himself to his feet. His face was white with shock as he stumbled backwards. 'He... he...

cheated...' pointing at Tan who had scrambled to his feet, and stood grinning with true madness on his face.

'MINH,' Peter's scream echoed in his ears. He could see tears running down his friend's face as it grew more distant, finally he realised someone was dragging him backwards from the arena leaving a smeared trail of crimson by his feet. *I was the last of my family, the only one left. Does it really all end with me?*

CHAPTER SIXTY-EIGHT

'MURDERER!'

Peter's voice echoed through the cavernous hall. Anger stung his throat, but pain was a feeling he'd come to know well.

In less than a second his enemy had covered the few yards that lay between them, the first blow smashed him across the jaw, the second thundered into the side of his head. A ringing in his ears plunged Peter's thoughts into chaos, and a heel in the chest slammed his body against one of the thick wooden columns that lined the chamber.

It took a moment for Peter to realise where he was. The dust tickled his lungs, narrow shafts of sunshine pierced the shutters above, illuminating the red and gold panels that ran from floor to ceiling. A trickle of warmth crept across his face and dripped down onto the cold, white tiles below, staining them with droplets of crimson. *Get up.*

Peter forced his body to its feet, every inch of him was crying out in pain, but he chose not to listen. The impossible twists of fate that had led him here couldn't all have been for nothing. *Could they? Remember your training,* he thought. *Calm your mind.*

Slowly, Peter exhaled, he felt the fear and anger leaving his body, rising upwards like a balloon through the shadowy rafters of the castle and out into the depths of the blue sky beyond. Every tiny detail of his surroundings lit up; the shimmer of the statues that lined the room, the earthy aroma of incense that burned on a stone altar in the corner, the whisper of a flute playing in the distance, and the iron sting of blood on his lips.

By the time his eyes focused, the enemy was hurtling towards him. Peter felt his weight sink through the soles of his feet deep into the earth below. His teeth gritted and muscles tensed. *Live or die, it all ends now. I'm ready.*

Peter's legs launched him into a charge. Tan's strikes seemed to move in slow motion, hitting nothing but air as his enemy weaved through the barrage of punches and kicks that enshrouded him. BANG. His palm connected directly under the chin of his opponent, stopping him like a brick wall. With his own body weight working against him Lord Tan's feet continued forwards, lifting clear from the floor. He smashed the ground and howled in a fit of rage, he clambered to his feet and charged again. Peter dodged his fists side-stepping the attack just as Hong had done back in the village. Five lightning fast strikes to Tan's ribs and a final blow to the head sent him stumbling sideways. With his head still spinning Lord Tan lunged again, throwing everything he had into his final *coup de grace*, a crushing front-kick towards his opponent's chest. Peter swooped down, spinning his head and shoulders so low his hair grazed the ground, his right leg arched upwards, and his heel smashed into the side of Tan's head with crushing force. For a moment his enemy stood motionless, his eyes glazed over, then collapsed back to the ground with a bang that shook the castle floor. *Not getting up this time are you?*

A wave of panic shot through Peter, he had been so consumed by the battle he had almost forgotten Minh, who was growing more and more pale at Tai's side by the second. He sprinted towards them.

'Is he alive?'

'For now,' Tai said. 'But he's lost a lot of blood, keep this pressed tight I need to find something to seal the wound.' He stood up and ran towards the doors.

'Stop,' yelled one of the remaining guards as though he had suddenly realised that it was still his job, but General Khang had already swung the doors open and the soldiers—that had been waiting with their ears pressed against the door—flooded in blocking Tai's path.

CHAPTER SIXTY-NINE

'What happened?' the first man through the door called.

'Lord Tan was defeated,' General Khang answered, knowing there was no way for him to deny it, lying out cold in the centre of the room. 'They have earned their freedom,' he said trying his best to hide a smile.

'Peter!' Sophie ran over towards her brother. She locked her arms around the back of his neck gripping herself tightly against him with one arm he continued to keep pressure on his friend's wound and the other rested on her shoulder.

'I'm so glad you're alive,' she said, 'I never thought I'd see you again.'

'Likewise,' he smiled.

General Khang turned back to where Lord Tan had been lying, just in time to see him scrambling dizzily towards his throne. He dragged himself to his feet hanging onto the sides of the chair.

'ARREST THEM!' Tan screamed, his face bruised, with a huge welt on the side of head. The closest guards, unsure of whose orders to follow, seized Peter, Sophie, and Tai forcing them to their knees as they struggled. General Khang waved another guard over to step in keeping the pressure on the injured man's wound.

Tan whipped the ceremonial, short-sword from the arm of his throne and in a half-run stumbled the length of the room towards the prisoners. *He can't be...* Khang thought, but the intent in Tan's eyes was clear. *He's going to murder them like animals while they're pinned down by* my *men!*

'COWARD,' Khang's voice boomed. The gold encrusted scabbard of Lord Tan's blade clattered to the floor and his arm arched back into the battle-ready position for execution. *Not in my name.*

Time seemed to stand still. The general realised his hand had been resting on the hilt of his own weapon since Tan first fell. As the warlord stumbled the final few feet, it released on impulse, the razor-sharp steel cut through the air with a swish and had returned to its sheath by his side in less than a second. Lord Tan's strike barely lifted, it was as though the power had been drained from his muscles. He kept moving, making it within inches of the prisoners, but his eyes were vacant. He dropped to his knees and his arm twitched as though it was still attempting to swing.

Lord Tan's head tilted to the side, and then rolled clean from his body, landing on the stone tiles of the hall with a dull thud. A second later his headless corpse followed, it collapsed to the ground, intermittently shaking. There was absolute silence; every set of eyes in the room was upon General Khang. He adjusted his robe, cleared his throat, and turned to the rows of his men to the rear.

'Today marks the end of this fool's tyranny. Every trace of his life will be scorched from the earth. WE BEGIN NOW!'

The room exploded in shouts and cheers. Khang thought about the time he had spent with Lord Tan when he was still just a boy, wondering how and when he'd become so dishonourable, wondering if there could have been any other outcome. *I spent too long wondering.*

He looked over his shoulder to Sophie, memories of his daughter laughing as they played together among the spring flowers flooded back. Khang's whole body was shaking. A wave of fear swiftly followed by relief engulfed him and for a moment he was a young man again. *You did the right thing. Your Karmic debt has been repaid.*

CHAPTER SEVENTY

Chi's face was white a ghost, she stood frozen in the corner by the throne, her bottom lip quivering as she struggled to comprehend the sight of her husband's corpse lying headless in the centre of the room.

'You'd better run,' Sophie mouthed from the far side, waving her hand as if to dismiss her. Chi slipped out into the corridor to the right of the throne and disappeared as she broke into a sprint.

'Get this man to a doctor,' General Khang ordered pointing at Minh, whose face was now sickly pale. Three guards wasted no time in getting him up, hanging onto their shoulders, whilst one continued to apply pressure. As they carried him off, Khang turned and addressed his own men.

'Those injured in battle should be treated with the same compassion you extend to your own men. A true leader is the one that chooses mercy over violence.'

'I can't believe you're here,' Sophie said holding Tai's gaze. His tanned face flushed as he answered, almost in a whisper.

'They were going to find you, I had to come too.'

Sophie put her arms around his neck, and he pulled closer her into him. As her face pressed against Tai's chest, she held her breath listening to the sound of his heartbeat.

'You,' General Khang said, stopping Peter with a palm on his chest as he followed the guards, 'You've killed and injured many of my men—this is something that cannot be forgotten.' He smiled, 'however, I am a man of my word and have respect for your martial spirit. I will give you until sun rise to leave the city and never return. After that you will be arrested on sight and tried for your crimes. Do you understand?'

'I understand. Thank you general,' Peter bowed deeply. Sophie was amazed, the brother she knew would never have been so polite or modest.

'Thank you Khang,' she whispered, staring into his eyes. 'You are a good man. I owe you more than you know… thank you.'

She bowed and turned back to Peter and Tai, 'Let's get out of here—too much of my life has been wasted within these walls. General, one more thing, could we take a carriage and horses?'

Peter's mouth was wide open in disbelief of her audacity.

'We will never turn over precious resources to enemies,' Khang snapped in reply, once again sounding like the military commander he had been when Sophie had first met him. 'You should be arrested for even asking,' he lowered his voice, '…but with all the confusion I'm not sure we'll be able to account for everything accurately before nightfall,' he said, trying to suppress a smile.

CHAPTER SEVENTY-ONE

Here we go again. The banging on Giap's wooden door frame was frantic. This time he found himself being led to the servant's quarters in the inner castle.

Giap managed to remove the blade and sterilise the wound before sewing it up with the precision that only a surgeon has mastered. *Now he's stabbing teenagers?* Giap thought bitterly as he worked.

'He's lost a lot of blood. Fortunately, the blade has managed to miss his vital organs. If we keep him well hydrated and the wound clear of infection he should recover. But it may take some time,' Giap said speaking slowly to the foreigner that watched over his friend.

'We don't have any time,' he replied. The young man's face was panicked, 'we need to be gone by morning.'

Just when you think you've heard it all. Giap could see from his expression that arguing wouldn't do any good. 'Very well,' he said with a sigh. 'I'll find you some medicines. One for the pain and one to keep it clean... first though, get a fire started, we need to seal the wound.' Giap handed him a piece of iron with a flat metal head and pointed over to a hearth in the corner of the room.

A few moments later, the patient had begun to come round, but was in excruciating pain. 'This final step is going to hurt,' Giap explained, 'but we need to seal the wound and sterilise that cut on your arm, to minimise the risk of infection.'

Out of his leather bag the doctor produced a glass bottle of clear liquid. It was his if-all-else-fails option, you didn't work through the number of battles Giap had seen without having a few tricks up your sleeve.

'Drink this.' He handed the bottle of opiate liquor to his patient. 'It's your anaesthetic,' he chuckled. The doctor helped lift the bottom of the glass bottle, making sure plenty of it poured down his throat. A few gulps in and the patient could barely hold his head up let alone feel much happening to him as the doctor started cleaning. As instructed, the foreigner had got a fire going using the tinder and flints in the hearth, and the iron began to glow red-hot.

Judging by the scars and bruises all over his body, Giap's patient was obviously no stranger to pain, but the iron plate pressed against his skin searing the wound shut was a different story. He screamed so loudly it almost burst the doctor's eardrums as he fought the instinct to cover his ears, instead keeping his grip on the plate. The alcohol soon did its job and moments later he was asleep and snoring. *Never fails*, Giap thought, and examined the wound. *Good work.*

CHAPTER SEVENTY-TWO

In the hours following Tan's death Peter, Sophie and Tai stayed by Minh's side.

Sophie listened whilst her brother explained their story, relishing the sound of her mother tongue. After so long spent without even hearing a word in English, it sounded almost foreign.

As they waited for the old doctor to return with medicine, Sophie slipped away. She entered the wives' quarters to find most of them sitting in the corner looking anxious and uneasy. They had seen the fear in Chi's eyes as she dragged in her half-awake son by the hand, frantically scoured the room for any or all of the valuables she owned before sprinting out again, ignoring all questions as if she was in her own world.

'What's going on?' Yen asked as Sophie ran into the room grinning.

'Oh.' She hadn't considered that they might not know. 'Lord Tan is dead... you're free.' She scanned the room and was met with mixed emotions of joy and sorrow, the two older women had been here so long they couldn't imagine any other life, whilst Yen, Beautiful-Nung and Lanky-Hao were struck with happiness. After a few minutes of panicked chatter the commotion calmed.

'I'm sorry for how we treated you,' Beautiful-Nung said with honest sympathy in her eyes, 'you were right to stand up to him, and us.'

'Goodbye.' Sophie nodded, 'good luck.'

By late afternoon Minh was awake, but still in a lot of pain.

'What should we do now?' Sophie asked as they sat on the floor of the makeshift hospital room.

'We continue with your plan,' Peter said, 'head east towards the coast and then talk our way onto a boat heading as close to home as we can.'

The room was quiet, *It's been so long,* Sophie thought, *where even is home?* After another minute she broke the silence. 'Tai, will you come with us?'

'Of course' he answered, 'I'd never have even left my village if I hadn't had come with you. Although I'd also never have become a criminal, or nearly been executed either.' He laughed, slapping Peter on the back. At that moment the door slid open and Khang paced into the room, he looked exhausted, but there was a glimmer of hope in his eyes.

'The soldiers throughout the province are falling back to the citadel. We are in a very unstable time, I suggest you make your move immediately, it is almost nightfall. Many of our men won't look favourably on you being here.' Peter nodded. 'I'll offer you some guards to take you as far as the lower citadel, then you are on your own.'

Khang called down the hallway and four men arrived at the doorway. Sophie recognized the soldier that had smiled at her on the evening she first escaped. *Was it only a few months? Seems like years ago.*

'Where is Chi?' she asked.

'It looks like she's run with the boy, desperate to save their own skins, the spineless witch. No honour,' he muttered shaking his head. 'Rest assured when they are caught I'll make sure the child is banished and she spends the rest of her life knee deep in pig shit on the swine farms.' Sophie sniggered, which in turn brought a smile to Khang's wrinkled face.

The guards heaved Minh onto a stretcher and within minutes the group had passed through the main gates and out into the streets of the citadel. Sophie never even bothered looking back. *It's the start of a new life,* she told herself as they walked into the fading light, *I really will never see this place again.*

The guards left them just before the corner where she had first escaped. They passed the handles of the stretcher to Peter and Tai then jogged off back the way they came. Sophie ignored the astounded expressions on the villagers' faces as they passed by, bells had been ringing in the castle all day and they all knew something serious was going on. Now this bizarre group of outsiders were walking out unguarded and free in the fading light. *A strange sight indeed.*

They located the stables easily enough and Sophie heaved the wooden doors open. She was first met by the warm glow of lanterns and then noticed Chi's panic-stricken face in the corner. She appeared to be trying to saddle up a horse, while Lord Cau hid behind the farthest stable.

'Oh it's you, thank goodness.' she said, breathless, sounding almost excited to see them. Sophie didn't say a word.

'You have to let me come with you, I can pay. Look!'
The desperation in her voice was palpable and her shaking hands fumbled to pull a cloth from within the folds of her dress. She produced a golden necklace dotted with blue stones from the bundle, thrust it into Sophie's hand, and grabbed onto her wrist. *Pathetic.*

'I always liked you Sophie, we were friends, come on. Let's go, quick,' Chi said, nervously gripping tighter and tighter.

'ENOUGH,' Sophie snapped. 'Get. Off.' She shook Chi's bony fingers from her arm, and the forced kindness on the woman's face melted away to reveal a bitter frown.

'You stupid little girl,' she snarled. Sophie started to turn and walk over to Tai who was already working on saddling up another of the horses. 'You'll regret this.'

Her voice grated like sandpaper, Sophie's anger boiled over and she spun on the spot smashing Chi in the face with her fist. She yelped in pain and cradled her face, slumped on the hay floor of the stables. 'YOU BROKE MY NOSE,' she screamed, staring down at the sight of blood pooling in her hands.

'Mother!' Lord Cau ran over and started to mop the blood on her face with his sleeve, while she gurgled inaudible curses at Sophie. Tai had freed two horses and was leading them out of the stable and into the harness of a carriage that was waiting nearby.

'Enjoy the pig farm,' Sophie called back staring down at the raging old wife and deposed heir on the floor of the stable. She walked through the door, slamming it and sliding the wooden deadbolt across the lock.

Nearly all of the guards were absent from the lower citadel and the two operating the main gate offered no resistance as one of "The Tigers" held a sword up to the senior officer's throat and demanded the doors were opened. As the heavy gates slammed behind, they were out into the darkness of the open fields and on the dusty track that headed east.

CHAPTER SEVENTY-THREE

As the carriage wound down from the mountains towards the coast, the landscape gradually morphed from rocky outcrops into flat lowlands. It had been four days before a faint taste of salt in the water signalled that they were getting close. Like a mirage, the horizon melted into the land in the distance, playing tricks on Peter who was always hopeful the coast was just around the corner. Minh was resting and recovering, whilst Tai took control of navigation and aimed east following the path of the sun that travelled overhead.

The next morning, distant calls from seagulls could be heard and thick ocean salt sat heavy in the air. *I never realised how much I missed it,* Peter thought. *The space, the freedom, the smell and the sound of crashing waves.* As he was reminiscing on the past and thinking about the future, the outskirts of a town sprang up around them. First a few farmhouses and fields, which appeared to be much larger and better built than those in the mountains, then small houses and shops that were selling all manner of goods. As they started to pass more and more people, Peter listened out for conversation but the change in accent made it hard to understand most of what was being said.

Within the hour—for the first time in its existence—the wooden wheels of the carriage hit the cobblestone streets of an actual road and violently shook up and down with every turn. Tai called out to a local boy, asking for directions as they passed, he gawped at the odd group of mountain folk and foreigners travelling in this aristocratic carriage, before waving his hand forward, indicating they were on the right track.

As they entered the gateway to the docks a couple of miles further on, both Tai and Minh were dumbstruck. It dawned on Peter they had probably never even seen ships, or even the sea, there were only small fishing boats that sat on the lakes and rivers in the highlands. Here there were more than thirty enormous cargo liners moored up at the port, with thousands of frenzied workers attending to them, it was certainly an overwhelming sight. Peter turned to his sister at his side, 'Excited?'

'I'll be happy never to see this place again. That's for sure'.

'So what now?' Tai called back from the driver's platform.

'Let's stop over there.' Peter waved towards one of the few empty spaces in the corner of the dock, 'I'll get out and go and look for some other foreigners or police or something and come back in a while.'

It was more than three hours before he returned. Minh had been transfixed by the ornate European-style and design of the ships across the dock and stared in wonder at his surroundings, while Sophie and Tai both slept, leaning up against the wooden walls of the carriage.

'Good news,' Peter said, startling them both awake.

'What is it?' Minh asked.

'I've found a Dutch merchant boat, they're leaving for Singapore tonight.'

Sophie blinked and glanced around, seeming exhausted. She raised herself up off the hard wooden seat. 'How's that good news?' she said groggily. 'It's nowhere near where we want to be...'

'Yes, but Singapore is a British Colony, they'll have a lot more ships going to Britain than here, what's our other option? Wait here with no money, water or food until we get captured again? We're still criminals remember.'

Sophie nodded, she was worried she'd wake up any moment back in the castle and just wanted to be as far from there as humanly possible.

'There's one problem,' Peter continued, 'the captain wants at least ten pounds,' he winced as he said it.

'Really?' Sophie said, angered by their extortionate pricing.

'That's what I said, but they'll have to supply our food and water, and they'll be risking a lot because none of us have any papers. Either way, they're leaving at dawn. I need to find the captain tonight with the money if we want to get on board.'

'We could sell the horses?' Tai said.

'This might be a little more valuable,' Sophie said pulling Chi's blue-jewelled necklace from her robe, and dangling it in the light of the afternoon sun, looks of disbelief soon parted into smiles, and finally laughter.

They led the carriage towards the quietest corner of the dock and unsaddled the horses. Peter and Tai then dragged them over to a market square just across from the quayside.

'HORSES FOR SALE,' they yelled in as many languages as they could until a local businessman offered them a pitiful handful of cash for the animals, less than a pound each, and rushed off before they could reconsider.

The three of them managed to carry a limping Minh a hundred yards into the town searching for a place they could rest, have a good meal after days on the road.

'This is incredible!' Peter practically yelled with excitement. 'I literally haven't had a meal like this in two years,' he said devouring his second bowl of noodles and chicken in warm, sweet broth. The money they had earned from the horses was burning a hole in his pocket and between the group they managed several more bowls, plates of meat, rice and bottles of beer.

This is heaven! I haven't actually got anything to worry about, Peter thought as he lay stuffed, and half-asleep on the wooden bench of the restaurant surrounded by his friends.

They watched the pink rays of sunlight slipping away behind the masts and chimneys of the boats, then after an hour or so of fully-indulged rest, the group tied up their few belongings and left towards the dock front. Peter went searching for the captain and soon found him drinking tea in a roadside shack, discussing the final provision count with the dock hands.

'Ah lad, did you get the money?' the old seaman asked him in a thick accent.

'No,' Peter said. The captain's face dropped, 'No money, no trip, this isn't a charity' he replied.

'I was hoping this would do instead,' Peter said dangling the necklace in front of the him. The captain snatched it from his hands and examined it closely for a few seconds. When he looked up, his face was fixed into a beaming grin.

'Ha-ha, my friend!' he slapped Peter on the back, and called out to a female assistant sitting to the rear, 'we're going to have a few more passengers now, so we'll need to take on more water and meat.' He turned back to his customer.

'Follow Mi here, she'll take you over to the boat and make sure you get settled alright.'

'Yes sir,' Mi answered, then finished translating his orders to the dock hands.

She pointed out the boat, which was about halfway down the quay. As they passed the corner where the others were waiting in the carriage, Peter waved them up. Sophie grabbed two small bags that carried a few clothes, her brother's sword and Minh's staff, while he and Tai supported their injured friend walking parallel to the waterfront.

Mi led them up the gangplank to the top deck of the boat, past a huge steam tower and then back down into the body, finally arriving at the door of a small and dingy cabin where they would be spending the next couple of weeks. The group lay about trying to get comfortable in the tiny room as the sound of porters and dockhands bringing cargo aboard echoed through the wood and steel beams of the boat.

CHAPTER SEVENTY-FOUR

Peter studied the cabin. It was pitch black but after more than two hours of lying in the darkness trying to sleep he could see clearly enough. Minh was snoring away in the lowest hammock, Sophie was above him in another, while Tai was lying next to him on the floor. It was hard, but Peter was used to nothing but ground beneath his body, and dry ground seemed like a luxury.

I can't believe it's over, Tan's really dead. Peter was happy, but at the same time another feeling swelled inside him. *Everything is changing again,* he thought, almost disappointed. *What will happen to the people here now? What happened to Hong?*

He climbed to his feet as quietly as possible, hoping a walk would distract him from the unsolved questions that troubled his thoughts. By the sound of things the ship was still being loaded, it rocked slightly back and forth as gentle waves lapped at its hull. The creak of wood and steel bending under the weight of a heavy load, echoed through the depths of the boat. Peter pushed open the flimsy wooden door that was barely hanging on to their cabin and stepped out into the hallway, he carefully weaved through the narrow corridors. *There's got to be a toilet here somewhere,* he thought; it had been months since he had been so well hydrated.

At the end of a hallway Peter came to a steel door, he tried the handle but it didn't budge. By the thick beams and rivets either side of the frame it looked as though it divided up parts of the boat. There were voices on the other side and the sounds creaking and banging as cargo was shifted. *Must be the hold*, he thought, bringing his ear closer to the cold metal.

Peter strained to hear the voices, they sounded familiar. The accents of the men cut through the background noise, they sounded just like Minh and Tai, *obviously from the same region.*

'...well seems like it's been madness there for the last few days, the general is rounding up all of the loyalists and putting them on trial,' one voice said.

'I heard he was helped by those rebels too, the group that went around attacking the soldiers?'

'The Tigers?'

'Yeah, that's it.' Peter smiled, without being hunted down, fame was actually kind of nice.

'Do you think that's them?' the first voice asked, 'the group that came aboard?'

'I don't know, I would expect them to be a bit scarier, they looked like a bunch of beggars.'

Peter sighed, his ego-boost had been short lived.

'I reckon it must be. Speaking of which do you know what ever happened to the other woman, the one that escaped?'

'I don't know, but I heard someone matching her description turned up in the south a couple of months after.'

'Oh yeah? Do you think we should we tell them?'

What woman? Tell us what?? Peter's heart was pounding like a drum.

'Best not to get involved, I don't think Lord Tan even knew.' The first man sounded worried. 'Besides, I don't know how I'd react if I was them, after all this time learning my mother was alive...'

EPILOGUE

The blade cut deep into his shoulder. Hong's reactions had worsened with age. He was forced to his knees with only his palms clasped together around the steel, holding death at bay.

It's only fitting I go out in prayer, he thought, kneeling at the foot of the altar with his gaze fixed upwards. Blood was dripping through his fingertips and his palms began to slip. The eyes of his enemy locked with his own as they fought a battle of strength, one the old man knew he was certain to lose.

The screech of an eagle overhead, circling for prey, caught the soldier's attention, and for a fraction of a second he glanced over his shoulder. *I pray and the mountain answers.*
In the moment of distraction, Hong released his right hand, his fingers curled, and compacted into solid stone. The blade slid deeper and with opposing force Hong's fist thundered into his enemy's abdomen. The soldier's grip on his sword loosened, his mouth opened wide as if he was trying to scream but unable, and a dribble of blood ran from its corner. He dropped to his knees.

With a shout of pain, the old man tightened his fingers around the blade. It cut them deep as he forced the steel from his body, but finally the sword cluttered onto the grass-covered stone of the former temple courtyard. Hong rolled across his uninjured side, slamming his foot into the soldier's head and ending the battle for good.

He lay on his back staring up to the sky and whispered a prayer to the spirits of this hallowed ground. Hong had done all he could, his disciples' fate was now of their own making. At last, after what felt like a lifetime of violence, the old man could rest. A deep sigh escaped his lips. Silence filled the clearing once again.

ABOUT THE AUTHOR

Augustus John Roe is an author, linguist and martial artist. He is originally from the United Kingdom, but splits his time between his home country and Vietnam, where he lives with his family. He writes young-adult and adult fiction, as well as non-fiction texts on martial arts and language. For more information about any of his work please visit www.augustusjohnroe.com.

Printed in the United Kingdom
First Printing, 2019
ISBN: 978-1-9995966-2-0

Westlake Press
69 Sutton Drove,
Seaford, U.K. BN25 3NH

www.WestlakePress.com